Summer's Secret Marigold

Titles in the Cornish Secrets Series:

A Secret Rose

Lily's Secret

Holly's Christmas Secret

Summer's Secret Marigold

Summer's Secret Marigold

Kirsty Ferry

Where heroes are like chocolate – irresistible!

Published 2022 by Choc Lit Limited
Penrose House, Crawley Drive, Camberley, Surrey GU15 2AB, UK
www.choc-lit.com

A CIP catalogue record for this book is available from the British Library

ISBN 978-1-78189-497-2

Printed and bound in Great Britain
by Clays Ltd, Elcograf S.p.A.

With thanks to Emma Dent (1823–1900) for leaving such a wonderful record of your life. But more for my Great Uncle John and my Aunty Nancy – partners for life, without the actual marriage bit. Quite scandalous in those days, I guess; but if you had known my uncle, he would have completely won you over and you wouldn't even have batted an eyelid…

Acknowledgements

It's been an absolute joy to write – and discover – Lady Elsie Pencradoc's story in *Summer's Secret Marigold*, the fourth in the 'Cornish Secrets' series. Elsie first appeared in *Lily's Secret* as a rather precocious eight-year-old, and then hosted a party, aged nineteen, in *Holly's Christmas Secret*. I knew that the fourth book had to be Elsie's story, and indeed that was the most frequent request from readers: what happens to Elsie? The truth of the matter is that I didn't know. I knew, however, that I would discover her story when I started writing, and I wasn't disappointed. I *did* know that Elsie was not going to be the sweet and innocent Edwardian girl people might associate with that time, but rather she would become one of the most notorious "names" of her era – in my fictional world, of course. Elsie was a girl who did nothing that was expected and everything that was shocking, and as you read the story, you can see how that all happened! Yet she remains one of my – and my readers' – favourite characters.

There is, I have to say, a scene at a masquerade ball, which literally jumped into my mind when I was contemplating writing *Summer's Secret Marigold*. It jumped into my mind from the pages of a book called *The Lady of Sudeley*, by Jean Bray. The book is a biography of Emma Brocklehurst who married John Coucher Dent in 1847 and lived for almost fifty years at Sudeley Castle in Gloucestershire. As happens in all the best fiction books, Lady Elizabeth Aschcombe, who opened the castle to the public in 1970, stumbled on a real-life trunk full of Emma's letters and diaries which had been hidden away for years, and the result was Emma's biography. One of the small, almost throwaway scenes in the Emma Dent book (but probably not that small or insignificant for Emma Dent, given the characters involved), was that one of Emma's closest friends, a gentleman called Sam Fielden, met his future wife at one of Emma's parties. Sam was "bewitched" by a lady called Sarah Yates, who appeared at the party as a Lancashire witch and stole, so it was said, not only Sam's heart but also most of the newspaper coverage for the event. As soon as I read that, I knew that a version of that had to be a pivotal scene in Elsie's story. And so it was. And so the story grew from there. I must also add that the wonderful gardens at my fictional Elton Lacy were inspired by the beautiful gardens of Hidcote, near Chipping Campden, Gloucestershire, now in the care of the National Trust.

As I say, I was as surprised as anyone as to how Elsie's story worked itself out, and I hope you will enjoy it too. To help bring it to life, I must thank the fabulous team at Choc Lit, my wonderful editor and cover designer, the splendid Tasting Panel who agreed the story could be released into the wild (Carol Botting, Emily Seldon, Margaret Marshall, Carolina Castro, Rosie Farrell, Lisa Vasil, Liana Vera, Carol Fletcher, Jenny Mitchell, Shona Nicolson and Sharon Walsh), and of course the readers who kept asking me about Elsie. Thanks also to my family who, as always, are supportive and helpful – and know when to avoid the snarling author-in-the-corner when need be, or to tame her with offerings of gin/coffee/chocolate, as and when appropriate. Thank you everyone!

Come to me in the silence of the night;
Come in the speaking silence of a dream;
Come with soft rounded cheeks and eyes as bright
As sunlight on a stream;
Come back in tears,
O memory, hope, love of finished years.

From 'Echo' by Christina Rossetti

Chapter One

Present Day

MAY

Sybill Helyer put down the phone with a sigh. Why did legal wrangles have to go on for so long? And there was no end in sight for this particular one. It was more annoying that the solicitor had contacted her at work. In some ways, Sybill almost felt like the phone call had sullied Wheal Mount, the Arts Centre she managed in Cornwall, with something she really didn't want to think about too much.

She loved her job, and what made it even more special was that Wheal Mount was now affiliated with Pencradoc Arts Centre, which was run by Coren and Kit Penhaligon.

She knew Pencradoc Arts Centre was more Coren's baby than Kit's. Kit was happy coming and going, but he had his own life in Marazion with his partner Merryn and his own studio, shop and workshop. In four months, Merryn and Kit would have their own baby as well.

She smiled a little as she thought of fair-haired, grey-eyed Coren – he was the eldest brother, the most serious and, if she was honest, the deepest of the pair. Very few people could get through the corporate exterior to the man beneath, and he had been particularly difficult to deal with when the brothers had first inherited Pencradoc from their Great Aunt Loveday. However, Sybill knew that a gentler man existed: she'd seen him on a few occasions, but he'd always closed up right afterwards. It was frustrating in the extreme. She had known him for several years now – and, if she was completely honest with herself, had loved him for almost all of that time.

Yet every time he appeared to be teetering on the brink of taking their relationship to the next level, he clammed up and it never happened.

Sybill shook herself out of her gloomy thoughts and glared at the phone. She had her own reasons for not pursuing things with Coren right now. But *please God*, when all this was done, she would be free and she could damn well try to do something about the miserable situation.

Her mobile phone beeped, alerting her to the fact she had a text message, and she turned her attention to that instead. She smiled wryly. *That* wasn't going to take her mind off things, was it? It was from Coren Penhaligon.

Coren pounced on the phone as soon as it rang. Sybill, returning his message. *Good.*

A quick smile flitted across his face as he saw her name come up on the screen, but he made the effort to sound professional as he answered.

He did suspect that there was the residue of that treacherous little smile in his voice as he began to speak though. 'Hey, Sybill. My favourite witch. Thanks for calling me back.' *Professional*? All right. Not professional at all. So *that* was a failure. He'd called her a bloody witch! Again.

'Your favourite *what*? Look, as I keep telling you, Coren Penhaligon, just because I'm named after a witch doesn't mean I actually *am* a witch! And anyway, what was I going to do? Ignore you? Or put a spell on you?' He was stupidly relieved to hear there was an answering smile in her voice, but that voice also had a tight little edge to it. *That wasn't like her*.

'Is everything okay?' he asked, leaning forwards, elbows on his desk, frowning. 'You don't sound like yourself.'

Sybill sighed. 'No, I'm fine. It's fine. Just dealing with a tricky customer, that's all.'

'Oh.' Coren relaxed a little and sat back in his seat. 'Anything I can help with?'

She laughed. 'No. Not really, but thanks for the offer. How can *I* help *you*? Going by your "SOS emergency" text, I'm guessing you're about to make my woes seem insignificant.'

'Ah – at least it got your attention. Thank you again.'

'No problem. What is it, then?'

'The latest exhibition Merryn has planned. You know the one I mean – the one she's been enthusing about for weeks? Well she's finally decided that it's definitely going to be based on a summer costume ball.'

'Lovely. But is it based on any *particular* costume ball? I know Merryn and I have had some conversations about all the different balls over the years. Our lovely Pencradocs seemed to quite like going to the things.'

'Yes. The one Elsie Pencradoc attended at a neighbouring property in 1911.' The Duke of Trecarrow, Elsie's uncle, was the head of the Pencradoc family at that time, and at one point, the Pencradocs had owned both Wheal Mount and Pencradoc itself. 'The party was at Elton Lacy – home to Sir Ernest and Lady Pearl Elton. Merryn wants our display rooms to sort of reflect the preparation that Lady Elsie would have put in to getting ready and all that stuff, before she went. I was wondering whether you had anything in your archives about it? Anything that we could use to demonstrate that it wasn't always just as easy as ordering a fancy-dress outfit from eBay and hoping for the best?'

'I doubt eBay existed in 1911,' said Sybill wryly. He heard her clicking at some buttons – her computer keyboard, he guessed – as she searched her database. There was a wealth of information at Wheal Mount from all aspects of the families' lives.

Coren had worked out that Lady Elsie Pencradoc would have been twenty-four in the summer of 1911. Her father, Ellory, had died before Elsie was born. Ellory had been the Duke in the late 1800s before Elsie's Uncle Jago had inherited the title. Jago and his wife, Alys, had lived at Wheal Mount, and Elsie, her mother Zennor, and her step-father, the artist Ruan Teague, had continued to live at Pencradoc with their family.

Coren shivered. He remembered when he and Kit had first come to Pencradoc and a portrait of Ellory had been in the hallway. It was the coldest, most unfriendly portrait he'd ever seen, and the thing had haunted him in more ways than one. Thankfully, that picture was long gone and had been replaced by a portrait of Ellory's first wife, Rose – she was much more appealing to look at and, as far as Coren was concerned, she more than deserved her place in the spotlight.

Coren's mind roved to the marble bust of Elsie at the bottom of the stairway. It had been created when she was a small girl and caused everyone who saw it to smile. She had grown into a talented artist and photographer, and as she was the double of Ruan Teague, tongues had wagged all her life as to her parentage. But, as Coren understood it, that had never seemed to bother Elsie.

Sybill's voice brought Coren back to the present. 'Ha. Here we go – yes. I've got some stuff that might help. Photos. Invitations. Ooh, and some letters from that time. Lovely. Okay – I'll have a rummage and I'll get back to you. There's quite a lot here that's new to me as well, to be honest. We had a student help us out on placement earlier in the year and she spent a lot of time up in the attics being guided by Tammy. It's one of the jobs on my never-ending list to have a closer look at what she noted. Most of it is Pencradoc stuff, so I'd probably have only gone and searched through the Pencradoc boxes if you'd asked me to, to be fair.' She sounded amused. 'This is very exciting, I must say!'

'Thanks. Shall I come to you to pick it up?'

'I'll come to you.' There was a definite smile in her voice now. 'You know how I love a trip to see you.'

'To see me?' He couldn't resist trying to have a bit of a joke with her, although it was quite rare for him.

'No! Well – yes. Yes, of course. But to see you at Pencradoc. You know what I mean! To see you … all, in general. To see you all at Pencradoc.'

'Ah, right.' He bit his tongue to stop himself adding any

further comments to that. If he did, he'd end up giving away more than he thought he should.

More than he thought was safe.

'Leave it with me. I'll let you know when I'm coming.'

'Thanks so much. I mean it.'

'I know.'

'Bye, Sybill.'

'Bye, Coren.'

Then she hung up and the line went dead. And Coren put his head on the desk and groaned. It never got any better. It never did.

1911

Lady Elsie Pencradoc let herself into her London home, shedding her coat, gloves and hat as she went. She'd had a frustrating day. The politics of the Slade School of Art, where she was currently working alongside her studies, had annoyed her greatly.

There was talk amongst some of the male students, who were inspired by the Post-Impressionists, about creating an exclusive group – for men, of course – based at the studio of Walter Sickert, who Elsie frankly didn't like very much. The Camden Town Group would consist of people like Walter, as well as Spencer Gore and Wyndham Lewis. The usual crowd, with a maximum number of sixteen at any one time. There were rumours of even allowing Duncan Grant in – who had only studied at Slade for one single solitary term – and the very sweet, but very deaf John Doman Turner, who Spencer taught via correspondence of all things. Elsie had only met John once in passing. He was very shy, but he had smiled at her. The others always said he was quite unsure of his talents. Spencer had joked that was because he worked as a stockbroker's clerk, and it didn't take a lot of imagination to do that really – but apparently the man *did* have talent, and Spencer received five shillings each time he responded, despite the fact some of his responses were, apparently, curses and complaints about John's work, but there it was.

Elsie sighed and picked up the letters from the hall table, shuffling through them for something, anything, of interest. Between Spencer's crowd, and the small number of Rupert Brooke's Neo-Pagans who still haunted Slade, Elsie wondered how anybody actually had time to *do* any art. Her thoughts on that particular subject extended to musings which included Gwen Darwin, and Gwen's lover Jacques Raverat, and how the pair had one foot in Duncan's Bloomsbury Group, and the other in Rupert's Neo-Pagans. How, Elsie thought wryly, Gwen and Jacques remembered the necessary rules and behaviour in each "group" was a mystery, for those crowds had very different outlooks on life.

She'd met Rupert as well – of course she had. Who hadn't, in that part of London, in the sort of lifestyle Elsie had chosen? At first, she had been stunned by his fair hair, his pretty words and his incredibly handsome face. She could see how easily a person could fall for Rupert and his poet's soul. But there was just something too intense about him – too dark, really – behind those beautiful eyes and, try as she might, she couldn't really think of Rupert growing into old age. She shivered.

Youth. That was what it was all about in Bloomsbury, in her world of art and artists. It was wonderful and she adored it, and it was a place she felt she fitted in perfectly. But she knew that one day she would have to go back to her family home in Cornwall and, horror of horrors, settle down.

She felt her top lip curl at the thought of it. There was only one man who she had ever considered settling down with – and, to be honest, she and Louis Ashby had drifted apart of late. She had to accept that this was her fault more than anybody else's, but it couldn't ever be undone and there was no way back from it. She could trace the fracture back to that one time; that one particular moment in their lives where everything had changed. And if there was anything in Elsie's happy, privileged Bohemian life that frustrated and upset her more than she cared to dwell on, it was the situation with bloody Louis.

Louis looked at the address on the top of the letter – he had memorised the damn thing anyway, but he wasn't about to take any chances. *Brunswick Square*. The place that Elsie had run off to. He took a deep breath and looked up, along the road, tracing the grand houses and garden squares out, until his eyes settled on the terrace ringed with metal railings which faced onto the neat square of grass, trees and shrubs.

He walked up to number two, checked the address once again, and took hold of the door knocker. With more confidence than he felt, he rapped hard and took a step backwards, not sure whether Elsie, being Elsie, would come to the door and answer it herself.

It turned out that she had a maid to do that for her.

'Ahh – hello. Is Elsie here? Lady Elsie?' Louis felt the colour flood his cheeks. He'd known Elsie all her life, so why did this particular trip feel so awful?

Of course, he knew why – he definitely knew why. But he needed to tell her in person.

'Yes, sir. Who may I ask is calling?' The maid looked at him questioningly.

'Louis. Louis Ashby.' He could have bitten his tongue off. If he'd said Noel or Ernie or any one of their other friends – even perhaps Laurie, her next youngest brother, or Clem or Enyon or Arthur, her other brothers – perhaps then he might have been assured of an invitation into the house. *Of course*, he reasoned, his mind racing, *the maid probably knows those people, but then they don't have the monopoly on those names. For all the maid knows, I might be a different man with the same name as one of Elsie's friends or relations ...*

'Shut up, Louis,' he hissed under his breath. He was confusing himself. All he knew was that he'd be lucky to be allowed to see Elsie. He pulled his hat from his head and raked his hands through his fair hair, frowning into the depths of the corridor that suddenly seemed very long and not too welcoming.

But it seemed luck was with him, and the maid came back within a few moments. 'Lady Elsie will see you now, Mr Ashby.' She bobbed a curtsey as Louis nodded and stepped inside, his heart racing and his ears burning with horror as he thought about what he had to tell Elsie.

The maid showed him into a room on the right-hand side of the hallway, and even if Elsie was nowhere to be seen, and even if he had been blindfolded and dropped in the middle of the property, he would have known it was she who lived there.

He was vaguely aware of walls covered with paintings and sketches; family photographs ranged across the mantelpiece and grouped together on various pieces of furniture; a camera discarded on a table; a paintbox on another table next to the window, a multitude of brushes haphazardly rammed into a jam jar next to it; a sketchbook open at a half-finished sketch of a smiling toddler, whose eyes sparkled with mischief as they looked out at the viewer; some scattered pictures of a young man he didn't recognise ...

But all of that faded into insignificance as he saw her, saw Elsie Pencradoc, dressed in her customary black, her hair wild and curling past her shoulders, her eyes deep, dark and slightly narrowed as she fixed that gaze straight on him. A silver locket hung around her neck, stark against the black of her frock, glinting with the light from the tall windows. The evening light caught her curls and the contrast between the blue-black of her hair and the paleness of her face was startling. Louis stopped just inside the door, unable to move, unable to do anything except stare at her and forget, for a brief moment, why he was here.

Chapter Two

Present Day

Sybill rummaged around in the storerooms at Wheal Mount – which were actually the old servants' quarters and the attics on the second floor – and found what she was looking for. It certainly took her mind off the phone call.

There was a photograph of Elsie, posed at the foot of the steps, arm in arm with a dark-haired, good-looking chap. He had a confident half-smile, which on anyone else may have looked arrogant, but his eyes told a different story. They were glinting with mischief, and he was dressed as a Regency gentleman. Elsie herself was dressed in a flowing black dress, a cloak and had a vague, dreamy expression in her eyes, and a weird little lopsided smile, almost as if she was barely concentrating on the moment. The photo made Sybill herself smile. Elsie looked a little drunk, to be honest.

'I guess that's the result of the Edwardian version of pre-event drinks, Elsie,' she murmured, sitting back on her heels and studying the photograph. Elsie had been wild and unconventional, and from what Sybill had heard, she'd been something of a social butterfly – it just made Sybill love her more. This was definitely a photograph taken on the evening of the Elton Lacy ball. The date on the back was 24th June 1911, and that tallied with the invitation and letter Sybill had filed along with the picture. It was a little frustrating that she didn't know who the young man was, but the most important thing was that Elsie was in the photograph. It was signed on the back by Ruan Teague, Elsie's step-father and a renowned artist, as well, which made it extra special.

There were several portraits of Elsie at Wheal Mount and also at Pencradoc by several different artists – not surprising, really, considering the circles Elsie moved in and the people she had met, both at her liberal arts college and at the Slade, where she had worked for a few years while she lived in London. However, it was refreshing to see this particular photograph as it seemed to show Elsie genuinely caught in the moment. Some of the portraits were a little – well – *avant-garde*, Sybill thought; some were largely splodges of colour, others were blocks and cubes making up Elsie's face. Sybill knew Elsie had studied and practiced during the time of Futurism, Cubism, Expressionism and everything in between. Privately, Sybill preferred the more traditional pieces, even though she felt obliged to exhibit all the different styles in the house.

In fact, she had some of these pictures ready to be sorted out for a display – if Pencradoc's exhibition was to be all about Elsie, an idea which Merryn had been very keen on, then Wheal Mount's feature exhibition could be too, and Sybill had decided it would be interesting to pull in Elsie's life at the Slade. That way, they could sell joint tickets for each exhibition and both properties gained from the other. It was a format they had trialled before and it worked well. Sybill just needed to know which aspect of Elsie's fabulous life Merryn was keen to focus on, and she could fine-tune Wheal Mount's Slade exhibition to suit. However, it was definitely easier for Sybill to pull portraits out of storage which simply depicted Elsie and let Merryn focus on the theme for Pencradoc.

Well, after some cheerfully exciting conversations between herself and Merryn to plan it all out, and that chat with Coren, now she knew the exhibition was going ahead – which was excellent. Sybill smiled at the photo of Elsie and her escort, flicked a speck of dust off the corner and gathered up the invitation and letter. Although Elsie's main residence had been Pencradoc, Sybill had most of the records and artefacts from Pencradoc at Wheal Mount.

The reason was simple. Sybill knew what she was doing

with them. Kit was only at Pencradoc with his wife, Merryn, part time, and Coren had been too ensconced in getting the place up and running to have any time to organise it. So Sybill had taken it all on board, and it made sense for her to keep all the historical artefacts with her records. In exchange, Merryn, who had worked at an art dealers in London and still freelanced for them from time to time, acted as a consultant at Wheal Mount too, and was happy to be called in whenever Sybill needed confirmation on things. Merryn would be coming to Wheal Mount soon to continue their discussions about the joint exhibition and see what Sybill had already lined up for the companion exhibition. There was, in particular, one unsigned item that defied Sybill's knowledge on these things, so she was looking forward to getting Merryn's take on it.

Sybill stood up and headed out of the room. She took one last look behind her before she locked the door … then looked again. She could have sworn there was a black shimmering shadow in the corner which briefly took the form of a person before melting away again.

Imagination. She shook her head and closed the door firmly.

Pencradoc had ghosts. Wheal Mount didn't. And anyway, as much as she believed in them, she didn't think that had been one at all …

'Sybill!' Coren stood up as the door opened and Sybill walked in. She had a Wheal Mount branded sustainable jute bag on her arm, and he smiled. 'You're advertising our rivals whilst walking through our grounds?'

Sybill grinned and handed the bag to him. 'Free marketing. No harm in that, is there?'

'None at all.'

'It's mutually beneficial. As I keep telling you. Oh, and watch out for my pet toad. He's in that bag somewhere, along with my grimoire. And my broomstick is parked outside. Is that all okay?'

'Yes, yes. My apologies. You're not a witch and I don't want to be turned into a frog. So, do you want a coffee? Then you can talk me through this little lot.' He gestured to the chair opposite his desk and Sybill sat down.

She nodded. 'Coffee sounds great, thanks. Anyway, I'd turn you into a toad, not a frog, and you could be friends with my little pet one. The one that's in that bag.' She nodded at the jute bag and looked so serious, Coren couldn't help but grin. 'Hey. I wonder if they had servants bring the coffee to them in the olden days?' Sybill continued. 'Instead of the boss making it. That's a thought and a half.'

'Apparently this was the old study in times gone by – Loveday used to tell us she'd come in here to play on the old typewriter until she was caught one day typing up a story on the back of some important documents. To me, it's a room where the man of the house could hide away and pretend to do work to avoid the demands of his family.' He smiled to show he was joking. He'd liked Loveday's stories of the olden days and had decided to turn the old study into his office once Pencradoc was more established as a business. Coren put Sybill's bag on his desk, then went over to the coffee machine, positioned on the deep windowsill of the room, and dropped a pod in it. While it was whooshing and steaming through the system, he turned and faced Sybill, leaning back against the sill with his arms folded. 'So, how's the provision going for the Slade exhibition?'

'Great! There's one thing in particular I would like Merryn to look at, as I'm not sure who the artists are. Elsie was working at the Slade well into her married life, and I think she was a popular choice of sitter for the students.' Sybill smiled, her gaze seemingly far away in Bohemian London, no doubt amongst the Bloomsbury Group and all their associated pockets of scandal. 'She was there beyond World War One as well, so there's a good range of artwork over about twenty years. She left London when the rumblings started about World War Two, so luckily she escaped the Blitz, and by then she was living back at Pencradoc with her family.'

'Not that your specialist subject is Lady Elsie Pencradoc at *all*.' Coren was amused.

He handed her the mug of coffee and she sipped it gratefully. 'Gosh, I needed that. As soon as you asked for the stuff, I dashed straight up here and didn't finish my own cuppa. Please feel sorry for me?' She blinked big brown eyes at him mournfully.

'I'm desperately sorry.'

'Next time, say it like you mean it.' She settled comfortably in the seat and crossed her legs. 'So, do you want to do the grand unveiling while I hug my Americano here, and I'll talk you through everything?'

'Sure.' Coren pulled the bag back across the desk towards him and opened it up. 'So, we've got a photograph, an invitation and a letter.'

He spread them out in front of him as if he was dealing cards, and Sybill nodded. 'Yes. So, they all relate to the 1911 Midsummer Costume Ball at Elton Lacy. You can see it's a picture of Elsie and her escort, and it's signed on the back by Ruan Teague. That alone makes it quite priceless. I know it's not a painting, but it is a piece of art he created, and it shouldn't be dismissed.'

'Quite right.' Coren studied the photograph. 'She looks tipsy.'

Sybill laughed. 'I think she is.'

'I've seen you look like that.' Coren cast a glance up at Sybill, and she blushed.

'I told you, me and champagne don't get on. You plied me with it!'

'It was a special occasion – I'd had that grant come through. It meant we could put some efficient heating in the house and get the roof fixed! Which also meant we could start opening up the retreat rooms – just as you suggested, Sybill Helyer!'

'True.' She grinned. 'What have you got next?'

'This.' He pointed to the invitation. 'That's pretty normal, though, for the time, isn't it? Goes well with the photo.'

'Yes, the date's the same as on the back of the photo. Twenty-fourth of June 1911.'

'Great. And I'm assuming this is the letter that went with the invite?' He tapped the expensive looking notepaper, covered with large, vibrant handwriting.

'It is. Well done. See how it was addressed to Elsie in Brunswick Square? That pins it down to being something quite special – if she brought it back to Pencradoc with her thirty years later and didn't just bin it, then I think it's quite meaningful. It came from Lady Pearl Arthur Elton. I think they were great friends by the tone she uses. It's hardly formal, and she also mentions Holly and Noel Andrews, who are, of course, Locryn's relatives.' Locryn owned an antique shop in Pencradoc village, and his partner, Sorcha, owned the Tower Tea Room at Pencradoc.

'What the hell does she mean by "Whooper-upper"?' Coren frowned at the unfamiliar word in the letter.

Sybill laughed. 'It's a fabulous phrase of the time that meant a bit of a party girl. I think it was like someone who thought they could sing but really couldn't, yet tried with enthusiasm.'

'An Edwardian karaoke queen.'

'Exactly.'

'I like the sound of Elsie.'

'Me too. Would *you* ever karaoke, Coren?'

'No.'

'Thought not.'

1911

'Louis. What brings you here? And why do you look as if you've seen a ghost? It's just me. Like always.' There was an edge to her words she didn't really mean to have there, but Louis was absolutely the last person on earth she had expected to walk into her home – and now he was here, standing in the doorway to her parlour, looking for all the world as if he was frozen to the spot.

'Elsie. I ...' His voice trailed away, and she noticed he was clutching his hat ridiculously tightly. He shrugged, his shoulders drooping despondently inside his overcoat. 'I wanted to see you. Business brought me here. To London. And I knew that you were here, obviously, so thought I'd come and see you.' He attempted a smile, which flickered and died whilst his eyes clouded over, as he looked somewhere – anywhere but at her, it seemed.

His fair hair was unkempt, as usual – as if he'd just raked his hands through it and left it like that. Knowing Louis, he had probably done just that whilst he was waiting to see if she'd let him in. Elsie thought wryly of some of her favourite stories – of vampires and demons and spirits – and how they needed inviting into a person's home. Had Louis come, like a demon in the night, to steal her soul away? It was all she had left, really.

But he was, and always had been, more "fallen angel" than "demon". She felt her own shoulders sag and that wave of black despair wash over her once again – as it often did when she thought about the pair of them.

'You're lucky you caught me. I just came home.' She waved at a seat and took one for herself, throwing herself into it as she always did. She'd already dispensed with her boots, but stopped herself from putting her feet up on the table as she also usually did. It just seemed too intimate, really, with Louis here. Which was also ridiculous, as he knew her in so many ways that nobody else did.

'I'm glad I caught you then.' He hovered – this man, who she also knew better than anyone else ever had – and looked uncomfortable. 'I hope that it's been a good day at the Slade?'

He phrased it as a question, so she was more or less forced to answer. 'Not too terrible, really. We've had worse.' She remembered the tantrum one of the more creative young men had thrown that afternoon, and how she'd had to take him out of the studio and tell him firmly to calm down before he went back in. She also remembered the look that Fabian Austen had given her as he walked past them; that half smile and the raised eyebrow that seemed to say, *rather you than me, but you're doing quite well.*

Fabian was one of the seemingly confident young men who worked out of the Slade – he was on a graduate fellowship route, just the same as Elsie. But, whereas one of Elsie's favourite things was to work with the students, Fabian always seemed rather removed from that – as if they were beneath his notice. Elsie knew that it was all just a front. Fabian was one of the kindest people she knew, but he wasn't a man who let anyone in too easily. Many of the female students – *and staff*, she thought wryly – had tried to break down his walls and become close to him.

Fabian brushed them all smartly, yet devastatingly attractively, away. Then, Elsie knew, his eyes would drift towards someone like Rupert and cloud over, knowing it was hopeless and he had to keep certain feelings and inclinations well-hidden.

Elsie sort of knew how he felt, which was maybe part of the unspoken bond they both shared. She wasn't interested in anyone and did her fair share of brushing men off – she couldn't possibly let anyone in; not so long as Louis was in her life. Not so long as there was, perhaps, an outside chance they could pick up their relationship again.

In her more logical moments, she knew it was unwise to think that – she had been the one who had cut him off in the first case, after all – but she was Elsie Pencradoc, and she had always dared to dream.

But seeing him standing in her house, almost close enough

to touch, pushed the thoughts of almost everything else out of her mind. *Almost* everything – not quite everything ...

'Please, Louis – sit down. Surely we're beyond standing on ceremony?'

As if to prove it, she went ahead and put her feet up on the table, then pulled a sketchpad across to her – it was almost a talisman, something she could do with her hands, as she tried to make sense of her feelings with him in the room, standing so very, very close to her.

She flipped the picture of the toddler over and started, almost unthinkingly, to sketch out a new picture. 'Louis. Sit.'

'Yes. I suppose.' He sat down then, and looked for somewhere to put his hat. He awkwardly laid it on the floor. 'I've missed you, Elsie.' The words came out in a rush, and she looked up quickly to see his cheeks flaming red.

'I'm sure you haven't missed me that much, Louis.' She scrawled at the hairline on the face she was creating on the paper before her. 'I'm sure you've been very busy.' She looked up and caught his eye. His gaze was fixed on her, his grey eyes unfathomable. Her pencil jumped from the area she was working on and smudged somewhere to the right of the subject. She tutted under her breath. *How does he still have this effect on me?*

'I have been busy – I can't deny it. I've been tied up in the estate and the business. I didn't realise how much was involved until I started working on it with my brother – although Drew's mainly doing the London part, as he lives a little closer to town than me.'

Elsie's pencil paused as her gaze roved across Louis' dear, familiar face, and she felt that lurch in her stomach as she quashed the feelings down. Hell, did she even truly know *what* she wanted any more?

'Father is making sure I know how to look after the place from the Cornish side,' Louis continued. 'I think he's enjoying letting go of it in some ways.' He smiled that crooked smile of his that always made her heart jump. 'I still have much to learn, as he keeps telling me.'

'And how are you ... otherwise?' Elsie darkened a shadow on her picture, rubbing the area over with her forefinger. She tutted again as she realised her hands were still filthy from her work at the Slade. *Ah well, never mind.* 'I haven't heard from you for ever so long. I have no idea what you're doing with your life now.'

'I'm not dead yet, if that's what you mean.'

Elsie jerked her head upwards at the tone of his voice; he sounded half-amused and half-angry. She flushed. Louis had suffered from a particularly nasty bout of bronchitis, which had turned into pneumonia then pleurisy a few years ago – she had been immensely annoyed with him when he hadn't attended a party she had hosted one Christmas, blamed him terribly in a letter she had written before she knew the real reason why, and felt dreadful when she found out that he had been genuinely very unwell. She also felt dreadful that she had thought he was simply avoiding her party with the excuse of a common cold.

The whole time after that period was something she didn't really want to remember, but it was impossible not to. She felt her own cheeks flame and dropped her head, leaning further over her sketchpad so he didn't see. *No such luck, though.*

'Ah, Penny.' He used the silly nickname he'd given her when they were children, based on her surname. 'Forgive me.'

'I never wished you dead, Louis,' she muttered.

'I know. But your letter implied I should have really been at death's door before I was allowed to miss your party. Am I allowed to quote from it?'

'Stop it. No. I've already apologised for all of that. I was a spoiled brat and I know that.'

'Fair enough. But really, I don't hold any grudges, Penny, I hope you know that. We were both young, and when you're young you're allowed to be a little silly. At least the letter you sent my parents is a little nicer. Mother was delighted to hear from you when Father was ill – they both said it meant a lot to them when they got it. And he's very well now, so that's one thing.' The hint of amusement was back in his voice now, and she risked looking up at him again. His eyes were warm, and finally she sighed and tossed the sketchpad aside as he began to speak again. 'And, Elsie, I'm not exactly sure how we got from ... there ... after that Christmas ... to ... this,' he continued, staring down at his hands. 'I don't like it, and I want you to know that I did try, Elsie – but you went away and you cut me off ... and I couldn't do anything else.'

'I know.' Elsie felt her mouth turn downwards. *It was deliberate*, she wanted to say. *I had to do it*. But she didn't. She said nothing, and that was why his next words made her ball up her hands into fists and dig her nails into her palms until she was sure they'd bleed or she'd scream.

'I had to come and see you, Elsie, because I wanted you to hear it from me and not from anyone else. I'm quite possibly getting married.'

Elsie stared at him, silent and immoveable, for what seemed like a decade.

He wasn't sure what he'd hoped for – perhaps that she would leap out of that chair and beat her fists on his chest, shouting at him and pleading with him not to do it. He would have made his decision there and then. He was only considering getting married out of a sense of duty – after Elsie had disappeared and made it quite clear she wasn't interested, his parents had vaguely earmarked a girl called Margaret, who they thought might be Quite Suitable, and they hoped that he would think the same.

He didn't.

Margaret Corrington was ice to Elsie's fire; happy, he suspected, to be wed to a gentleman in Louis' position, to be able to entertain her friends in a large, comfortable house without particularly caring who the poor husband was. She was also an acquaintance of his sister-in-law, and he had heard from her that Margaret had hinted she would expect the best of everything, and would definitely want a separate parlour in her marital home; a sanctuary free from small children, household animals and her husband. That wasn't necessarily a bad, or indeed an unusual thing, but the way Louis' sister-in-law, Felicity, had wickedly mimicked the comment had made him bite back a smile.

He had himself briefly wondered whether Margaret would be the sort of woman who expected the marital duty to be carried out once a week until she became pregnant. If the duty resulted in the birth of one or two children, that would be her job done, and she and her future husband would sadly end up living perfectly separate lives.

Louis hoped not, but in his darker moments couldn't help comparing this imagined life to the one he had always hoped for with Elsie; a happy house, full of laughter and children, and making love long into the night and early in the morning. Margaret would never come close to Elsie, but he didn't actively dislike Margaret, just as Margaret didn't actively dislike him. She just wasn't Elsie and never would be, and the brutal truth was that, yes, they could probably manage to live reasonably comfortably alongside one another, but there was no way either of them could love the other in the way that Louis imagined would make a truly happy marriage.

He felt the letter he had taken with him to Elsie's London home, the letter she had sent to his parents, uncomfortably close to his heart; saw in his mind's eye her familiar neat handwriting, which he had always marvelled over. Elsie was chaotic and wild, but her copperplate letters were perfectly formed – it was one of the foibles he couldn't quite match with her personality. He looked back at that face, the one that was still staring at him silently – a face that was too thin, too pale – and saw her lips pressed tightly together as she took in his news.

'Very well,' she said with just the slightest tremor in her voice. 'Thank you for telling me. I do hope you'll be very happy together, whoever you choose.'

'You know her,' he admitted. 'It's Margaret Corrington. But she is not …' His words petered out. He wanted to say "she is not my choice" – but he simply couldn't bring himself to speak ill of the girl when she wasn't even there to defend herself. Instead, he amended his words. 'Look. Our family has known Margaret's family forever, so everyone is convinced it's a good match. But you know who my real choice would be, Elsie. I can stop it. I can stop the whole thing … if you just tell me to.'

There was a beat as she took the information in, and all he wanted to do was pull her into his arms and tell her if she only said the word he would stop the whole hideous train-wreck from ploughing ahead.

'Margaret *Corrington*?' Elsie's eyes were suddenly wide and disbelieving. 'My *God*. I'm surprised she's even entertained marrying into your family. She—' Elsie bit her lip and flushed. 'She was close to your brother for a time, was she not? Practically betrothed. Yet my cousin Clara said …' But then she shook her head and closed her eyes, seemingly attempting to steady herself with a couple of deep, shaky breaths. When she spoke again, her voice was low, calm and dangerously brittle. 'You'll understand if I don't attend the wedding, I'm sure. And now, I think you'd better go. I'm expecting company.' Her knuckles were white, her fists clenched as she got to her feet and stood stiffly before him. 'Have a safe journey home, Louis.' She nodded briefly and turned away from him, dipping her head towards her sketchpad.

Louis nodded, even though he knew she couldn't see him. 'Yes. I understand. Goodbye, Elsie.'

'Goodbye, Louis.'

Then she roughly flipped the sketchpad over, so the book was open but the picture wasn't visible any more and leaned heavily on it, pressing her palms on the book as if she could crush the life out of it.

He stood up, bowed mechanically, and walked out of the room. It was as he left the house and took several deep breaths outside, a few houses along, that he saw a young, dark-haired man striding along the street. His hands were in his pockets and he was walking straight towards Elsie's house. Even from a distance, he had an air of arrogance around him.

As the man came closer, Louis' stomach lurched. It was the man in the sketches littered around Elsie's drawing room. Sure enough, the man went straight to her door and rapped smartly. Within seconds, the door was open and he was inside.

Louis watched a moment longer, then turned away. He focused on the ground beneath his feet; putting one foot in front of the other, just to get him away from the peaceful garden square. But at the back of his mind, there was one thing that he thought he might hang on to; he'd had a brief glimpse of the picture Elsie had been drawing. And it was of himself.

Elsie would never destroy a picture, he knew that of old, and it was almost her habit to draw people as they were in the room with her. So if she'd drawn him, at least, in some way, he'd be with her for a little longer.

On the train home, Louis barely saw the scenery pass the window. He had no business in London – none at all. His only business there had been to find Elsie and tell her what was potentially happening.

It had made him feel indescribably worse.

Chapter Three

Present Day

Sybill stayed in Coren's office chatting a little longer. She loved coming here – sometimes she could hardly believe that until Pencradoc had become an arts centre, she'd never even set foot across the doorstep.

She'd been working at Wheal Mount Arts Centre for years, ever since she'd had a holiday job there as a student. She'd progressed from being the person who sat in the doorway handing out maps to tourists and smiling a lot because she didn't know very much, to having sole responsibility for ticket sales in the kiosk, to being part of the archival team, to becoming the main exhibition and event planner, all the way up to her present post as manager, and she'd loved every minute.

Her own managers had been pretty good with her when her life blipped, and she'd been determined to repay them by being the best she could absolutely be. Her reward, it seemed, was to now be in charge of the place she loved so much, and to be able to work alongside the team at Pencradoc Arts Centre.

Wheal Mount was a friendly place, and she couldn't help but think that was because it had retained the joy and love from the original owners, Jago and Alys Pencradoc. She had been especially entranced by Lady Elsie, Jago and Alys' niece, and cousin to their lively family of four blonde girls. The girls were all carbon copies of fair-haired Alys, with the dark Pencradoc eyes that Kit, Coren's brother, had inherited – but not Coren. Coren had grey eyes, with long dark lashes and … yes, she really should stop thinking about Coren's eyes and concentrate on what he was actually saying to her.

And he was saying: 'So, which artists do you think you've

got ready for display for Elsie's portrait collection? Just so I can add it to our marketing materials. Or I can get Merryn to add it to our marketing materials. That's probably more realistic.'

'What? Oh – sorry. Loads of the Bloomsbury Group, of course. I like to think of her sitting in one of their salons, drinking wine and posing for their pictures. Just imagine it. She'd not bat an eyelid. Her family was so liberal and unconventional, all those entangled Bloomsbury relationships would be like water off a duck's back. And we've got a William Coldstream dating from the late twenties, so Elsie would have been in her forties. Still a stunning woman. A Helen Lessore from a similar time.' She thought for a moment, recalling the raft of artworks. 'A Winifred Knights sketch, just a small one, from the First World War. A Rex Whistler, of *course*. He was so good at society beauties and all those Bright Young Things – I doubt the fact Elsie was a little older than his set would have stopped him choosing to do one of her too. Who else? Jacob Kramer. A Paul Nash, even though he was better with his landscapes. They must have been like ships in the night. He only stayed a year.' She smiled briefly, thinking of the chunks of shading that depicted Elsie on Nash's canvas.

'I don't know much about Nash – wasn't he a war artist?' Coren looked vaguely impressed at the famous name.

'He was. And a brilliant one too. Yes, I don't think it's any accident that Elsie was at the Slade just at the time they opened the doors to those students – Ben Nicholson, Stanley Spencer, Mark Gertler, William Roberts, Dora Carrington, Christopher R. W. Nevinson, Edward Wadsworth—' Sybill reeled the names off, counting them on her fingers as she spoke. 'They were a "Crisis of Brilliance", or at least that's what Henry Tonks said. He was the Professor of Drawing there at the time. You'd never get that amount of talent together there again.'

'Sounds pretty impressive!' Coren grinned.

Sybill laughed and shrugged. 'It was. Add Elsie Pencradoc to the mix, and it's a dream come true. She loved it when they introduced stage painting in 1929. In fact, I'd be inclined to say that she was instrumental in pushing for it. She was certainly delighted enough to tell Lily Valentine all about it in one of her hugely rambling letters. We've got that ready to display too – just as an addition. Honestly, if Elsie walked into Wheal Mount in the near future and saw herself plastered on all those walls, I think her ego would explode.'

'Just as well she's not likely to then. It might get rather messy – what with exploding Elsie everywhere.' Coren's face split into an even wider smile. 'Kit and myself might be a little more down to earth about it. It'll be weird seeing so many images of her in one place, though. I know we're related to her, and there are photographs and portraits all over Pencradoc, but I think what you have will trump us any day.'

'But you'll have the more human side of her here – you'll bring to life the girl who came to Cornwall for a fancy-dress party with her friends one midsummer, and dressed up as … well. I'm not entirely sure what she's dressed as. A witch, perhaps? Whatever she is, she's a gothic beauty.'

'A gothic beauty. Yes. That describes her pretty well.'

'I think so. But I'm still inclined to think of her as a witch – perhaps it's because I'm named after one myself, as you so frequently remind me.' There was a flicker of a smile from Coren, followed by an apologetic shrug that made him look young and bashful, and her heart melted yet again. *God*. She needed to get a grip. 'Anyway. I'd best go.' Sybill stood up reluctantly. She would be happy to stay for much, much longer and talk about all of this with Coren – but she knew not everyone shared her passion for art. Coren was very much more the business mind of the Penradoc partnership. She looked at him, feeling another wave of affection for him. He'd basically given up a successful career in something international and high-powered to come and make Pencradoc

Arts Centre work. And now he was located in deepest Cornwall, working with his brother and his sister-in-law, and there was nowhere else for the buck to stop beyond him.

He must have seen her looking at him rather intensely, and he smiled properly, seemingly amused at her furrowed brow and buttoned-up mouth. She knew she looked like that when she was thinking deeply.

But Coren? Coren was gorgeous in every single way, from the lock of fair hair that flopped over his forehead, to his serious grey eyes that sometimes twinkled with mischief, to that slow, sexy half-smile that he really didn't seem to know made her knees knock together embarrassingly under the desk opposite him ...

She loved him to distraction. She really did.

'I'll walk you out then,' he said. 'Unless you want to summon your broomstick?'

'No, a walk will be fine. Thanks.' She hesitated. Should it be this easy to leave? Shouldn't he even try to delay her, even just a tiny bit? If she was even halfway right in her hopeful idea that he had deep-buried feelings for her, shouldn't there be a glimmer of reluctance to see her go ...?

But this was Coren. So – no, basically. No.

'Come on then. I could do with stretching my legs.' Coren made a big production of standing up and stretching. Then he pasted what he imagined was a rictus grin on his face. *God*! How much more awkward and stupid could he make this moment?

He knew the drill. He should distract her, offer her another coffee. Engage her more in conversation about the things she clearly loved.

But he couldn't. And the reason *was* rather stupid. He indicated she should leave the room before him and followed her out, then fell into step beside her. As they walked, he glanced at the wall in the main hallway where the portrait of Duchess Rose now hung, taking the place of her husband, Ellory – the portrait Coren had hated so much.

Coren was sure the damn thing had been the direct cause of the worst behaviour he had ever been guilty of. He just didn't like it. He didn't like the way it made him feel, the way Ellory seemed to possess him, and the way that he'd begun to think and act and be like Ellory. Thanks to Merryn – and he still bore the scar on his hand to this day, where she'd stuck a knife in it to stop him attacking Kit – he'd come to his senses, and he'd made a huge bonfire of the damn portrait when they'd all got over it.

The *stupid* thing he kept questioning was, what if Ellory's influence still lurked within him somewhere? What if all the apparent ghostly stuff had been more to do with Coren's personality; a well-hidden dark core that made him treat everyone he loved so appallingly for his own gains?

He glanced now at Sybill and felt his eyebrows draw together in a frown. He was undeniably attracted to her, but was he even capable of letting her in? What if he began to behave like that again? He hadn't been able to stop himself the last time, and even now, a few years on, he was still horrified at what he'd done – what he'd become.

Kit was all loved up with Merryn, and, ironically, even though the brothers spent more time together now than they had done for years before they inherited Pencradoc, he felt somehow removed from his brother. He couldn't forget what he'd done to him, and it had almost caused a rift that might never have healed.

And now Kit and Merryn were going to become parents. They had moved on, quite happily, it seemed, from all the events before. He, on the other hand, almost felt he had retreated into himself, and although he would like nothing more than to take his relationship with Sybill to the next level, would it even be a good idea? Would he not just destroy that as well?

Merryn had, quite bluntly, asked him what he was playing at and why he wouldn't ever give it a chance with her. He had responded that it was a bad idea to get involved with someone you worked with. At this, she and Kit had looked at one another and rolled their eyes in mutual agreement of Coren's blatant stupidity.

For God's sake!

He dragged his gaze away from Sybill and opened his mouth to say something trite as he walked her to the door, when two things happened almost at once.

Firstly, Merryn came through the door, holding an open tourist leaflet and reading it without looking where she was going. Secondly, as Coren put his hands out automatically to stop her crashing into him, he realised they'd stopped next to the marble bust of Elsie at the bottom of the staircase. Elsie had been just a child at the time the bust had been made, but her expression was wonderful and her curls as wild as they were on any of the later pictures of her. "Little Elsie", as everyone called her, encapsulated everything that was vibrant about the girl and foreshadowed the woman she would become.

'Careful! Next time I might just let you walk straight into me.' Coren squeezed Merryn's shoulders gently, then let his hands drop to his side. From where they stood, he noticed someone had draped a locket on a chain around Little Elsie's neck and placed a garland of orangey-yellow flowers around her head.

'Oh! Crikey. Sorry, Coren. I was miles away. Hey, Sybill! Good to see you. I was going to call you again, actually.' Merryn grinned and brandished the leaflet. 'So, it's good that you're both here. Oops. What's that Elsie's got?' She pointed the leaflet towards the bust. 'Jewellery. And pretty flowers too. Gorgeous girl. Aren't some of the visitors sweet, dressing her up when they pass?'

'Hello Merryn – wow. You've blossomed.' A strange look

flickered in Sybill's eyes, then she seemed to pull herself together and grinned back at Merryn – maybe a little too brightly. On second glance, Coren saw that his sister-in-law had indeed expanded since the last time he'd taken much notice of her condition – which was a while ago now, he realised. It was great news for Kit and Merryn, of course it was, but it was one more thing that he needed to think about. Maternity cover. How the hell did he work *that* one out? He felt his eyebrows pull closer together as he thought about it.

'We need to get your maternity cover sorted,' he said, maybe more abruptly than he'd intended. He didn't think he'd meant it to come out quite like that. He opened his mouth to apologise to Merryn, but saw that she was simply looking amused rather than offended. He apologised anyway. 'Sorry.'

'That's okay. I'll help you write the job description. I've got someone in mind, to be fair. No worries. Anyway – it looks like someone lost their necklace, and someone else found it and popped it there for safekeeping.' She brandished the leaflet again at the bust of Elsie, then looked at the leaflet in some surprise, as if she'd just realised she still needed to clarify why she was looking for them both. Coren saw Sybill's eyes follow the pointing leaflet, and then she deftly unhooked the locket.

Then, seeming to fumble around and not quite know what to do with it, she slipped the locket in her pocket and made a big show of moving her head from side to side to try and follow the leaflet that Merryn was now waving hypnotically, left and right, in front of their eyes. 'Yes. So. Elton Lacy has an open day this weekend – one of those charity garden ones. You might want to try and go there to see the place where Elsie had her ball.'

'Merryn, when did you become so butterfly-minded?' Sybill sounded curious and amused at the same time. 'Flitting from lost property, to leaflets, to stately home visits, and reading when you're not looking where you're going. That's not like the organised Merryn I used to know ...'

'Five months ago?' Merryn offered and had the grace to look abashed as she brandished the booklet at her baby bump, before passing the leaflet over to Coren. 'Think about it anyway. See you later.' She wandered off in the direction of the offices and waved over her shoulder to them as she disappeared down the corridor.

'Elton Lacy.' Coren raised his eyebrows and looked down at Sybill. 'Do you want to go? For research. Obviously. Business trip and all that.' He shrugged. 'I've never been. It's a pretty successful hotel and wedding venue now. Still owned by the family by all accounts.'

'So is Pencradoc.' Sybill appeared to be looking almost wistfully after Merryn, her eyes seeming to follow her friend's crazily uncoordinated pregnancy gait, then she turned to Coren and nudged him playfully. The contact, brief as it was, sent a shiver up his arm, and he consciously moved away slightly.

'True.' He nodded. 'It just doesn't seem that way sometimes. But of course it is.' He half-smiled at her, careful not to catch her eye for too long. 'I think it's worth investigating Elton Lacy, though. Spying almost. We've had a few enquiries as to whether we'd ever have weddings at Pencradoc. I'm not exactly against the idea.'

'It would be good if you could make that happen.' Sybill nodded thoughtfully. 'Not that the Teagues are the best advert for marriage. Living in sin, after all! They supported that whole-heartedly, I think.'

'They still got married eventually. Maybe they just wanted to be sure.'

Sybill laughed. 'Four children sure, and that includes Elsie. It always amuses me. Anyway. Yes. I'd love to come with you. A business trip sounds lovely.' She smiled wryly. 'Well, to some it might not, but I'm looking forward to it. When is it?' She nodded at the leaflet. 'Not that it matters. I can make myself available.'

'Great.' Coren flicked through the booklet until he came to the correct page. 'Saturday.' He looked up at her and raised his eyebrows. 'Are you still able to make yourself available?'

'Yes. Oh, Coren. What are we like? The pair of us? Nothing better to do on a Saturday than business research, eh?'

'It's one of our busiest days. We should probably both stay on site. No. Forget it.' He raised his hands in defeat and shook his head. 'We shouldn't go.'

'Yes, we should.' Sybill suddenly took hold of his forearm and brought it down to her level, grabbing the leaflet. 'It looks nice there,' she said, nodding as she flicked through it. 'We should definitely go. No arguments.'

'No arguments.' Coren was still reeling a little from the shock that had run up his arm when she'd touched him again. *God. This wasn't good.* He was wildly attracted to her, and he couldn't trust himself to take it any further – yet he'd basically asked her to spend the day with him.

Who was he today, and would the real him come back, please?

1911

Elsie stood in the room for what seemed like an eternity, not moving, listening as he left and the door shut quietly behind him. As she heard his steps echoing through the hallway and the front door close, she rushed to the window and looked outside, peering out between the curtains so she could see him walk down the street, out into the tree-lined square and disappear into the distance. His shoulders were hunched up inside his overcoat, his hands deep in the pockets. He looked defeated, and she bit her lip so hard that she tasted blood.

Trying not to sob, Elsie turned her back to the window, leaning her hands behind her on the windowsill. She looked around the spacious room, not seeing it, not seeing anything except him, just as he had been there moments ago. Shy, nervous, waiting for an invitation to sit down. The stilted, terrible conversation they'd had. The way he'd leaned towards her as he'd set out the plans for his future.

How had it ever come to this?

She moved her hand briefly and fiddled idly with her locket, and then her gaze alighted on the pile of letters that she'd picked up on the way in this evening. She took a deep breath as she remembered that one of them had Pearl's handwriting on the envelope. Pearl was her beautiful American friend who had married her old friend, Ernest, and was now a mother to four adorable children. Pearl's letters were always cheerful. She could almost hear the gorgeous New York accent coming through the page.

Pushing herself away from the windowsill, she headed over to the letters and sifted through until she found that one. She searched in vain for a letter-opener, eventually settling instead on a palette knife which she used to rip the envelope open.

Instead of the long letter she'd been expecting, there was an invitation inside, along with a single-sided sheet of paper with few words scrawled upon it.

We would so adore it if you would come visit us, the note said. *We're having a party, and Holly and Noel are coming, so, my darling, you have no excuse to refuse. Even my sister and brother are popping across from Paris where they've been taking in the sights! I'm so desperately excited at the thought of having Viola and Sam here, you wouldn't believe it. And we will see you very soon as well! Oh – it's a fancy-dress ball, so be prepared to dress up and be all "afternoonified" as Holly says! A Midsummer Costume Ball. What fun! Of course, it's a few days late on Saturday the 24th June, but we know how deliciously busy you are, so decided to delay it simply for you, chuckaboo! You're our favourite whooper-upper and it wouldn't be a show without Punch.*

Elsie stared at the words until they began to blur into one

another. Well – it wasn't exactly what she would have chosen to do, but it might help take her mind off things. She flipped the invitation over and read it.

According to the date, she had around a month to come up with a costume for the fancy dress ball. 'Oh dear Lord.' She closed her eyes in despair. 'What fun.'

'"What fun" is what, dear girl?'

She opened her eyes, jumping at the amused voice that suddenly came from across the room. 'Fabian! I didn't hear you come in. You gave me a shock.'

'I told Gladys not to introduce me – said you were expecting me. My fault. Looks to me as if you had a shock before I even got here. Everything all right?'

'No. No, not really.' She bit her lip before her voice started to wobble. 'Home things. Things from Pencradoc. You know.' She shrugged.

'Hmmm. Home things. I see.' Fabian's gaze drifted to the overturned sketchpad and he raised his eyebrow. 'May I?'

Elsie shrugged again. 'If you must. Just a sketch. Nothing exciting.'

Fabian half-smiled and flipped it over. His eyes widened for a second, and he looked across at her. 'Just a sketch? I think not. I think that's a portrait full of emotions. Is it him?'

Elsie could do nothing but nod. Fabian knew the story, so there was no point in lying to him. 'Yes. He was … just here, actually.'

'I'm sorry I missed him. But he's a long way from home.'

'Business in the city, apparently. I don't know.' She wasn't going to elaborate on Louis' potential marriage. She couldn't quite bring herself to verbalise that to anyone right now. 'But I do know I just received this.' She brandished the invitation, trying to steer her friend off the subject of Louis. 'This is the "fun" I was referring to. A ball. A Midsummer Costume Ball. Hideous. I can't even smile at Pearl's silly language today.'

'Darling, you love parties!' Fabian laughed and sat down

on the seat Louis had vacated not so long ago, throwing himself into it, all arms and legs and curious eyes, waiting for her to elaborate.

'I do. But *ugh*. I'm just not in the mood, I suppose. Unless!' She strode over to Fabian and leaned down, putting her hands firmly on his shoulders. 'Unless you come with me. You can escort me, because God knows I'll need an escort, with all my friends being desperately in love with one another now, and it's an excellent way to introduce you to Teague properly.'

'To Teague?' Fabian's eyes widened, and for a moment he looked very young and quite star-struck.

'To Teague.' Elsie laughed. The famous artist Ruan Teague was her step-father – although Elsie suspected the familial link was a little closer than that, but it wasn't something she could say out loud to most people. 'I've told him all about you and he's keen to meet you – if anyone can introduce you to the right people to make things happen, he can. I know you want to specialise in Society portraiture, and he will know exactly what you need to do and who you need to work with. Trust me.'

'Trust you.' Fabian nodded mechanically. His mind was obviously with Teague in another realm somewhere, talking about portraiture over a decent brandy. 'I will. Thank you.'

'Good man.' Elsie brushed some imaginary dust off his shoulders and kissed the top of his head fondly. 'Now, Fabian Austen, let's have a cup of tea and a good gossip, shall we?'

As she headed over to the wall to ring the bell, her smile slipped a little. Louis' news had upset her and she was still reeling, both from seeing him and from hearing what he'd had to say.

It was simple. She loved Louis, heart and soul. But they could never be together. Not after what had happened four years ago. In fact, she could never be with anybody.

'Did you see Elsie then?' Louis' mother asked the question

politely as she sipped her tea and laid the next row of cards out for her game of Patience.

'Yes, she's just the same old Elsie.' Louis sat down opposite Lady Ashby. 'Although perhaps a bit wilder looking.' He half-smiled at the memory.

'I swear that child is a witch.' Lady Ashby smiled as she moved some cards around. 'Always has been. Like an ... enchantress.' She wiggled her fingers around in a mystical manner, and Louis couldn't help but laugh.

'An enchantress. Of course.'

'Is she going to Pearl and Ernest's party?' His mother looked up at him questioningly. 'I've been told they're holding a costume ball. I do believe there's an invitation for you over there, dear.' She waved vaguely in the direction of a side table.

'I wouldn't know. I suppose she might have been invited.'

'You might perhaps consider taking Margaret with you? It could be another opportunity for her to meet your friends – I don't think she's met many of them, has she?'

'No.' Louis stood up and headed over to the table. He picked the invitation up and studied it. Margaret had never really shown any inclination to want to meet his friends. She had declined every other event they'd been invited to. 'Perhaps. It might be quite fun to attend this one. A Midsummer Costume Ball.'

'You could go as a pair. King Henry and one of his queens. William Shakespeare and Anne Hathaway. King Arthur and Guinevere. So many to choose from.'

'Possibly.' A brief image flitted across his mind – he in the guise of King Arthur, but by his side, Elsie as Morgan le Fay. Far more exciting than Margaret dressed as Guinevere. 'Elsie and I went to another ball, and we did the Arthurian theme then. I don't know if I would care to do it again.'

He meant, of course, that he didn't want to try to recreate that with anyone else but Elsie.

He couldn't. He just couldn't.

'Oh! Of course.' His mother nodded. 'That was the summer before she left for London, wasn't it?'

'It was.'

Another reason why he didn't want to try to recreate it – how could you ever improve on the perfect evening? Although she had disappeared to London afterwards, so perhaps it had only been perfect for him.

Elsie may well be an enchantress, and that was probably why he couldn't explain any of it away any more – no matter how hard he tried.

Chapter Four

Present Day

Saturday came eventually, after what felt like approximately a century's wait to Sybill. She was ridiculously excited about it – far more so than she should have been for something that was just a research trip.

Coren had offered to meet her at Elton Lacy to save her travelling to Pencradoc first, but she had politely declined the offer, offering instead to come up to Pencradoc so they could go together. So here they were. She was driving, and he was sitting in the passenger seat flicking through a few pages he'd printed out from the Lacy website.

'It's got private gardens, which only the wedding parties are allowed to use – stops people who are just at the restaurant or something wandering in there while the weddings are on.'

'Does it actually say that?' Sybill flashed a quick sideways look at him and grinned. She was rewarded by one of those funny little half-smiles that were all too rare, and therefore even more precious when they occurred.

'Not in so many words. But I am well versed in reading between the lines in these things. I guess those are the gardens they've got open today.'

'Do you think you'd ever open a restaurant at Pencradoc?' Sybill was curious.

'God, no. The tea room is enough. It's not what we're about at all. We're not a conference centre or a hotel or anything like that.'

Sybill nodded. 'Right answer. A restaurant makes it more formal, doesn't it?'

'It does. Takes away the spirit of it.'

'I'd not allow one at Wheal Mount either. Our tea room is also enough.'

'Good. I'd not come to your restaurant.' He flashed her a quick teasing look, and she laughed. 'Well, here we are anyway. It's pretty full already. They've even got a Man directing traffic to car parking spaces!'

'A Man, indeed. You know, I can almost hear that capital "M" at the beginning.'

'It was said with a capital "M". Here we go. All parked up. Put your papers away. You look like a complete spy.'

Coren actually laughed at that one. 'Shhhh. I won't tell if you won't.'

'I won't. Don't worry.'

They got out of the car and followed the winding pathway up to the house. 'Wow. Look at that! I think we could put Pencradoc in the left wing and Wheal Mount in the right, and still have space left over,' Sybill said, as they rounded the corner and saw the immense, imposing house before them.

'It's bloody huge!' Coren appeared stunned. 'God. I'm glad Pencradoc isn't this big. It would have taken Merryn a year to do our inventory and six months to find any interesting portraits ...' His words tailed off and he seemed quick to change the subject. 'So. This house had American dollars poured into it, yes?'

'Yes. I think they extended the original building even more when Pearl Arthur came into the family in the early 1900s. I know she and her husband had several children, but I'm not sure it warranted an extension of that size.'

'Who knows? I don't want to think of their heating bill though.'

'Ever practical.' Sybill was amused. 'Come on. Let's pay our way and indulge in some espionage.'

So they did. And the espionage, it had to be said, was rather fun.

Sybill almost felt like she'd been transported to some other life as she found herself ignoring the official map and heading wherever she fancied, laughing and talking with Coren as they made their way through the grounds. He seemed more relaxed today and was happy to follow in her wake. They walked through garden rooms, linked by clever pathways lined by topiary and colourful plants: the red garden, the box garden, the lavender walk … the list went on. Here and there were follies and gazebos: a temple to the four winds, a banqueting hall, a Roman garden set out to look like a forum with broken columns and statuary, an Egyptian garden, a Swiss garden …

'Oh!' Sybill suddenly came to a halt at a beautifully classic archway covered in honeysuckle and climbing roses, warmed by the early summer sun. The scent was incredible and she sniffed appreciatively. 'This is rather special.'

'As special as Rose's Garden?' Again, Coren quirked that funny little look at her and she couldn't help but laugh.

'No. Not as special. Don't worry. Rose's Garden is super-special.' She patted him on the arm, meaning only to confirm that the Gothic rose garden at Pencradoc, designed by Duchess Rose in the late nineteenth century, was indeed super-special. Instead, she removed her hand quickly as an electric shock zinged up through her fingers.

She shoved her hands in the pockets of the smart dove-grey cardigan she'd slung on that morning as an afterthought. She'd only worn it in case it got a bit chilly in the gardens, despite the fact it was supposed to be summer.

Her fingers curled around something small and oval and cool to the touch. The locket – the one from "Little Elsie".

'Oh my, Coren. I'm so sorry. I'm an absolute thief.' She pulled the locket out of her pocket and was about to offer it to him, when he looked over her shoulder and pointed through the honeysuckle arch.

'What's that?'

She followed his gaze, and it was almost as if cotton-wool or a heavy mist descended on them, muffling the sounds of the garden – the sound of the bees disappeared, there was no breeze rustling through the leaves above them, no sound of the water spilling out of the fountain into the Bathing Pool that was in the garden room they were looking at.

Instead there were two shapes, and the whole garden room seemed to reflect a strange trick of the light, making the shapes appear almost like moonlit silhouettes. To Sybill, the image looked like a man and a woman sitting on the edge of the pool. The woman was dressed in what looked like a black cloak, the man in eighteenth-century finery. The woman turned suddenly and plunged her feet into the water, and the man reached out. Then, just as quickly as they had appeared, the area brightened, the shadows lifted and the sounds of summer were with them again.

Sybill blinked and rubbed her eyes. When she opened them again, the edge of the Bathing Pool was empty. There was nobody there at all. What a strange little place this was – totally muffled and private and hidden away from everything.

Maybe the people who'd been there had slipped away down another pathway. Maybe they'd been Lacy staff, taking a break from publicity photos perhaps. They'd sort of looked as if they'd been having a cigarette break, after all.

'Where've they gone?' Coren asked the question aloud, but there was no reply from Sybill, who stood looking stunned beside him, clutching something in her outstretched hand. It seemed she had been interrupted from passing whatever it was across to him.

'I–I don't know. There *was* someone there, wasn't there?' Sybill looked up at him.

'I thought that there was – in fact—' Coren suddenly felt as if someone rushed right past him and involuntarily he jumped aside, turning to see who it was. There was nobody there – but there was a trail of stems twisting and turning, flowers nodding, as if in the wake of a pretty strong breeze. He shivered, and as a feeling like a fist of ice punching into his chest came over him, he gasped.

'No … no, I think we're mistaken.' Sybill peered along the pathway, then took a couple of tentative steps. 'No. Nobody there. Gosh. Oh!' It was her turn to jump to the side. Then she shook her head. 'Glad I've never seen a ghost, or I'd think that was a ghost in a hurry. Or that maybe those people were ghosts. Oh well. Pretty sure ghosts don't look that … solid … anyway.'

Coren didn't answer. Sybill had been involved with Pencradoc long enough to enjoy the tales that Merryn gleefully told her about the Pencradoc ghosts, but she was clearly unconvinced they could look as real as a normal person and act like one too.

Part of him wanted Sybill to remain blissfully unaware of the dark secrets that sometimes haunted Pencradoc, and just to revel in the beautiful place it was nowadays. But another part of him wanted her to know the stories for what they were – and the fact that he completely believed in the strange goings-on at that place.

But it seemed Sybill's mind had moved on. 'Why don't we have a look up there? It seems lovely and peaceful.' She headed further along, and after a moment's hesitation, just in case any ghosts were lurking nearby, he fell into step beside her.

'Anyway. Here!' She half-turned and brandished her hand again. 'If I don't give this to you right now, I'll pilfer it again.' She shook her fist and then sat down on the edge of the Bathing Pool. 'Come on. Have a seat.' She smiled up at him and patted the ledge. 'Glad those two didn't leave their cigarette butts lying around.'

'Okay.' Coren hesitated and looked around. He was certain he'd seen some people in here, but there was absolutely no trace of them. And no scent of tobacco either. They might have gone out of another exit, but he certainly hadn't seen them leave. They'd just … disappeared.

Unless, as Sybill had said, they'd just moved away down

the other path and he'd missed it. Still, the feeling unsettled him a little.

He decided he was being ridiculous and sat down next to Sybill. She opened her hand and he saw the locket lying on her palm.

'This is the one from the other day – when we saw Merryn and she told us about this open day. I had the same cardigan on. I must have just put it in my pocket and got distracted. Did anyone query it? I'm going to feel really bad if someone's been asking for it and I had it all along.'

'Nobody's said anything to me. Perhaps they haven't missed it yet. No harm done anyway. I'll take it back with me tonight and put it in lost property.'

'Thanks.' Sybill dropped the locket into his palm, and as their hands connected, he had a flash of an image in his memory – something half-remembered, the feeling of that very same locket in his hand. Their eyes locked for a moment.

Sybill cleared her throat and drew her hand away. 'Do you think we should open it?' she asked after a moment. 'Just to see what's in it?'

He didn't miss the fact she was flexing her fingers, and then she clasped her hands together as if steadying them. Her knuckles were almost white through her skin, she had them clenched together so tightly.

'Perhaps we should.' Then, and he didn't know what made him do it, he handed it back to her. Her hands separated and she took hold of it again. They were shaking a little now, but she nodded and bent her head to the piece of jewellery.

And when she opened it, it was as if a sob caught in her throat and she snapped it shut, thrusting it back into his hands before standing up and hurrying away from him as fast as she possibly could.

'Sybill!' Coren stood up and ran after her. He reached her just before she disappeared through the gap in the honeysuckle arch and touched her shoulder. It stopped her from bolting, and she turned around to face him, an odd expression in her eyes.

'I can't look at that again. I can't.'

'Why not?' Coren was confused. He opened the locket, keeping it out of her line of sight and frowned. There were two perfectly lovely little watercolour pictures inside it; one of a man and one of a toddler. The man looked kind. He was half-smiling, his hair was fair like Coren's, his eyes the same grey. The little girl was quite clearly his daughter – she had the same eyes, the same nose. Only she had a little heart-shaped face, and her hair was wild and dark and curly, refusing to be tamed into bunches either side of her chubby cheeks. She was grinning out at the viewer, confident and cheerful ... and strangely familiar.

'These are beautiful. Such careful work. Antique, I'd say – someone must really be missing them. I know I would if it was mine.'

Sybill shook her head. 'Antique? I don't know. She – she looks like. Well.' She blushed a furious crimson and tried to smile, but it wobbled off her face. 'She looks like my daughter.'

1911

After Fabian had left, Elsie found she couldn't settle at all. Making a decision, she marched through the house and out through the back door. She grabbed her bicycle and wheeled it back into the house, bumping it across the wooden floorboards to the front door. She pulled the door open and bounced it down to the path. There was no need to explain herself, and she pushed off, cycling the three miles or so north west towards Regent's Park, Primrose Hill and Chalcot Crescent.

She reached the tall, graceful house with the pillars either side of the door and the little wrought iron balcony across the first floor, and there she dismounted elegantly and rang the bell, her heart pounding as it always did when she visited here.

The door opened and within moments she was inside the chaotic, friendly house of her great friends, Lily and Edwin Griffiths.

'Elsie!' Lily came towards her, holding her arms out and Elsie stepped into the older woman's embrace gratefully. Lily had once been an actress and had married Edwin, an ex-soldier, when Elsie was eight. Edwin was a friend of Elsie's Uncle Jago, the Duke of Trecarrow, and the couple had come to Pencradoc shortly after they were married. Sixteen years later, Edwin and Lily were settled with their family in picturesque Primrose Hill. Their oldest boy, Albert was an awkward, blushing fifteen-year old, lost in his music half the time, and was unable to hide his hero worship of Elsie, who treated him much as she treated her younger siblings. Lily and Edwin also had a fourteen-year-old daughter, Evie, a twelve-year-old boy, Edward, and then there was little Marigold, only three years old, spoiled and indulged by every single one of them. 'How lovely to see you! We didn't expect you until tomorrow. Haven't you just had a ghastly day at work?'

Elsie smiled, loving Lily's gentle Irish accent. 'It wasn't too ghastly. Some rather tempestuous natures and a few tears, but what can one expect, immersed in such creativity all day? I can be rather tearful and tempestuous myself at times.'

'Can't we all?' Lily kissed her on the cheek and led her by the hand into the reception room. 'You just sit down and let us look after you for a wee while.'

'Thank you.' She let her shoulders relax. Since Louis' visit, they felt as if they had been hunched up around her chin somewhere.

'I'll get you some tea and cake, shall I? Then you can talk. You look as if you need to talk.' Lily frowned and reached forwards, touching Elsie's hand. 'What is it? Is it Louis?'

Elsie laughed shortly. 'You're so perceptive. Yes. Yes, it is. Lily, he came to my house today.'

'Your house!' Lily was shocked. 'Oh *acushla*, my darling. Why was that?'

Elsie blinked away a silly tear or two, mainly on hearing Lily's old pet name for her. 'He said he had business in the city. But I think he just came to tell me he's getting married. There now. I've said it. Ha! Why doesn't it sound so terrible when I say it out loud? When I *think* it, it truly drives me batty.'

'Did he really say he was getting married?' Lily raised her eyebrows, clearly used to Elsie's grandiose declarations.

'Well. No. Not quite. He just said it was possibly on the cards.' She pulled a face. 'To Margaret Corrington of all people. Ugh. Awful, awful chit of a woman. Could tell him a few things about her. Really could.'

'You can stop it happening. You can just ... *tell* him.' Lily looked at her appraisingly. 'It might be time?'

'No. No, I can't.' Elsie shook her head, and poor Lily looked defeated. It wasn't the first time she'd suggested that course of action. Elsie had always been very clear about why she couldn't tell Louis *anything* – what would it do to him, to his reputation, to both their families?

'Well, *acushla*, it's your decision.' Lily smiled a little sadly and stood up. 'I'll go and get the little one, shall I? She's upstairs, busy with Evie's old dolls' house, I believe.'

Elsie clapped her hands. 'Wonderful. I say, can I go up and surprise her? I just want to pick her up and give her the biggest cuddle in the world.'

'I'm sure you can.' Lily smiled and walked over to the bell. 'You go up, I'll sort tea and cake out. Be as long as you like. Bring her downstairs if you want to. She'll love it – tea and cakes like a big girl. I'll get some milk as well. She can have that.'

'Thank you.' Elsie smiled at Lily, her heart flooding with love for her one-time idol, and now the woman she entrusted with her darkest secrets.

Elsie crept upstairs, her heart thumping as she made her way along the corridor to the nursery. There, she knew the little girl would be amusing herself with Evie's old toys. At Pencradoc, there was a nursery full of little girls' treasures, and Elsie knew the child would love to explore the trunks full of dolls and shelves of books, the old dressing-up boxes that still made Elsie smile when she thought of the plays and pageants she had organised over the years with her siblings and cousins. *One day*. One day, she would take Marigold there and show her it all.

She'd let her run around the grounds and slide down the banister of the grand staircase in the hallway, just as she had done herself when she was younger. She'd let her sit in the kitchens and eat apple pie, hot out of the oven with lashings of clotted cream. She'd let her do all those things and more.

Elsie pushed open the door to the nursery quietly and peeped inside. Sure enough, Marigold was sitting cross-legged in front of the doll's house, a doll in each hand, making them have a conversation. Her dark, curly hair was tamed with two ribbons, but she still looked dishevelled and slightly untidy, and as if she'd had a very good day indeed.

'Boo!' Elsie said loudly, and Marigold squeaked in delight, turning round, the dolls held aloft.

'Mama! *Mama!*' She scrambled to her feet and ran across to Elsie, flinging her arms around her legs. 'Mama! Are we going home today? Because I have to tell Aunt Lily if we are.'

Elsie nuzzled the wild, curly hair, so like her own. 'Well, now. Show me what you're doing here, then we'll go and have milk and cake. And then we can decide. How about that?'

'How about *that*,' the little girl echoed, and rubbed her nose on Elsie's best black skirt.

Margaret was having tea with Louis and his family. Her mother had decided to pay a visit, with Margaret, of course, and Louis noticed Mrs Corrington's small, keen eyes darting around the morning room, assessing the value of everything the Ashbys had on display; from the family silver on the dresser, to the portraits of long-dead Ashbys by Reynolds, Gainsborough and the like, to the inlaid walnut writing desk in the window which had been his grandmother's. Margaret, on the other hand, sat primly like a little blonde doll – not a hair out of place, not a smudge of dirt on her pink dress. And not a bit of life in her face.

He took a fresh look at her and couldn't help comparing the little doll-like creature to the spirited Elsie. He could almost understand why his older brother, Drew, had disappeared one summer and come back married to the vibrant Felicity instead, just when the families had initially begun to ponder a potential match between the pair. Drew and Felicity were happily ensconced in Surrey for now. They'd come back and live here at Ashby Court when they had to, and when Drew had to take over – but in the meantime, their father was busy ensuring Louis knew what to do around the estate in terms of caretaking. They were all hopeful that it would be several years before Drew had to come back here permanently, and were grateful that Sir Aubrey Ashby was fighting fit once more after his short bout of illness.

As they sat there today, Louis couldn't help thinking about all the times Elsie had been in that very same room, had sat in that very same seat, giggling and chattering, her eyes sparkling, her laughter ringing throughout the house.

'—Midsummer Costume Ball. Am I right, darling?' Lady Ashby's voice jolted him out of his reverie, and he smiled politely, trying to think what the context of that comment might be.

'Midsummer Costume Ball. Quite.' He nodded, wisely, he hoped, and sipped his tea which was in a ridiculously small teacup patterned with blue flowers.

'It will be delightful for you to attend, I think. I used to love costume balls when I was younger.' Lady Ashby smiled at Louis. 'My favourite outfit was that of a mermaid.'

'A mermaid?' He was astonished and looked at his mother

in a new light. She was only in her mid-forties, hardly ancient, but he couldn't for the life of him imagine her dressed as a siren of the sea.

'Well, I didn't have a fishy tail, of course,' she continued. 'Rather a blue, green and silver dress, cleverly designed to look as if it was flowing somewhat, with a sort of train at the back that one could flick about if one wished by way of loops of fabric around one's thumbs. Your father went as Neptune, Louis. We made a wonderful pair. He even had a trident and a crown of shells.'

'I see.' Louis fought back a smile. It was rather hard to imagine his somewhat staid father in the guise of Neptune – never mind his mother dressed as a mermaid to escort him and flick her sparkling tail around the ballrooms of Cornwall. Elsie would love that story; she would—

'I preferred not to attend those sort of gatherings.' Mrs Corrington was disapproving. 'However, Margaret is excited to attend this one. Despite it being arranged by ... an *American*.' She mouthed rather than spoke the last word.

'Pearl and Ernie are very dear friends of ours – of mine, I mean.' Louis couldn't help himself. They *were* great friends – Elsie had always welcomed Pearl into the fold and swept them up into her orbit quite happily. He knew they had stayed in touch with Elsie, and he realised then that, yes, Elsie would probably have been invited. She just *would* have been. It was ridiculous to assume otherwise. Of course she may choose not to come, which would be understandable.

He remembered the last ball they had attended together, and the image of Elsie laughing up at him, the scent of champagne faint on her breath.

Involuntarily, he smiled at the thought, then quickly rearranged his expression to one of more solemnity. His father would be proud.

'I am looking forward to going,' he said in an earnest tone, nodding into his teacup.

'And Margaret is looking forward to going with you,' said Mrs Corrington firmly. 'It's time she was introduced to your friends – to more of the local … *families*.'

Louis looked up in surprise, and involuntarily caught Margaret's eye. *Really?*

'Yes. I'm quite willing to attend the ball with you, Louis. Thank you. I most certainly need to meet more of your circle. After all, our paths may cross quite a lot more in the future.' She blushed prettily, looking even more like a little porcelain doll.

Louis nodded again, equally seriously. But he couldn't for the life of him remember actually asking Margaret to go at all …

And the only reason he thought Mrs Corrington wanted Margaret to get to know Pearl and Ernie was because Pearl and Ernie were the wealthiest "*family*" for absolutely miles around.

Chapter Five

Present Day

Sybill hadn't meant to say that. In fact, it was something she'd never said to anybody. Ever. Her daughter? She had to remind herself she didn't have a daughter – not a living one anyway.

'Your daughter?' Coren was understandably shocked. 'Sybill? I ... I ...' He shook his head. 'I don't know what to say. I didn't know you had – had a – daughter ...' His voice trailed away and she waited for the inevitable. The backing away from her. The clear lack of knowing what to say. *Oh well. Best get it over with.*

'I don't. I don't have a daughter.' She shrugged. 'But I had one. Technically, she died before she was born. I don't want to go into it. She didn't survive past twenty-four weeks. I don't know what went wrong, but, whatever it was, she didn't live.' She sat down on a bench, her knees buckling as she collapsed in on herself and hid her face in her hands. 'Sorry, Coren. You shouldn't have had to find out like this. I shouldn't have told you.' She shook her head, her face still hidden. 'She would have been ten now. It was a long time ago.'

There was a beat, and she waited for Coren to cough, to clear his throat, to go, "Well now. Okay. Fancy that." Or to add something else trite in the same sort of conversational way.

Instead, she felt him sit down next to her. His arm wrapped around her and he pulled her towards him. He didn't say a word as he gently guided her face into his body and let her find a place to snuggle into. She just sat there, her face buried in his shoulder, as she sobbed away the hurt of the last few years.

When she'd calmed down, she drew away and looked up at him, conscious of the fact that her face must be red and blotchy. She knew her nose was leaking most inelegantly, and her eyes felt as if they were swollen to three times their normal size. She saw that his eyes were damp too, and he looked as if he would willingly join her if he let himself go.

'I'm so sorry,' she said. 'It normally doesn't come over me like that.'

Coren shook his head. 'You go ahead and do what you need to do. You don't need to apologise to me.' Then, to her surprise, he leaned forward and kissed her forehead, before brushing her damp hair away from her face.

'Thanks. God.' She shook her head and straightened herself up. 'I do owe you an explanation, though. I can't just dump all that shit on you and expect you to ignore it.' She tried a watery smile and was surprised to feel it stay on her lips for a few seconds. So she took a deep breath, ready to talk to him. 'I got pregnant to my boyfriend after we'd only been together for a couple of months. It wasn't planned but it happened, and we decided to make the best of it. We got married, rented a house and were all set to try and do the grown-up thing of having a family. Marco's Italian. He's a sculptor and he was only over here working for the summer – at Wheal Mount, of all places – but we just clicked. And it was romantic, and he was a bit exotic and desperately good-looking. I was twenty five and probably old enough to know better – but I got as carried away as he did. We got a bit wild, and I took things I probably shouldn't have taken, and I drank more than I should have drunk. And then I found out I was pregnant.' She shifted uncomfortably. 'At the time, we swore that it was fate and it was meant to be, and it wouldn't have happened if it wasn't meant to, and all of that stuff. It was one crazy, mixed-up, messed-up summer. I hate to say it, but too much of it's a blur now. We thought we were invincible. We ended up cleaning up our act and getting married.

'Like I told you, I lost her at twenty-four weeks. We called her Lucia. We'd literally been married three months, and then suddenly what was there to hold us together? No baby. No family ties. No reason to stay married, really. We muddled on for a bit, tried to make the best of it, but we just drifted apart and fell back into our old ways to try and forget. We eventually came to the painful realisation that we probably weren't meant to be together after all. Marco took it all pretty badly as well ... we did love each other in our own way, and Lucia *was* his daughter too. I came home from work one day, and he'd gone. He'd packed his bags and returned to Italy, leaving me a little note that told me how much he loved me and her, and that he just needed some space to clear his head. He promised he'd be back – but of course he didn't come back. It's been long enough now, and I think we've both finally decided to do the proper grown-up thing and cut each other loose. That's what I was dealing with when you called me the other day. I was on the phone to the solicitor. I can't keep hold of Marco and he needs to let me go too. We owe it to one another ... gosh.' She rubbed her face and pressed the heels of her hands into her eyes, taking a deep breath. 'Wow. So now you know.'

'I do. And thank you. Thank you for trusting me.' There was a quiet moment where Coren didn't need to say anything, but Sybill knew he was silently working it out in his head, giving her time to breathe as he did it. 'One more thing, though, if you don't mind me asking. You said this little girl looked like her? Like Lucia? How ...'

Coren didn't finish the sentence but Sybill nodded anyway, realising what he wanted to say. 'Yes. It sounds really crazy, but I dream of her. I dream of her running around the grounds of Wheal Mount – and she's even at Pencradoc now, because I dream of her there too.' She felt a bit silly saying that, but somehow she knew deep down she didn't have to feel silly because Coren would just accept it. 'She's just like that little dot there – the girl in the locket. Obviously, I don't know exactly what she would have looked like, but I know she would have had crazy, wild hair just like that, just like mine, and I always see her with her hair tied in bunches, the same as that little girl. She's got the same smile, the same little cheeky face.' She felt like she was going to lose it again and took a deep, steadying breath. 'So, when I saw that little thing in that picture, I couldn't help but associate her with Lucia. Now do you understand why I started to run off?'

'I do.' Coren's voice was soft. 'It explains a lot.'

'Yes.' Sybill nodded and felt herself grow red again. It explained a hell of a lot. It explained as well, for example, why she'd never tried harder to take it further with Coren. Part of her felt as if it was still tied to Marco and Lucia – if she let them go, what would be left of her? And if she didn't let them go – then how could she ever move on with her life?

Marco had sort of made things easier. He'd been over a few weeks ago, turned up on the doorstep, and said they needed to sort things out once and for all. They'd talked, they'd cried, they'd even almost made love – but, bizarrely, something had stopped her from doing that, from making that final farewell to a man she had shared so much with – and she knew exactly what that something was. It was time for Sybill to put the lid on the box, and package Marco and Lucia away in a little corner of her heart where those precious few months could be cared for safely. She had to allow herself to walk away from the past once and for all.

Because the whole time she had been with Marco, trying to thrash out the details of their dying relationship, all she wanted to do was run to Coren.

Coren was conscious of the weight of the locket in his hand. How could one small object do that to someone as strong as Sybill? He glanced down at her and wondered afresh about how much a person really knew another person. He'd been half in love – well, completely in love – with Sybill for years. But did he really know anything about her?

The answer was, of course, he knew about as much as she had been prepared to share. But funnily enough, now he had been entrusted with her deepest secret – the fact that she had lost a baby almost six months into a pregnancy – he felt as if he didn't need to ask anything else of her. Whatever there was in her life that she wanted to share, she'd do it in her own time, and nothing would be quite as difficult as telling him that story.

And Marco! Of all things, he'd never expected her to produce a husband out of thin air. *Hang on—*

'So, forgive me for asking, but with regards to Marco ... does all that mean you're still married to him? That you've been married to him all this time?'

'Yes. I suppose it does. We loved each other once. We don't love each other like that any more. It's all going through its death throes at the minute.' She pulled a face. 'Bad analogy, but it does feel like that – another end to something. It was hard to make the break because of Lucia. But now – now I think it's the right time.' She looked up at him, and for a moment his heart stuttered. There was something in her eyes that hinted at the reason behind that, but he was too afraid to ask.

Too afraid to let her in – because what about bloody Ellory?

He looked away, and his eye caught the garden map sticking out of Sybill's pocket. She'd shoved it in there when they'd hurried into the Bathing Pool area through that honeysuckle arch. 'May I?' He indicated the map, and that little spark in her eyes dimmed as she looked away.

'Of course.' She handed it over and folded her hands in her lap.

'Thanks.' He unfolded it and read through some of the text. 'Oh – look. That looks fun.' He pointed to something on the map and smiled at her. He felt truly terrible that he was so reserved when he was with her, and often he had wondered why she hadn't just slapped him when he was being his most aloof. It wasn't an attractive trait, and despite what it looked like, it didn't come naturally to him. Anybody who had known him pre-Pencradoc would have barely recognised him now.

He was lucky that Kit was so tied up with Merryn and the impending baby, or he would have definitely said something by now. God, that was another thing, wasn't it? Seeing Merryn drifting around the estate at the minute was probably killing Sybill.

Involuntarily, he moved closer to her and put his arm around her, squeezing her quickly in a hug. She looked surprised and, if he was honest, why wouldn't she? The thought did make him fight back a smile.

'What looks like fun?' She hadn't moved away from his embrace, which was a good sign.

'This. They're doing tours of the Lacy so potential guests can see which rooms are available for the weddings.'

'Ohhhh.' She began to smile. It was a wobbly smile but a smile nevertheless. 'I can see where this is going.'

'Me too. Are we or are we not here to spy on the Love Rivals?'

'The *Love Rivals*?' She snorted a laugh, then quickly turned it into a cough. 'I like it.'

'Good. I mean, I'm up for it if you are? We can tag along on a tour, spy a bit more. Only if you feel like it though. I mean – that's a hell of a thing you've told me this morning.' He was suddenly serious. 'I can understand if you just want to call it a day and head back.'

'I don't want to call it a day.' She shook her head vehemently. 'Oddly, I feel a bit better now, you know.' She glanced at the locket and studied it. 'Actually. May *I*?'

'Yes. Of course.' He handed it over to her, then watched as she opened it and felt his heart break a little for her as she traced the face of the little girl with her forefinger.

'It's not her. Of course it's not. I'm sure hundreds of little girls look like that.' She took a deep breath and closed the locket, handing it back to him. 'It was just a shock, that's all. I'd like to know who it was though.'

'And the man? Do you think it's her father?'

'Perhaps.' She flushed. 'I didn't look too closely at him. He looked pretty familiar though – one of many people who had their miniatures painted like that, back in the day. I see them all the time in my line of business. Come on – if you want to do the tour, we'd best head that way. We can catch the twelve-thirty one – then I'll buy you a cup of tea and a scone, and we can jeer at them and tell them Sorcha's are better.'

'I like your style.' Coren stood up and held his hand out. 'Come on. Let's go and be James Bond for a bit.'

Sybill giggled, and it was a lovely sound. 'The way we're behaving, I think we're more like Bond villains. All this subterfuge.'

'But isn't it fun?'

'It is!'

He took her hand and hauled her up off the bench. Then, despite the seriousness of the conversation they'd just had, they hurried off towards the Lacy, laughing all the way.

1911

Back at Brunswick Square, Marigold was settling down for the evening in the drawing room, curled up on a comfy chair and singing a song to a doll, as Elsie, restless as ever, pottered around picking up stray pieces of artwork and shuffling sketches together, thrusting them into a satchel to take to the Slade on Monday. She had a few of her favourite pictures in her office there, and she involuntarily picked up the one of Louis, then wondered what she really wanted to do with it.

'Who's that?' Marigold had clearly grown bored of her doll and scrambled out of the chair to wander over to Elsie. 'He looks nice. But he's not Fabian.' She shook her head solemnly. 'You have more pictures of that man in our house, don't you?'

'I do. But no, he's not Fabian. He's someone I don't see a lot of any more, that's all.' She stuffed the picture in her satchel. It was the best way to hide it from a curious child. 'I say – I've been invited to a party. Isn't that exciting? And do you know what? I have to dress up!'

'Oh!' Marigold's grey eyes widened, the picture of the nice man apparently forgotten which was, of course, Elsie's intention. 'I like to dress up.'

'I know you do, my darling. What do you think I should dress up as?'

'A princess.' The answer to Marigold was simple; didn't everyone want to be a princess?

'Yes. That's an excellent idea.' Elsie smiled at her daughter. 'Now, I think it might be time for bed, don't you?'

Marigold began to shake her head, then a yawn escaped and she rubbed her eyes. 'No. No, I don't think so.'

She yawned again and Elsie, laughing, scooped her up. 'I think so. Come along. I'll read a story to you and tuck you in.'

'All right.' Marigold relented and snuggled into Elsie's arms. 'I do like coming here to sleep,' she murmured. 'But I like Aunt Lily's home as well. They are all very kind.'

'They are.'

'I know you are busy and they have to look after me a lot of the time. I am very lucky. I have two houses.'

Elsie's heart twisted a little. If only the child knew which other houses she had – Pencradoc, for a start. And she'd adore the other family home at Wheal Mount as well – but the timing had never been right to introduce her to either of those places. And she was afraid to admit that, as time went on, it seemed to be a worse and worse moment to do so. How the hell could she introduce a three-year-old to the family and merrily admit that she, Lady Elsie Pencradoc, had fallen pregnant at the age of twenty and not confessed that fact to a soul apart from Lily, Edwin and Fabian?

It was the most difficult decision she'd ever had to make,

to keep it all a secret, and despite the fact that the black, bottomless guilt often overwhelmed her, she told herself it was for the best that nobody knew at home. Her reputation was devilish as it was – she had never been conventional, never *wanted* to be conventional, but her parents and her siblings, not to mention Louis and Louis' family, didn't deserve to suffer for her mistakes. She simply couldn't do that to the people she loved most in the world, and have her actions and choices reflected back on them in such a way. The Margaret Corringtons of this world had enough ammunition against her. They didn't need more of the stuff to throw at her little family.

It was almost unthinkable, and even now she felt herself grow hot when she remembered how she had fled to London as soon as she knew she was pregnant, and how she had charmed her way into the Slade after Marigold was born – so she at least had an excuse to stay in London, to be close to her daughter and Lily, and to be well away from everyone else who knew her.

'Louis! Louis Ashby! We've found you.' There was a voice from behind him, and he turned and looked up, closing the newspaper he had bought to read as he waited in the Bodmin tea shop for Margaret.

'Pearl. And Holly. How delightful to see you.' He stood up and smiled, indicating that the young women, Elsie's great friends and by default part of Louis' social set as well, should sit down at the table. 'Please. Allow me.' He pulled out two chairs and stood while they made themselves comfortable. In Holly's case, it seemed to be a little more difficult easing herself into the space. It looked as if she was due to have the baby quite soon, and appeared very grateful to be seated. 'And how are you ladies today? Can I tempt you into a pot of tea and a scone at all?'

'Well, now, that's exactly what we came in here for,' said

Pearl, smiling widely. She'd never lost her American accent, and the sound of it made Louis grin. Her four-year-old twins would sometimes lapse into the accent as well, despite having a perfectly correct English nursemaid to learn from. The other two children were too young to have much conversation, but Louis knew they would inevitably grow up with the same wonderful speech patterns.

'How fortunate that I'm here then. Let me organise that for you.' He waved a waitress over and ordered, then sat back in his chair, happy to have the company of people he didn't have to try too hard with; people he could just be himself with.

And people who knew Elsie, who might be able to talk to him about her.

'Are you here alone? It's a crying shame if you are. You should be glad we came along.' Pearl took a sip of the tea Louis had poured out for her and replaced the small cup in the saucer. 'Holly and Noel are staying with us at the Lacy for a little while. We thought we'd come here and have a little treat while the boys do other, very intense, things which don't interest us much.'

'That sounds delightful. And no, I'm not alone. Well, yes. At the minute I am. But no. Not really.' He frowned. 'What I mean to say is that I'm waiting for Miss Corrington to return from her shopping trip.'

'Miss Corrington? *Margaret* Corrington?' Holly looked horrified. 'What on earth are you doing waiting for her? She's dreadful.'

'Truly dreadful.' Pearl nodded in agreement.

Louis hid a smile, but it wasn't really amusing, was it? If he married Margaret Corrington, then the women he was with today would smile and be polite and do everything to pretend they were happy she was in their circle – but really, he knew the truth of how they felt without having it confirmed so bluntly by his friends. 'She's not *that* dreadful,' he tried valiantly.

'Oh, she is.' Holly nodded and shifted in her seat. 'She's extremely dreadful. And she's not Elsie, which is why we have to dislike her – on principle, of course.' She gave Louis a very hard stare which almost had him quailing. 'We'd dislike *any* female companion of yours that wasn't Elsie. But that little pink scorpion is quite definitely the worst of the bunch. Why, Noel almost based the witch in his book on her. But then he said the witch had to have some redeeming features to make her a more well-rounded character, and I said he couldn't use MC at all.'

'MC?' Louis realised straight away that they were Margaret's initials but wondered why Holly referred to her as such. And why she was deemed a pink scorpion? 'Pink scorpion is rather harsh, don't you think?'

'No. It's not harsh enough. And MC is short for Miserable Creature,' offered Holly with a mischievous smile. 'I don't think she has ever smiled at me or spoken to me, no matter how many times we have met.'

'It's because she dislikes your Liberal Background,' Pearl said solemnly. Louis could almost hear the capital letters which Pearl intoned into that phrase. Holly had gone to the Liberal College of the Arts with Elsie, and Louis knew she had been on a few Suffragette marches to support votes for women. She was also married to the highly successful novelist, Noel Andrews, whose fame and subsequent wealth had sky-rocketed when he had produced a fairy-tale book to rival *Alice's Adventures in Wonderland*. Holly was also an esteemed illustrator in her own right. In short, she was everything a certain sort of woman might despise – independent, outspoken, free-thinking and not content to sit around looking vague and pretty, agreeing with everything a gentleman said whilst sipping tea. Although, to be fair, Holly was sipping tea right now, her silvery blonde hair neatly pinned up and held off her face with a velvet hairband. But she had mitigating circumstances in the fact that her pregnancy made her look far more demure and domesticated than Louis knew her to be.

'And also, I've been informed she called me a "Brash Dollar Princess",' added Pearl, scowling. 'Just because I'm American and married someone with a title. What she fails to see is that Ernest and I do actually love one another.' She glared at her scone and ripped a piece off, chewing on it angrily as she apparently thought about it. 'She'll despise Viola and Sam – my brother and sister. They'll be at the ball too, by the way. Stopover from Paris on the way home. Hey, Viola might end up married over here, one never knows. Currently, she's more interested in Ragtime dancing than settling down. Turkey Trots. And Grizzly Bears. And what's that other one, Hol?'

'Bunny Hug.'

'Bunny Hug. That's it. Ragtime.'

'Ah,' said Louis. There wasn't much else he could say really. In truth, Pearl *had* come from America, brought to England by her family to marry a titled gentleman in straightened circumstances and inject his estate with her fortune. But in Pearl and Ernie's case, they genuinely did love one another, as she said, and it was clear to anyone who knew them. And Holly *was* extremely liberal in her outlook – not something a traditional girl like Margaret might warm to at all.

In fact, Holly was a lot like Elsie. Or, at least, what Elsie *had* been like. The Elsie he knew now was almost closed off, and Louis had definitely felt a wall go up on the few times he had seen her over the last few years.

'So, that is why we deem her a miserable creature,' finished Holly. 'She actually tried to call Pearl "brash" to Clara – you know, Elsie's cousin – we think it was to try and get in with the Pencradocs and engage in some gossip, but Clara is extraordinarily loyal and told *us* what she'd said! We're polite to MC, of course, but please be advised, dear Louis, that if you're not going to marry Elsie, or even Clara, which would be bad enough – it's a joke, don't look at me like that, she was quite fond of you when she was younger until Elsie chased her off – then we really don't want you marrying Margaret.'

'I haven't actually said *anything* about marrying Margaret! But the problem is, the person I *do* want to marry doesn't want to marry me.' Louis was almost surprised to hear himself voicing the words, especially to Holly and Pearl.

'Would that be Lady Elsie Pencradoc, by any chance?' Holly sounded amused and Pearl hid her smile behind her teacup. 'Come to the costume ball. See if she happens to turn up as well. She hasn't refused to come yet, so we're taking that as a positive sign.'

'It doesn't matter. I'm not confessing to anything or promising to be anywhere. Let it be said that she is not at all interested – she had a chance just a few days ago to say the word and change my mind. But ... she didn't.' He shrugged. 'So that's an end to it.'

'No!' Holly suddenly surprised him by slapping her palm on the table, causing him to jump. 'No. Look. Louis.' She leaned forward as best as she could. 'What the hell are you? A man or a mouse? Fight for it! Damn it, *fight* for what you want!'

'Excuse me?' A cold voice interrupted them. 'I'm not sure if it's particularly seemly to shout in a tea room. Louis, I'm not staying here to be embarrassed by women's rights rally cries. Come.'

'Margaret!' Louis whipped his head around and saw her standing there, her blonde ringlets positively fizzing on her shoulders. Quickly, he stood up and bowed. 'Really, we're not embarrassing anyone. Come and sit with us and indulge in a slice of cake. It would be lovely for you all to ... to ...' His voice fizzled out. *To get along? To not hate each other? To understand why I almost feel I'm being railroaded into marrying you ...?* Because really, there was no proof, except for some spurious gossip, that Margaret had said *any* of those things, was there? This coldness, however, was a side of Margaret he hadn't seen before, although Holly *could* appear quite outspoken if you weren't used to her ...

'No, thank you, Louis. Let us leave.' Margaret turned so she was facing away from Holly and Pearl. 'Mother is just coming. I said I would come in here in readiness to order her a hot drink, but I do not think she would appreciate the customers they allow in.' She held her arm out and stuck her chin in the air, indicating that he should take her arm and lead her out of such a den of iniquity with great speed.

'It's all right, Louis. Go.' Pearl looked up at them, her eyes flashing angrily. 'I'm not sure we want to be mingling with certain *clientele* either.'

'Yes, please just go, Louis. Can't be doing with women who don't agree with women's rights, you know.' That was Holly, her eyes glinting equally dangerously.

Louis looked helplessly at his friends, and they both nodded in confirmation, two pairs of steely eyes on him. He knew the looks weren't *about* him exactly, but it made him feel quite uncomfortable regardless. And, if he was honest with himself, he did rather wonder where Margaret's attitude was coming from right now.

'Very well.' He bowed to Pearl and Holly again. 'Your party – I *will* be attending. I will see you there, if not before.' Then, almost reluctantly, he took Margaret's arm and allowed himself to be swept out of the shop.

He wasn't surprised, as he walked away from the table, that he heard Holly's voice going, '*Squeak, squeak, squeak.*'

He did see the humour in the situation, but he still couldn't help cringing. What on earth was he doing? Margaret began chattering sweetly about a hat she'd seen, her little face upturned and eager as he made agreeable noises, and he found himself wondering if he'd dreamed the whole scenario they'd just left behind.

But his mind wasn't on hats or cat-fights between women, which he knew were part and parcel of their existence – hell, he'd been around Elsie and her sisters enough growing up.

He was thinking about Elsie and about how he could fight for *her*.

He had gone to Elsie's London house, and the whole thing had failed spectacularly. The only other line of attack he had open was the costume ball. And if both he and Elsie went to that, and nothing was resolved to his satisfaction, then he might as well retreat into a hole in the skirting board and eat his own body weight in cheese.

Chapter Six

Present Day

'And this is the Garden Room,' intoned the guide. Sybill assumed she was the wedding planner, but she really looked a bit snooty and not very approachable. If she was contemplating getting married – well, married again, being honest – this woman, Bianca, would have put her off straight away.

'I feel underdressed, even for the tour,' muttered Coren in her ear. Everyone else seemed to be in their Sunday best. They had obviously come for the tour and wanted to make a good impression, whereas Sybill and Coren had clearly been stomping through the undergrowth, and she felt very sweaty and dirt-stained.

She stifled a laugh. 'Me too.'

'I should have come in a tux.'

'And me in a prom dress.'

It was Coren's turn to stifle a laugh, and the fact he had laughed made Sybill laugh again – but, alas, rather too loudly, as it drew Bianca's attention unpleasantly towards them.

'I'm sorry,' Bianca said, as Sybill wondered how she could actually focus on them when surely her upturned nose was in the way. It really was the epitome of someone looking down their nose at someone else. 'Did you have a question?'

'Yes.' Coren surprised her by speaking up. He surprised her even more by taking her hand. 'I was wondering how far in advance a person must book up for a Lacy wedding?' He was guileless and Sybill was impressed. 'My fiancée here,' he raised her hand and squeezed it in front of Bianca's nose, 'was amused because I said the lead-in time must surely be several years in advance.'

Bianca visibly softened as she perhaps anticipated a

booking coming her way, and her thin lips cracked into a very small sort of smile. 'Not quite a few years, Mr ...?'

'Harker. Matthew Harker.'

Sybill bit her lip against another snort of laughter. Really, this was incredibly unprofessional – Coren had just mentioned the name of one of their friends, Matt, who lived far enough away to be most likely unknown here, and who wouldn't be looking for a wedding any time soon as he'd already had one with Merryn's friend, Cordelia. Matt was a teacher and also delivered classes and workshops at Pencradoc during school holidays.

In fact, Matt and Cordelia had been one of the couples to query whether Pencradoc would be hosting weddings. When the answer had been "sorry, not yet, but we'll do what we can for you, you know that, don't you?", they'd decided to go ahead and get married elsewhere, but they'd had a celebratory picnic a week or so later on the lawns at Pencradoc, catered for by Sorcha.

Still, Coren's slight identity theft had been a smart move. Very smart – and a good way to stay anonymous. Coren Penhaligon's name was well-known around this area for the work he'd done on Pencradoc Arts Centre. His face, a little less so. Coren didn't "people" very well, as Merryn kept telling him when she was teasing him.

'Well, Mr Harker, we would suggest a "lead-in time" as you say of approximately a year. We do get booked up rather quickly for weekends, so we could perhaps say a little less than a year if one wished to wed on a weekday.'

'Wonderful.' Coren nodded seriously. 'Something to think about. Let's see the rest of the rooms then,' he continued smoothly. He was clearly hoping to prevent Bianca from urging him to book up right now for next summer.

'Certainly.' Bianca's smile slipped away again with the deflection of the booking, and she turned smartly on her heel and led the small group of people through the house again.

'This, here, is the morning room – fabulous for, well, *morning* weddings—' she paused while her guests chuckled obligingly '—and this is the drawing room. We can make the wedding flow from one into another throughout the day, if the wedding party so wish – but obviously, that would be two lots of room hire.' She smiled around at the party, who chuckled again, but slightly less convincingly this time.

'I *really* don't think I want to get married in this place after all, *Matt*,' Sybill muttered, leaning up to whisper in his ear. 'Can't we just do it at Pencradoc?'

'Sure,' he whispered back. 'We could be the guinea pigs. Cheaper to organise anyway.'

'Definitely. Mates' rates.'

'Mates' rates. Hey – look at that. What's going on there?' He tugged her slightly towards a partially open door and pointed discreetly. As they looked at it, a weird light began glimmering from behind it, and there was the subtle sound of music and laughter, clinking glasses and conversation.

'I don't know. But … I want to know.'

'Me too.' And, just as the music subtly streamed out from the room and seemed to curl itself around them, they broke away from the tour group and slipped through the door together.

Sybill found that she was still holding Coren's hand but, as they stood in the room, a scene began to unfold before her eyes. She blinked, feeling faint and disorientated, and looked around her.

Coren wasn't beside her any more; she hadn't even felt his hand move away from hers, but she was on her own. She looked down and saw a black, glittering gown, felt the skirt brushing the floor as she moved. There was a weight on her shoulders she recognised as a cloak, and a slight pressure on her throat. She raised her hand and touched a velvet choker there, and felt the slightly scratchy sensation of what she somehow knew was jet against the skin of her forehead.

She heard voices. One of which was her own:

'I'm Lady Elsie Pencradoc. But tonight I'm a witch.'

She looked up – there he was, right in front of her...

'You're Morgan le Fay.'

'And you're King Arthur. Surprising.'

'Not really.'

'They'd go together quite well, wouldn't they?'

'They would. They do.'

'They don't. They can't.'

'They did before.'

And then the whole scenario shifted, and she found herself back in her modern-day clothes, staring at Coren who looked just as shocked as she did.

'Sybill? Are you okay?' He reached out and put his hands on her shoulders. She was staring ahead quite blankly, then she blinked, and it was almost as if she had returned from somewhere far away. He had an awful feeling that he might know exactly where that place had been.

Because he was, quite deliberately, standing with his back to the rest of the room, and because whatever else had happened there, he knew, he damn well *knew*, that there wasn't meant to be a ball going on there today, and that there shouldn't be a crowd of people dancing and laughing. And, of course, there wasn't a scene playing out in front of them, where two figures stood out from all the rest, staring at each other as still as statues whilst something unspoken occurred between them and the dancers moved around them – despite what he thought he had just seen.

And he knew as an absolute certainty that one of those people had *not* been Sybill, no matter what it had looked like – no matter that it had looked, for a moment, as if she had been bathed in a silvery, shimmery moonlight, swathed in black with only her pale, heart-shaped face visible beneath a cloud of dark curls and a black hooded cloak.

It wasn't Sybill at all. It was someone else, standing in the exact same place Sybill was, in a different time altogether …

'Coren. Yes. Yes, I'm fine. It just felt a bit …' She shrugged, seemingly unable to continue the conversation.

'You don't need to explain. Come on.' He took her hand and almost pulled her out of the room. They were just in time to tag onto the back of Bianca's group as they disappeared out of another door.

'Follow me – this next area is the ballroom.' Bianca's voice was commanding and soared above the murmured voices of approval. 'It's the perfect place to have an evening reception, and one of our most exclusive rooms.'

'I don't think so.' Coren saw that they were heading towards another door which he knew would lead into the room he and Sybill had just been in. 'Come on. We can slip out that way.' He indicated a corridor which had an "Exit" sign attached to the wall.

'No. No, I want to go back in.' Sybill tugged him back. 'I don't know why, I just want to. It's the ballroom, Coren. It's where Elsie dressed up as …' she hesitated '… as Morgan le Fay.'

'Morgan le Fay?' He stopped and stared at her. 'But we thought she was just a generic sort of witch?'

'She *was* a witch. But she was Morgan le Fay. She was *that* witch.'

'Lucky guess?'

'You could maybe say that.' Sybill ducked her head and refused to meet his gaze. He opened his mouth to reply, to protest, to query – he wasn't sure which. He knew, however, it probably wasn't the right time to mention the origins of Sybill's name, even in his usual teasing fashion.

Then he heard voices close by him:

'Elsie and I went to another ball at Pencradoc. We were King Arthur and Morgan le Fay there too.'

'You are correct, my liege.'

A deep, amused laugh. 'Shut up, Penny, you duffer…'

'Woah.' Coren spun around, trying to see who it might be, despite knowing full well it wasn't anybody earthly speaking to him. He had that shivery, heart-pounding feeling that told him something otherworldly had crept up on them and, for a few moments, they had shared the same space.

Please God – not Ellory. Not him!

'Ellory? Pah! As if. No. It's just us.' The girl who had apparently spoken sounded pragmatic about that fact. Then there was another laugh, a feminine one this time, one that would have been infectious and made everyone else laugh too, had it been heard under different circumstances.

'Coren?' Sybill was whispering his name urgently. 'You've gone pale. Do you need to leave? We can if you want.'

'No. No.' He looked around again and instinctively tightened his hold on her hand. 'Who's Penny? Have you ever heard of Penny?'

'Penny?' Sybill blinked in astonishment. 'That's Elsie's nickname. We've got a few bits and bobs in the records where she's referred to as that. Why?'

'*Elsie*? Sybill, I—'

But it was too late. Bianca's keen gaze had found them, straggling as they were at the back of the group, and she waved them over. 'Come closer, please. Step into the room. I can't have guests straying too far from the tour.' She treated them to a thin smile and a poor joke. 'We might lose you in the west wing and that would be dreadful.'

Coren had no choice but to follow Bianca's instructions, but whatever she said about the ballroom, he didn't hear. He was too busy staring around it, imagining it in a very different time, during a very different event. It almost seemed as if it was real. In fact, it seemed as if someone was showing him what it had been like; almost as if, for whatever reason, the ballroom they showed him, the events of that evening, had been a significant stopping point on that person's journey through life.

'Elsie Pencradoc. You didn't tell me you came from *quite* such a privileged background.' Fabian stood in the driveway of Pencradoc, staring up at the imposing grey building.

'It's not a bad old place.' She shrugged and pulled her black cloak around her, staring up at it with him. It was Friday, the ball was tomorrow, and she had left it as late as she dared to come home.

It had been, as it always was, a horror to drag herself away from Marigold and London, but she knew the little girl was in the best hands she could possibly be in. Marigold knew her mama was going to the "grown-up party", and it was terribly boring and no place for little girls. She was happy to be back with her extended family on Primrose Hill, and had said farewell with numerous wet kisses and slightly sticky hugs.

'*Acushla*, why does she always come back like a street urchin?' Lily had asked, laughing, as Marigold ran into her arms and rained kisses on her, before insisting that Uncle Edwin picked her up and sat her on his shoulders.

'Because we have fun,' Elsie had answered simply, and it was true.

'"Not a bad old place",' Fabian echoed. 'Quite.'

'Quite. Now, come on, let's go inside and you can meet everyone.'

'That sounds daunting, darling.'

'Mama and Teague are quite easy to get along with. And I'm not sure all my siblings are around, so you might be lucky and avoid one or two of them.' Elsie shrugged. 'Laurie will be off doing something estate-like, or perhaps at Wheal Mount with Uncle Jago – he's the eldest boy, so is sort of Duke in training, although he's really no blood relation to the Pencradocs. But he's twenty-three and quite sensible, so even if he was here, you'd get along with him. Then Isolde and Medora are, I think, travelling in the Lake District on a painting holiday. They've always been thick as thieves, those two. Clem's almost twenty so he's at university, which means we might be spared him. He's quite annoying because he thinks he knows absolutely everything and really he doesn't. So, to be fair, it might just be Enyon and Arthur who are here, and they are practically human now they have learned that a grunt does not suffice as an answer to everything.'

'You've got a large family,' Fabian said, clearly impressed. 'I have an older sister. We don't really get along.' He pulled a face. 'Because of one thing and another.'

Elsie patted his arm. 'Isn't it a good thing I love you then? I've got four cousins as well – Jago's daughters. Clara, Mabel, Lucy and Nancy. Imagine how noisy this place got at Christmas and birthdays when we were all here together. My cousins all look like Aunt Alys, all beautiful and golden. Not like me.' She shook her head. 'We're all dark and brooding. Me, especially.' She scowled. 'Anyway. We should go in.' She pulled the cloak further around her, as if, even three or four years later, someone might guess she'd had a child.

Her stomach turned over as she remembered the Christmas she had come down here whilst she was expecting Marigold. She was almost six months pregnant, and luckily was hiding it well. She drifted around in black Regency-style dresses and voluminous shawls for those three days at Pencradoc – high-waisted, many petticoated, bell-shaped creations – and told everyone she was reading the Romantic poets, and wanted to imagine herself as Lady Byron, or Caroline Lamb, or Mary Shelley. And Elsie, being Elsie, had carried it off.

Medora, an impressionable girl of sixteen at the time, had swooned over the fact, named as she had been after Byron's alleged daughter and a character in his poem, 'The Corsair'. She had proceeded to trail Elsie throughout Pencradoc, wanting to talk about poetry all the time, until Elsie had to shout at her to go away before locking her bedroom door to keep the child out. She then had to face the disapproving looks of Isolde over Christmas lunch, but she was used to that so it didn't really bother her much. The rest of her family had nodded in vague agreement at her caprice, and went back to being noisy and enthusiastic whilst also trying to stop Arthur eating too many candied fruits and sweet treats.

She'd stayed away from Pencradoc after that, mostly due to the fact that it wasn't long before she couldn't hide the pregnancy any more. She'd told her family she was going on a visit to France to study some of the Impressionists and hadn't seen them again until the summer. Lily and Edwin had helped her engage some discreet temporary staff at Brunswick Square. After Marigold had arrived, the staff had changed, Marigold had been accepted as a part-time member of the Griffiths' family ('What difference will one more child make?' Edwin had said, hugging Elsie to him as she wept with gratitude) and Elsie had picked up the pieces of her life as best she could. She also packaged up the Regency dresses and sent them to Medora with a smart little bound copy of 'The Corsair' and a copy of *Wuthering Heights* as she knew the girl also adored that story. Elsie was quite fond of her younger sister, despite what she sometimes said, although she tried not to think of the fact that the original Medora had fallen pregnant before she was twenty and brought even more scandal on her poor family.

So things had worked out – sort of – in Elsie's otherwise charmed life, but still she hesitated before stepping over the threshold of Pencradoc. It just felt different this time: as though all the carefully constructed boundaries and walls and yes, lies, were about to come crashing down around her ears.

'Yes, we should.' Fabian said and nodded, bringing her back to the present. 'I can't tell you how excited I am to be seeing Teague. I have my portfolio in my trunk. Hopefully he'll at least be able to tell me where I require improvement.'

'Have you brought the picture of me along?' Elsie nudged him playfully. She'd sat for him, telling him he was more than welcome to practice his skills on her, and she'd been pleasantly surprised by the likeness. It was a different style to what she was used to – she had, after all, grown up with the Boldoni-like portrait of her mother Teague had painted before they were married hanging pride of place in the sitting room. Fabian's work was more like that of James Tissot: jewel-bright colours and sharp details of confident women knowing exactly what they wanted out of life. Elsie was instantly recognisable in the painting, her pointed chin thrust upwards, her dark eyes staring boldly at the viewer, challenging them to like or dislike her – it was up to them, and she would remain self-assured whichever way the dice fell.

'I have.' Fabian's cheeks reddened a little. 'It's quite worrying, showing someone like Teague my interpretation of his daughter—'

'Shhhh.' Elsie pressed her fingers against his lips. 'Secret. Remember?'

'I remember.' He made to bite her fingers playfully, and they laughed as she tweaked his nose.

'Now. In we go.' And Elsie pushed her shoulders back, stood tall and strode forwards into Pencradoc.

Louis was riding his horse across Bodmin Moor, digging his heels in as he made it gallop so he could feel the wind against his cheeks, simply so he could feel *alive*. His lung condition wasn't so bad today, and he took great gulps of air, enjoying being able to breathe freely for once. Give it a few more months and the wretched bronchitis would be back. He knew he would be struggling again over the winter with it, damn it all to hell. He had even more reasons to curse it, because that was why he had been unable to go to that Christmas party of Elsie's four and a half years ago. By the time he had recovered enough to see her, it was springtime, and then it had been summer … and then she had gone.

'Dammit!' he shouted into the deserted moorland and dug his heels in harder, giving the horse its head and letting the great beast take him as fast as bloody possible across Bodmin Moor. Perhaps he would be lucky, fall off and kill himself, then he wouldn't have to miss Elsie so bloody desperately any more.

It had been two weeks since he had seen Pearl and Holly in the town, and nobody had heard from Elsie until a few days ago when she had written Pearl a lengthy letter and confirmed her attendance.

Ernie had wasted no time telling Louis this fact when they were enjoying a brandy after dinner one night at Ernie's home, and that had made Louis more determined than ever to go to the ball.

'I hear you're bringing a friend,' Ernie had said, raising his eyebrows. '*Your* friend, so Pearl says. Nobody else's friend.' Margaret was conspicuous by her absence at the dinner party. Holly and Noel were there, of course, and the three men were enjoying their drinks in the dining room without talk of children and childbirth, while Pearl and Holly were in the drawing room, discussing in great detail Holly's ever-increasing girth and what would be the most appropriate costume to wear for a woman in such an interesting condition.

'Please. She *is* just a friend. An acquaintance, even. Yes, I will be bringing her to the ball, because it's time she met everyone and tried to get to know them a little more.'

'Before you marry her, you mean?' Noel looked at him askance.

'I'm not ...' Louis gave up. *He might. He might be marrying her*. It was expected, and the more this dragged on, and the further removed from Elsie he was, the more that prospect became a possibility.

'Oh, he's protesting. I wonder how long he can hold out against his bride-to-be's numerous charms,' murmured Noel.

'Or hold out against her mother,' responded Ernie, which caused both of Louis' friends to snigger in a most ungentlemanly fashion into their tumblers.

Today, on the moor, he was scowling as he remembered that conversation. '*Fight for her*,' Holly had urged, and by God he meant to – but he had to see the girl first. The more he thought about it, the more he refused to accept that the dreadful meeting in London had been his last chance to make things right with Elsie.

Another horseman appeared on the horizon, and Louis looked up as the rider waved at him and then turned the horse towards him. As the young man came closer, Louis raised his arm in acknowledgement and shouted a greeting to Elsie's brother, Laurie.

'Laurie, my good fellow! What are you doing out on the moor?'

'I could ask you the same thing.' Elsie's brother, as with the rest of her siblings, looked very much like Elsie, and something in Louis' heart twisted as Laurie smiled a smile so similar to his sister's that there was no mistaking the relationship.

'I'm just out for a ride. Enjoying the summer.' Louis shrugged. 'Father and I have been organising some work on the orchards, and I left him to discuss cider with the gardener.'

The horses fell into step with one another and Laurie grinned. 'By that, I suspect you mean he decided to sample some.'

'I couldn't possibly say. I left them in the potting shed and hilarity was ensuing, so I thought discretion was the better part of valour and made myself scarce.'

'Good man.' Laurie nodded. 'I was at Wheal Mount earlier doing much the same thing. I haven't been back at Pencradoc long, but I needed to get some exercise. I don't enjoy spending too much time indoors and I'll have to be civil at dinner, so I wanted to get away from it all before that happened.'

Laurie shared a streak of the same wild spirit Elsie had. However, whereas she was artistic and expressed things through images, he was poetic and painted pictures out of words. He was a quiet young man, but Louis suspected that just underneath that he was seething with some sort of passion he kept well-hidden, at least for now.

'I'm sure your family are used to your demeanour, Laurie, and won't think anything the less of you for remaining quiet tonight, especially if you've been travelling and working.'

Laurie nodded and stared out across the moors. 'That would normally be the case, but El's back and she's brought a friend.' He curled his top lip ever so slightly. 'Fabian Austen, I think. He seems a decent enough chap, but by all accounts he came up with El specifically to see Father – so I'm wondering what all the fuss is about. I think he's going to Ernie's ball as well. And because he's a friend of my sister, I have to be polite and talkative, and that's why I'm taking some time for myself right now.'

'What?' Louis stared at Laurie, horrified. 'She's here? Elsie's *here*?' *Well, of course she is*, the logical side of him said – *of course she is if she's going to that bloody damnable ball!*

'Yes. Didn't you know?' Laurie looked at him curiously. 'Hmm. Apparently not. Yes. She's here. I think she's going back to grubby old Londinium on Sunday. Says there's something she needs to do before Slade on Monday. Heaven knows why she puts herself through all that. She can't stay still or settle for one moment. Always been the same. Anyway, which way are you going, old chap?' He slowed the horse down at the point where Louis would normally turn left to head back to Ashby Court, and Laurie would take the right to Pencradoc.

'Oh! Actually, I was going to call in at Pencradoc,' said Louis, making a split-second decision. 'I was planning to pay a social call, see how your mother is. See if the girls are back from the Lake District. Ask Enyon how his cricket is going ...'

'You weren't planning on doing anything of the sort,' replied Laurie mildly. He looked at Louis and smiled. 'But you might as well come back now with me and see her. See what you make of this Fabian chap.'

Louis felt himself blush to the roots of his hair. Was it so obvious that he had loved Elsie for years and still hoped to have a chance with her? Even when she had brought another man home to introduce to her family? To see Teague, of all people? Hang on – to see *Teague*? Elsie's step-father?

There was only one reason he could think of that would lead to a man travelling all the way down from London to Cornwall with a girl and ask to see her guardian. *Good God.*

'Yes.' He almost choked on the word. 'Yes, I'm coming with you, Laurie.'

'Jolly good,' said the younger man. He dug his heels into his horse, and they began to move off again. 'I thought you would.'

Chapter Seven

Present Day

'That's somewhere I actually think I love, but don't really want to revisit in a hurry.' Sybill felt unsettled and restless, and was at the point where it was difficult to even string her thought processes together. Far from being the lovely day out she had anticipated, Elton Lacy had stirred up all sorts of emotions and thoroughly wrung her out.

Yet, despite that fact – and in the good old English tradition of believing that a cup of tea solved everything – they had managed to polish off a cream tea in the light, airy café after the tour around the house.

'I don't think I'll be getting married here.' Coren was deadpan. 'Bit out of my price range.'

'We could perhaps just rent one of the garden spaces?' Too late, the image of her sitting on the bench spilling her heart out to Coren bounced into her mind. 'Or maybe not.' She looked down at the cup, picked the teaspoon up and drew some squiggles in the sugar she'd spilled in the saucer.

'Maybe not. I know what you mean though. It's a nice place. But it's not right for me, you know? I think it's beautiful, and it's friendly enough as a building – but it's not Pencradoc or Wheal Mount, is it?'

'No. That ballroom ...' It was time she addressed the elephant in the room. 'I'm not quite sure what happened in there. It was very ... atmospheric, shall we say?'

'A little too atmospheric. Rather ... immersive.' They were silent for a minute, and Coren re-folded his linen napkin carefully along the creases.

'I'm glad you agree. I thought I was going mad.' Sybill forced a laugh. 'I used to see some strange things in my ill-advised Marco phase, but I was never a guest at an Edwardian ball.'

'And is that what you think you saw?' Coren was serious. 'I mean it.' He flushed and she looked at him, surprised. Coren never seemed fazed by anything. He was one of the most practical, business-like, efficient people she knew. Rather like herself.

She knew her efficiency hid all sorts of deep-rooted anxieties and memories, and she suddenly wondered if Coren was like that as well. Maybe he was as damaged on the inside as she was.

'Well.' She exhaled a long breath. 'There were no soft drugs involved today. No alcohol. But there was definitely something odd in the ballroom. I wasn't even me. I was wearing a costume like Elsie's in that photograph we have. Good old Morgan le Fay.'

'And King Arthur?' Sybill snapped her head up and focused on Coren. 'Who was King Arthur? Who went with her as her other half?'

'Nobody. I mean, obviously somebody did – the mystery gorgeous friend she was photographed with. But he definitely wasn't King Arthur, was he?'

'No.' Coren was silent. 'I think I'd quite like to know if she ever went to another ball dressed as Morgan le Fay, you know? And met up with someone who dressed as King Arthur.'

Sybill shrugged and pushed her teacup away. 'We can look. I mean, we can check the archives – *I* can check the archives – see what we've got at Wheal Mount. There might be something there. Another invite, another photograph. Something that might give us a clue.'

Coren nodded and pushed his cup into the centre of the table to meet Sybill's. 'Yes. We'll do that. But seeing as you need to drop me off at Pencradoc anyway, do you want to check what we've got first? You don't have to. Not today, if you don't want to. But it was just a thought.'

Sybill caught his eye and was surprised to see something almost pleading in his gaze. This was Coren Penhaligon, for

God's sake. But he looked nervous. He looked, in fact, like he had experienced something just as odd as her, but it had shaken him up even more deeply than it had her.

'Yes.' She nodded. 'That's a good idea. We'll have a look when we get back home.'

Home? It was only as they stood up to go that she realised she'd said that. Home! What an odd thing to think. If anywhere, Wheal Mount was where she should feel most at home – but, surprisingly, she didn't feel like she did any more.

Pencradoc was more like a home to her now. And that was also a truly strange realisation.

As they drove back towards Pencradoc, they crossed Bodmin Moor. Coren knew that Pencradoc, Elton Lacy and Ashby Court made three points of a triangle across this part of the moor. He knew also from the histories of the families that the Eltons, the Ashbys and the Pencradocs had moved in the same circles and been close friends. That was one of the reasons, he supposed, that Elsie had kept the invitation to the ball at Elton Lacy out of the hundreds she must have attended.

As he gazed across at the landscape, his mind began to drift and he saw figures riding across the moor towards them, the horses flying silently across the green expanse.

He leaned forwards, certain that there was something strange about the figures, and pointed out of the window. 'Look. See those two?'

'See who?' Sybill glanced in the direction of his finger and shook her head. 'Nope. Don't know what you're looking at, to be honest.'

'Those two. On the horses. Their clothes—' The pair certainly didn't look as if they were dressed as modern riders would be. The girl, who was right out in front, was wearing a long dress and her hair was streaming behind her with no sign of a riding helmet. The man was dressed equally strangely – again, there was no riding helmet and his outfit looked old-fashioned and out of place, even on the timeless moorland of Bodmin. Coren turned his attention to Sybill. 'Can't you see them? Just there.' He looked back out of the window, his finger still pointing, then he stopped speaking and stopped pointing. 'Okay.' He ran his hands through his hair nervously. 'They've gone. They've bloody gone. Stop the car, Sybill. Please. Can we just stop the car a second. I need to get out ...'

'Oh!' Sybill indicated to pull in to the side of the road, and Coren unfastened his seatbelt and threw the door open, almost before she had even stopped.

'They were there. I swear it. They were *there*. Right by the side of the road – heading that way. Ashby Court's over that way, isn't it, Sybill?'

'Ummm ... yes, I think so.'

'Ashby Court.' He nodded and got out of the car. 'I thought so. Right. And that way is Pencradoc. Okay.' He shut the door behind him, walked off across the grass and barely registered the engine shutting off, and Sybill's door opening and shutting just afterwards as she hurried after him.

'Coren. Where are you going?'

'Over there. Over *there*.' And indeed, he was focused on heading towards a little cluster of shrubs and trees surrounding a small hidden clearing. He didn't know why he was going there, he just was. 'We're in the middle here, aren't we? Between Ashby Court and Pencradoc.' He swung around to face Sybill, knowing for sure there was some connection between the three properties. Something important that was happening, or had happened, and it was making itself known to them in too many different ways today. Some sort of floodgate had been opened, and he didn't quite know how. 'It's within walking distance even, I'd say. Just a couple of miles as the crow flies. You'd just get there quicker on a horse,' he continued.

'As I understand it, Elsie used to travel quite regularly to

Ashby Court. And Louis Ashby did the same to Pencradoc. They were really close growing up.'

'Louis and Elsie.' Coren stopped and turned, then laughed. 'Of course. Louis and Elsie.' He studied Sybill for a moment, saw her long dark hair blowing around in the slight breeze. Then he thought back to the pictures he'd seen of Elsie and took a step towards her. He reached out and touched her cheek, trailed his fingertips downwards so his hand came to rest on her shoulder, then he drew it away. 'You've got a look of her, you know? Of Elsie. But her hair was a lot wilder than yours. In every picture I've seen of her, it was just a whole load of curls.'

'I straighten this lot every day.' Sybill looked a little wary. 'If I leave it, it's curly as hell.'

'That figures.' He nodded. 'I hate to say it, but I think whoever we found at the Lacy found us here as well.' There was a beat, and the atmosphere was suddenly charged.

They moved towards one another at exactly the same time, and before he knew it, they were kissing. But this was a proper kiss, not just a friendly kiss, and he realised they were both helpless to stop it happening. It was almost as if something was urging them onwards and wasn't going to be content until they'd given themselves fully to one another, right here in the middle of Bodmin Moor.

The only thing he could do was to try to stop it going any further. Because, by God, he knew this wasn't going to end with just a kiss if he didn't put the brakes on.

'Sybill … Sybill. *God*. I could do this all day,' he murmured, and drew away from her with a great deal of effort. He laid his forehead against hers and closed his eyes. 'But I can't. I can't let it happen. We can't do this. Not today. Not after everything that's gone on.'

'I know.' Her voice was tight, shaky. 'I know exactly what you mean, Coren.' Yet they were still clinging to one another as if their lives depended on it. 'One day. One day, maybe we can. But no. Not today.'

And, with a huge effort, they released each other and stood staring at one another, not quite sure what the hell was going on. Coren reached out a finger and caught the tear that was gathering in the corner of Sybill's eye. 'Not today,' he confirmed softly. 'And maybe we shouldn't look for anything else Elsie related today either.' It tore him apart to suggest that; he would have loved nothing more than to spend extra time with Sybill. But they seemed to both knew it was the least sensible thing they could possibly do on that early summer Saturday.

Sybill nodded. The fact she agreed hurt him more than he thought it really should. 'Maybe not. I'll take you back, shall I? Back to Pencradoc. Then I'll just go.'

'Yes. It's probably for the best,' he said softly.

But he knew it wasn't. Not really.

1911

Elsie had, as expected, been welcomed with open arms by her parents and excited chatter from the two youngest boys, both clamouring for her attention. Elsie wasn't as decorous as Isolde and, strange as it may seem to anyone who didn't know her well, had her feet more firmly on the ground than Medora. The "little ones", as she still thought of them, always favoured their eldest sister for these reasons. Clem, Enyon and Arthur knew that Elsie would be the one who rolled around the grass with them, or tore her skirt to shreds by climbing trees and, even though she was a bossy child and told them in no uncertain terms what they should and shouldn't do, they thought she was the "bee's knees" as Clem had once told her when he was very young and feeling exceptionally affectionate.

Clem, however, was now verging on twenty and studying to be a lawyer, which the whole family thought was very odd. However, Clem said he thought lawyers would make a jolly good living, so had decided to try to be one. There was a private series of wagers around the siblings as to how long his enthusiasm would last, but it didn't seem to be waning any time soon.

'Mama. Papa. How lovely to see you!' Elsie always called Teague "Papa" – he was "Teague" to anyone outside of the family though. It was quicker than calling him "Step-Papa" anyway. 'This is Fabian. My friend from London. He's very much looking forward to meeting you properly.'

'It's so lovely to see you, darling,' said her mother, hugging her closely. 'And we're delighted that Fabian could come. We really are.'

'I'm very much looking forward to meeting Fabian as well.' Teague smiled at Fabian, who was, it had to be said, looking a little star-struck again. 'I've heard many good things about your work from Elsie. Have you brought along some portraits?'

'Yes, sir. I have. I hope you'll do me the honour of giving me some criticism.'

'Absolutely. I'll let you get settled, then I'll see you in the study. Just knock on the door when you're ready. I tend to work in there as the light is good, which will be ideal for me to see the detail in your paintings.'

'I think this is quite the best portrait, Papa. Isn't it?' Elsie whipped Fabian's picture of her out of the portfolio case and waved it in front of Teague, whose eyes widened in apparent amazement. It really was a good portrait, even if Elsie said so herself.

'Thank you.' Fabian looked even more impressed. Elsie hid a smile – he was as excited as a child at Christmas.

Zennor took Teague's arm. 'Just give us a call when you're ready, as Ruan says. I'd quite like to see your artwork too.' Then she smiled, and they headed out of the room with Fabian staring behind them.

'My God, Elsie. I've just met Ruan Teague!'

Elsie let out a peal of laughter and put the portrait on a

nearby table. 'I can tell you're impressed. Just wait until he's dozing in the garden after a huge Sunday lunch. You'll be less than impressed then.' She took his arm and drew him towards her, hugging him 'Thank you for coming down. I know it's a tedious journey.'

'The end result will be worth it. I can't believe quite how nervous I am. What if he challenges me? What am I to say?'

'Just be yourself, darling, and he'll love you as much as I do—'

'My vile eldest sibling! Welcome home, Prodigal Pencradoc!'

'Laurie!' Elsie spun around to face her brother. The pair of them had always been particularly close, and she dropped Fabian's arm to rush into Laurie's embrace. 'Oh my goodness. You're here too. How splendid.'

'I'm not the only one.' Gently, he extricated himself and took her hand. Turning around a little more, she faced the door and saw him there. *Him.* Louis.

She thought she might be sick.

'Louis. I … I didn't know—'

'Neither did I.' He stared at her for a long moment, his grey eyes unreadable. His glance flicked to Fabian and back to Elsie. He cleared his throat and held his hand out to Fabian. 'Good afternoon, sir. Louis Ashby.'

There was the briefest flicker of recognition on Fabian's face, and he held out his hand hesitantly in response. 'Good afternoon. Fabian Austen.'

'Quite.' Louis nodded quickly, then put his hands behind his back. Elsie knew that the smile on his face was forced; it didn't quite reach his eyes. 'Well, I just came to call on you all to see how you are. I can see you're busy. Other things to do. So.'

'So.' Elsie stared at him helplessly. She loved him. She still loved him with all her heart and she wanted to yell and scream because of her self-imposed exile from him. Life could be quite unpleasant at times, she acknowledged. But this was unavoidable. It had to be the way it was and there was no going back.

Louis stood there awkwardly for a moment, not really knowing what to do. He wasn't that good an actor. He couldn't just sit down, have a cup of tea and make pleasant conversation with the woman he loved and the man who clearly wanted to marry her. Why else, he asked himself again, would Fabian Austen want to see Ruan Teague?

'Thank you for coming down. I know it's a tedious journey.'

'The end result will be worth it. I can't believe quite how nervous I am. What if he challenges me? What am I to say?'

'Just be yourself, darling, and he'll love you as much as I do—'

The conversation echoed around his head as he stared into her dark eyes for a moment that seemed like an eternity.

He felt Laurie's hand on his arm, pressing gently, and he turned to look at him. Laurie was only an inch or so shorter than him, despite the fact he was three years younger.

'Come on, old boy.' Laurie nodded towards the door. 'I'll show you what I meant about our orchards. You know? When we were talking earlier?'

Louis could remember talking about cider, and he recalled briefly mentioning something about his father and his orchards, but there was nothing he needed to clarify about the Pencradoc orchards at all; regardless, Louis was grateful for a chance to escape. 'Yes. Yes. Good idea.'

'Let El sort herself out. I think we fell over at least three trunks in the hallway.' Laurie looked across at his sister and made a mock-salute. 'I'll see you later, vile sibling. Nice to meet you, Mr Austen.' He smiled quickly and manoeuvred Louis into the hallway.

Louis looked over his shoulder as they left. Elsie was still standing there, her arms sort of outstretched towards him, but then they dropped and her shoulders slumped. Fabian Austen picked something up – a portrait of Elsie, he saw – then put his arm around her.

He'd seen enough. 'Yes. Thank you, Laurie. Good plan.' He shook the younger man off gently and propelled himself, one foot in front of the other like an automaton, out of the door and away from Elsie Pencradoc.

Chapter Eight

Present Day

Sybill endured a miserable couple of days, but by Tuesday she couldn't stand it any longer. She had deliberately thrown herself into work – the way she always seemed to cope with anything she felt she was losing control over, but today her desk and her office weren't enough to contain her.

She headed into the space they were creating for the portraiture exhibition and spent some time with the pictures that had already been hung, walking around the room, noting if the labels were attached to the right pieces, checking the spellings were correct and all the other little details that might get overlooked.

She hesitated in front of one that showed Elsie as a younger woman – early twenties perhaps, her pointed chin thrust upwards, her dark eyes staring boldly at the viewer, seemingly not caring whether they liked her or not. This was the image of the "Elsie" who Sybill felt most connected to. It was as if she was saying, "yes, so I made mistakes. And so what? You might not approve of me or my lifestyle, but you know what? I don't much care what you think, to be frank. I've accepted who I am and what I've done, and it wasn't always the right thing – but I did it, it happened, and you can't change the past."

Sybill shivered. It resonated with her so much, and it was frustrating that this was the one she didn't have a name for as far as the artist was concerned. What she had told Coren was a slightly watered-down version of her life with Marco. There'd been extremely wild, happy, carefree days, and also unbelievably dark days, some of which she'd only been able to get through by self-medicating with whatever she'd had to hand. The life they'd shared had been unreal. More a nightmare than a dream, but they still clung onto it – for Lucia's sake, she guessed. And part of her did still love him, but it was a different sort of love – a friendship, a love that was born out of sharing one of the worst experiences a couple could go through. But she would never love him in *that* way again; the way she thought she might love Coren if they only gave each other a chance.

But staring at a century-old picture and fantasising about things that might or might not happen was not going to get her very far. Instead, she decided to go into the storerooms and see if she could find anything that might help Coren in his quest for King Arthur.

Reluctantly, she turned her back on the exhibition room and locked the door after her. There were signs up telling people they were rearranging the displays, and the glass panels in the doors were covered so visitors couldn't peek through them, but it was safest to keep the room locked, just in case.

She smiled and nodded automatically at people she passed in the corridors, staff and visitors alike, then took the stairs two at a time up into the attics. She stepped into the room that harboured a lot of Elsie's old treasures. Tammy, Sybill's assistant, had recently taken a placement student under her wing, and they'd been working quite a bit in there, but the student had left three months ago. Sybill had definitely been in there since, but what she saw today made her gasp. Neatly folded beside an open trunk was what looked like a dress. Sybill was certain that dress had not been out of the trunk in all the times she'd popped in. Fair enough, she had only done a cursory sweep and check on the place, always meaning to come back up and go through everything properly – but, to her knowledge, nobody else would have had need to be in there taking stuff out of trunks. It was a real shock to see the dress left there.

It wasn't any old dress either – the bodice was tightly laced, and when Sybill tentatively went to pick it up and shake it out, she saw that it was a long black gown decorated with crystals. It looked extraordinarily familiar. In fact, Sybill realised with a start, it was the exact same dress that Elsie had been photographed in. The exact same dress that she had found herself wearing in the ballroom at Elton Lacy.

Sybill's heart began pounding and her hands shook as she looked around for a hanger to put the garment on. Regardless of how it had got there, and that was something she didn't quite want to think about right now, it was far too precious to leave lying around on the floor. When she had located a hanger and attached the beautiful item to a picture hook on the wall, she went back to the trunk and peered into it.

As she looked closer, she saw that the trunk contained books – but, on closer inspection, she realised they were not just books, but sketchbooks. On the front of one of them, written out in blue ink in a fancy script, were the words *Lady Elsie Pencradoc Artwork, 1900*. Sybill's stomach turned over, and she plunged her hand into the trunk, pulling out sketchbook after sketchbook, all dated from the early years of the twentieth century, with more than one for most years. It was as if Elsie had decided to create some sort of art journal for each year, right up until 1907. There was only one book for 1907, then she picked up multiple books again from 1908.

The books were, as one might expect, full of doodles, paintings and notes – mainly about Elsie's large family and close friendship group. Here and there, pictures of her friends and family laughed out of the pages; sketches of landscapes, of Pencradoc and Wheal Mount; the tower tea room as it had been many years ago, looming up out of the Wilderness Gardens nestled on double page spreads with a bird or a rabbit or a dog randomly scribbled in the corner, almost as if Elsie had been trying to get an angle correct or simply capture the moment.

Elsie's journals were chaotic, unordered and beautiful. Sybill sat down on another trunk and flicked through them, her sense of awe increasing with each one.

Some of the pictures jarred though. Sybill realised it was because the fashions were not contemporary with when the book was dated. One full page portrait in the 1908 journal was of a girl looking over her shoulder, holding a book and wearing something more suited to the Regency days. *Medora Teague*, the title said. *Miss Byron takes the floor.* The view was the one that could be seen out of the morning room window at Pencradoc – the picture was so good, Elsie had even managed to breathe life into the gardens beyond. Medora was one of Elsie's little sisters, and Sybill had to acknowledge that she was a beauty.

A portrait in 1911 showed a heavily pregnant woman draped in a white tunic. On the next page was another girl clutching a basket of fruit while dressed in something more fitting to the seventeenth century.

'Oh!' Sybill suddenly understood. 1911 – the Midsummer Costume Ball at the Lacy! That explained the Grecian tunic and Nell Gwynne, or whoever she was – she certainly rocked the "King Charles the Second's buxom-orange-seller-of-a-mistress" look. Medora was a different story – that was more like a family picture, a girl coaxing her sister to draw her ... or maybe a girl coaxing her sister to be drawn. Sybill would never know.

But there were three pictures that caught her imagination more than most. One from 1907, one from 1911 and a further undated one, which was tucked in a pocket on the inside back flap of the 1907 book.

On one of the 1911 pages, beside Nell Gwynne and the lady wearing the Grecian tunic, was a picture of a man. He was turned away from Elsie, looking away into the distance. But there was no mistaking that he was dressed very much like King Arthur.

The same man – or at least a man wearing the same costume – appeared in the 1907 sketch. But it was the other loose undated one, tucked into the flap, that made Sybill catch her breath. She stared at it for a while, looking at all the bits and pieces that were placed around the scene, and remembered something quite important: there was often a story to be found in a picture, if one only knew where to look for it.

Coren was busy looking over some figures. Merryn's visitor surveys showed there was a consensus of opinion that a second-hand bookshop might be a nice thing to have in one of the gatehouse buildings. It had been something they'd thought about for a while, but the gatehouse in question needed some building work done on it, and there was some damp proofing to be sorted – otherwise, Coren was sure they'd be selling nothing but soggy pulp. He was also number-crunching his way through licences and insurance and all the other things they'd need to produce to become a wedding venue.

The figures weren't even registering, and that was highly unlike him. He was too distracted with the thought of Sybill standing on Bodmin Moor, her hair whipping around her face, and the feel of her lips on his.

This was no way to continue to run a business. He really needed to get a grip and—

'Coren. Sorry to barge in on you like this, but I've found something I think you need to have a look at.'

He snapped his head upright, the figures for damp proofing and wedding insurance already forgotten.

'Sybill! Come in. God, it's good to see you.' Had he really said that last bit out loud? Apparently he had, as he saw her flush, then she half-smiled.

'It's good to see you too,' she replied softly. 'I haven't had a very good couple of days. And one of us needed to visit the other, so …'

'I haven't been great the last couple of days either. And I was trying to think of an excuse to come down, but I didn't think bringing you damp proofing quotes was quite an exciting enough thing to make the trip.'

Sybill pulled a face. 'Not quite. I wouldn't have let you in if you'd just come brandishing damp proof quotes.'

'I might have had more luck with the wedding venue quotes, I guess. What are you brandishing instead? Should I let *you* in?' He was stupidly pleased to see her, he really was.

'Something more interesting than damp proofing. Sketchbooks. More to the point, Elsie's sketchbooks. I've just brought a couple. There are more at Wheal Mount, but these ones are the most important right now, I think. Also—' Sybill flushed '—her dress turned up. Her Morgan le Fay costume. I'll get it checked over for moths and stuff, and you can have that too. Have you got a tailor's dummy or a mannequin to display it on? Just thought it would be quite nice.'

'I'm not sure if what we have would work.' He really wasn't. That was Merryn's department. 'I think we've got something like that. But Merryn will know what's best to use. Is it okay if I get her to contact you to sort it out for you?'

'Why wouldn't it be?' Sybill gave him an odd look.

I don't know – maybe because she's even more pregnant now than she was, and you might not actually want to see her? But he made sure he didn't say *that* out loud.

'No reason.' He shrugged. 'Anyway, sit down. Let me get you a coffee and you can show me the books.' He didn't really want a coffee, but if he made one it would keep her in the office a few minutes longer.

'Great. That would be lovely.' She sat down and crossed her legs, and they chattered inconsequentially while the coffee brewed. The whole time, Coren was thanking his lucky stars that it seemed almost normal between them – that the fact they had experienced such a strange, emotional day on Saturday hadn't got between them as they had both thought it might.

That was a positive sign anyway.

When the coffees were made, he brought them over to the small coffee table and sat down next to her. He was aware of the warmth of her body, her thigh very close to his and the scent she always wore – oceans and fresh air, with an undercurrent of greenery. She had already opened one of the books and had it on her lap.

She looked up at him and smiled. 'Thanks. So, this is the first one. Who do you think this chap is dressed as?'

Coren looked at the picture and sucked in a breath. 'Wow. King Arthur? Would you say?'

'I would say.' Sybill nodded. 'We can't really see who this chap is because he isn't looking at Elsie, and she hasn't written his name on it either. Which is highly frustrating.'

'Highly.'

'So, this book is 1911, and all she's done is scribble the date underneath it. Look.'

She moved the book closer to him, and he saw Elsie's distinctive handwriting declare the picture to have been drawn on 24th June. 'That's the date of the ball we've been basing these exhibitions on.'

'Yes. And I'm not sure who this chap was, but I've a feeling he's this guy.' Sybill moved the book onto the coffee table and opened up the next one. 'This is from 1907. It's a much better picture of him. Again, it's dated around about midsummer. And this time we have a name: Louis.'

'Louis. Of course. It makes sense.' Coren looked at her. 'The great love of Elsie's life. Louis Ashby.'

'The very same.'

'Well, at least that answers the question as to who King Arthur was,' he murmured.

'Oddly, that's the last picture in the book, even though

there's about half a journal left to play with – unless you go right the way to the end, then you see this.'

With a sort of flourish, she flipped the book to the last page. Tucked inside a small pocket, much like the pockets Moleskine journals have, was a larger folded piece of paper, undated and unsigned. Coren had to blink and move away from it. The picture was so detailed that it took him a moment to scan all around it and try to separate out all the elements. It didn't look like Elsie's usual style, but then nobody ever said Elsie followed a particular path, so who could really say?

'Good grief. That is one busy picture. Makes me think that there was a lot going on in her mind when she did it. Even that letter on the mantelpiece – look at it! It jumps right out at you, almost like it's inviting you to pick it up and open it. I know nothing about art, but even I can see it's a bloody astonishing piece of work.'

'Yes. I agree. Isn't it fantastic? It's pen and ink, and an ink wash I'd say. She's spent some time on it. But I'm not actually sure what we're supposed to be looking at. I've had a good look at it, and I think it was Christmas – look, there's a wreath on the fireplace, see? So maybe the letter is a Christmas card. Or an invitation to a Yuletide Ball – how splendid if it was.'

Sybill was right about it looking festive – each holly berry seemed to glow glossily through the wash, each spiky leaf carefully situated. But, weirdly enough, the focal point of the picture was a study of a sketchbook. The book was propped up on the artist's knee as if that was the view she could see. She seemed to have her feet up on something, bare toes beneath a long skirt. However, there was also a reflection of the artist in a mirror, so she was visible from a different angle. From that angle, her dress was bunched and draped strangely across her body.

'Is she ...?' Coren didn't really want to say it and certainly didn't want to assume.

'Pregnant? I think so. Or she's had a huge lunch.' Sybill

pointed to the mantelpiece. 'Look at the detail though, the things she's got on display. Ornaments and all sorts. But that card or whatever it is definitely stands out, doesn't it? And then if you look over at the window, there's a winter scene outside. So detailed. Is there anything else that stands out for you?'

'Yes! Those photos on the windowsill.' Coren suddenly said. 'I recognise them. They're copies of the ones I've seen in photo albums. Aunt Loveday had them. She often used to show them to me and Kit, and tell us who everyone was. God, I can't believe that the detail in there is so fine that I can make out what they are! Whatever nib she used must have been tiny.'

'That sounded far too artistic for you to say!' Sybill looked at him in sort of amused astonishment. 'For someone who self-admittedly knows nothing about art, you must be picking things up all the time. Well done.'

Despite his own astonishment at the picture, Coren smiled. 'Thanks. You know something else? That room. I recognise the view. I'm pretty sure it's the teaching room on the first floor that we run Matt's classes from. I don't suppose you've got time to come upstairs with me, have you? It's got me desperate to find out a bit more, if we can. I'd like to go and see if it all matches or if I'm just mistaken.'

'Hmmm.' Then, suddenly, that spark was back in her eye. 'Me? Come upstairs with you? Well, now. It's the best offer I've had in weeks. Yes, Coren. Lead me to that bedroom. I'm as intrigued as you are.'

'Great.' And he smiled again, stood up and held his hand out. He was delighted when she took it so he could pull her out of the seat.

And she didn't let go until they'd walked across the room and opened the door. The smile was still on Coren's face from that brief touch, even as they ascended the staircase, the sketchbooks still gripped carefully in Sybill's other hand.

'Oh God. Oh Fabian.' Elsie stared after Louis and her brother.

'Is that him? That's Louis Ashby?' Fabian was staring as well.

Elsie shot him a quick look. 'Yes. Yes, that's him.'

Fabian nodded slowly. 'He looks nice. Looks just like your sketches in fact. You've caught an amazing likeness of the man – very handsome.'

'Oh God, *Fabian*!' Elsie rolled her eyes and punched him gently in the arm. 'I love you, despite of and because of your proclivities. But don't you dare fall in love with Louis. Not him – I mean it.'

'Calm down!' He looked down at her and laughed. 'I wouldn't dare. I don't think he'd feel quite the same anyway. The way he was looking at you – believe me. Nobody else exists in the world for that one.'

'Well, someone else will have to.' Her voice was steadier than she thought it might be, although her fists were now clenched so hard that her fingernails were digging into her palms. 'Margaret Corrington will just have to exist for him. I can't.' No – her voice was not steady any more. Not at all. In fact, even in her distracted state, she quite thought it might sound rather shrill.

'Come along. Elsie—'

'No!' She shook her head. 'Just no. Now.' She took a deep breath and switched on a smile. Turning to her friend, she dusted down his lapels and looked up at him. 'The study is along there, and so, of course, is Teague. Go. Now. And leave me to be miserable, please.'

Fabian stared at her for a moment, then quickly hugged her. 'All right. Has anyone ever told you you're a bully?'

'Frequently. Good luck. I'll get my bags unpacked and see you soon. A nice quiet family dinner tonight before the rambunctiousness of the ball tomorrow. Such fun.'

Fabian laughed and then took a deep breath. 'I'll get the rest of my work, and I'll go and see him.' He nodded decisively. 'Mustn't forget this one, must I?' He winked, slid Elsie's portrait into his portfolio and marched out of the room.

Elsie kept the encouraging smile on her face until he was out of sight; then, once the door had closed, she hurried over, locked it firmly, and then curled up on the sofa to weep quietly for a little while.

Louis didn't sleep well that night. Every time he closed his eyes, he saw Elsie's face. And worse than that, he saw Fabian Austen's face as well, saw Fabian Austen put his arm around Elsie and look at him, studying Louis curiously as he stood there in the doorway.

That meeting had made his mind up. There was no escape – he might as well marry Margaret and be done with the whole thing. He'd never be happy with anyone who wasn't Elsie, so he may as well be miserable with someone who was potentially prepared to marry for convenience and live a separate life thereafter. It would be worse, surely, to actually shackle himself to someone who truly cared for him, because he knew that he could never, ever reciprocate that affection.

No. Margaret would have to be the one he settled for. He sat up in bed, feeling slightly sick. It wasn't fair on either of them really, but what choice did he have? Here, in the soft misty light of dawn, it seemed logical.

He'd do it tomorrow – today, even, looking at the time – at the ball. He'd take her outside, make his intentions known to her and then speak to her father as soon as possible after that. He thought back quickly over the time he had known her, wondering if he'd ever implied that he would want to marry her.

Hand on heart, he couldn't think of one time where he had been anything more than friendly and polite, and he definitely hadn't encouraged Margaret. Rather, her mother had pushed the girl into his sphere, presented her under his nose at any given opportunity and, thinking about it now, encouraged a relationship built on nothing more than expectation.

In some ways he felt sorry for Margaret. She was little more than a chattel, something her parents presented to eligible men, like a piece of shiny waxed fruit on a silver platter. She didn't seem to have any female friends who genuinely liked her, and, if Holly and Pearl were to be believed, Margaret thought she could buy friendship with gossip, insinuating herself into other peoples' lives with tittle-tattle and stories. Yet she'd never done anything overtly to make him dislike her, and he was very much of the opinion that one speaks as one finds.

But she wasn't Elsie, and she never would be – however, if Margaret was available and willing, it would perhaps do them both a favour if he married her. It would take his mind off the unattainable love of Elsie, give him someone else to think about – it could even save Margaret from her overbearing mother and arrogant father.

But he knew that Mrs Corrington's influence was strong, and the waxed fruit never fell far from the tree in his experience. *Oh God. What on earth am I committing myself to?*

She just did not, and never could, hold a candle to the blinding light of Elsie Pencradoc.

'Damn it.' Louis threw the covers off and got out of bed. He walked over to the window and stared out at the early morning. It was a little before four o'clock, and the sun was already seeping across the horizon. The solstice had passed a few days ago, but the sunrise didn't seem to know that and was still surprisingly early.

Or maybe it wasn't early at all. Maybe Louis was just the one who was ridiculously early. Whatever, he couldn't just lie here and ponder. He had the urge to get outside and feel the world coming to life around him. He felt stifled, and that was possibly much to do with the fact that, after tonight, he would no longer be able to dream that he and Elsie would ever be together. He'd practically be engaged.

The thought of that was enough to spur him on and get him into his clothes quickly. He headed out of his room and hurried through the house, only seeming to exhale when he finally stepped outside and found himself in the cool morning air.

He closed his eyes and raised his face to the sky. Then he took a couple of deep breaths, opened his eyes and focused on the world outside of Ashby Court and Margaret Corrington.

Chapter Nine

Present Day

The room that Coren took them to was a room that Sybill knew well. When Matt came to teach his workshops, he always seemed to gravitate towards this one. He'd used many of the teaching rooms in the past but, over time, this particular one had more or less become his domain. It was a large, pleasant, airy room at the back of the house, and as such was quiet and conducive to work.

Sybill had come to try out a watercolour Christmas card workshop one year, and produced a couple of wintry landscapes and a robin sitting on a snow-covered post-box. It had been the first time she'd picked up a brush in ages – ever since Lucia had died, when she thought about it – and the smell of the well-used watercolour paint palette had enthused her all over again. It made her forget real life for a little bit as she got stuck in to glazes and washes, her hands seeming to create the pictures out of nowhere. She'd always loved messing on with a paintbrush and drawing materials; art seemed to come naturally to her, although it had always been more about enjoyment rather than talent.

As she remembered how the festive pictures seemed to paint themselves with very little help from her conscious mind, her stomach lurched a little. If this place *had* been Elsie's bedroom, then might Sybill have even felt Elsie's presence back then? Channelled a little bit of her talent and enthusiasm? For she was pretty sure, now she'd seen the sketches in Elsie's book showing Louis dressed as King Arthur, that the feeling she'd had in the ballroom at Elton Lacy had definitely been something to do with Elsie in that Morgan le Fay costume.

She shivered a little, despite the warmth of the room, and put the book down on a desk. She wandered over to the window and peered out. The estate stretched out before her, and she knew that in a moment she'd have to look at Elsie's book again and try to match the landscape with it. But for now, her eye was drawn to a spot further down in the courtyard; a shadow seemed to appear by the corner of the orangery – it resolved into a man, who was striding purposefully towards the house, keeping to the shadows of the trees, and she leaned forwards.

'Coren – see that? Should that person be here? I don't think it's Kit and that bit's not open to the public is it?' She touched the windowpane as she pointed at the man and, as her fingers connected to the cool glass, an image burst into her mind that made her catch her breath.

Before she could think about it any further, she threw the window open, hitched up her skirt and clambered out. It was a route she had taken many a time. A tree grew close enough by for her to reach across, grab a branch and shimmy her way down the old trunk. From there, she could drop onto the roof of the orangery and shin her way down the drainpipe onto solid ground at the back of the house.

It was just as she dropped onto the flagstones that she heard his voice: 'Elsie Pencradoc. Fancy meeting you here.'

'Who?' Coren's voice was in her ear, his body next to hers as she stared out. She blinked and took her fingers away from the glass, hoping that he wouldn't notice her hands shaking. 'No – I think you're seeing things. There's nobody down there.' She moved closer to the glass again, almost forcing herself to look out ... but he was right. There were some shadows of the tree branches, that was all, and something that looked like a piece of gardening equipment propped up by an apple tree. Maybe she had been mistaken after all; a cloud rapidly scudding across the sun would make any shadows appear to move quickly across the landscape. That must have been it.

But she didn't have too long to dwell on that fact or to try to convince herself that she had been mistaken, because

Coren was speaking again. 'I'm pretty sure this is the view from that busy drawing, you know. Shall we have a look?'

'Yes. Good idea.' She tore herself away from the window and headed back over to the desk. 'So – we need to fold it out fully and have a good look at it.' She spread the artwork out on the desk and tried to resist smoothing it down. She didn't want to risk smudging any of the fine details. And now she saw it in a better light, the detail, even on the trim of the dress where it draped over the artist's feet and tumbled to the floor, was incredible. 'Oh!' Suddenly she connected something. 'Look. In the sketch of Medora.' She quickly found Medora's picture and laid the open sketchbook alongside the larger piece of work. *The trim – beads of some description*, Sybill thought, *had the same pattern in both pictures*. Obviously, they weren't as detailed in Medora's picture, but the shape of the pattern was evident, and it seemed for all the world that the dresses were one and the same.

'But it's a really old-fashioned style of frock for the day!' Sybill said, comparing the two. 'So when exactly was this one done—' She tapped the corner of the large picture '—compared to this one?' She pointed at Medora. 'Is she just wearing something from a dressing-up box? After all, there does seem to be a theme of costumes and pretending to be someone you're not going on in some of these drawings. Is there anything in the landscape you think might help us? A different tree or a view anywhere, perhaps?'

She glanced up at Coren, but he was frowning. 'Yes, I agree with you when you say "pretending",' he said. 'Almost as if they're giving the impression of being something they're not – or at least showing that different face to the world. But remember who we're dealing with here – this is Elsie Pencradoc. One of her closest friends was an actress. Her family were probably the most scandalous in the county, and Elsie wasn't far behind in the scandal stakes herself. She lived and worked in London, she studied at the Slade, she had all these fabulous contemporary friends from Bloomsbury and everywhere. I'd say that what you see here is pure Elsie. I think, if we can get a close enough view of that little letter, or whatever it is on the mantelpiece, it might very well tell us a date so we can pinpoint when the picture was done. The more I look at that letter, the more it seems to me as if it's almost been placed there deliberately – you know, with the words on it facing us? That's not something she wants to hide. Damn – I wish I had a magnifying glass or something. I wonder if Matt has one around here?' He looked about him, his brows furrowed as if he was thinking deeply about something.

'Why don't you check the supplies?' Sybill nodded across to a built-in cupboard, one of the original features in the room, which she had spotted on her first visit here. Surprisingly, it wasn't very deep but it did its job, and she knew Matt kept things in there to help his classes run smoothly. 'In the meantime, I think I'll try to establish the angle she drew it from.'

She pulled a chair over and set it in front of the window, making a guess as to where it would have been. She moved it around a bit, trying to think of perspective and the distance from the window based on the artist's feet – she was pretty certain it was Elsie's work, but it was so different in style to the Elsie Pencradoc art she was familiar with, that she didn't want to assume too much. Having said that though, why else would it be in one of Elsie's sketchbooks? But, then, Elsie had so many famous friends. Who was to say one of them hadn't been here for a visit and just whiled away a few hours doodling?

It was one hell of a doodle though.

When Sybill was satisfied that the view seemed to match, she pulled over another chair – she had the idea she could sit in the first one, put her feet on the second one, and see if they could match the rest of the room. After all, the furniture had all gone now, the mirror in the corner; even the wainscot had gone, along with the big fireplace, all lost to plaster and wallpaper years ago before anyone thought about keeping the original features in these old houses.

It was sad, but it was still the original window, and Elsie would recognise that at least—

Sybill cut the thought off before she revisited in too much detail the experience of before, when she had seen that strange shadow and seemed to recall all those odd images when she touched the window. Instead, she resolutely sat down in the chair. Slipping her shoes off and putting her feet up on the other one, she settled into position, adjusting the books on her knees as if she was going to draw something.

A feeling of elation suddenly burst through her as she looked at the picture in front of her and the view before her.

It matched – it really did. Even to the corners of the room and the shelf along the wall, which was all that remained of that wonderful mantelpiece.

'Well, it was a long shot, but a lucky one.' Coren had found a collection of magnifying glasses that were high up on the top shelf. One of Matt's classes was plant and nature drawing, and Matt had previously explained that it was sometimes good to really get up close to something to understand how it was structured.

It was logical, but Coren had never been one for peering at things and studying them too closely. He always felt that in his role, time was of the essence. He was always busy and he was a rubbish artist anyway. But, in this particular case, he was glad his friend Matt didn't think in the same way as him, and he was certain that if they could focus in on that prominent item on the mantelpiece, it might give them a better clue as to the date of the picture.

'Here we go.' He swung around, brandishing a magnifier and stopped dead. Instead of the room he'd been in and the woman he had come into the room with, he saw it as it might have looked one hundred years ago. The vintage decoration was intact, the fireplace was crackling with flames, a festive, green wreath draped along it and an eclectic amount of – well – *stuff* was lying around: hair combs and ribbons on a dressing table; a big, warm-looking cloak draped over a chair; a pile of what looked like gifts, sitting on top of a half-packed trunk; a rumpled bed, seemingly hastily made, with some cards on the coverlet, the top one proclaiming *To Lady Elsie Pencradoc, A Wish for Christmas, 1907*. There appeared to be a wintry world outside the window, and, where he knew Sybill had been dragging chairs around, there was now a woman sitting on a *chaise longue* at the end of the bed, her bare feet resting on the red velvet arm, her arms moving swiftly as she drew on a large piece of paper. She was dressed in black – apparently in the same dress that Medora had worn in her portrait. It was bunched up beneath her bust, rising over the small mound of her stomach, and it fell to the floor in a swathe of black fabric.

She was bent over the work, her hair pulled back into a messy sort of bun, with wild curls escaping down her back and a black comb stuck in the side, adorned with feathers and black roses. He couldn't see her face properly, so intent was she on her work, but from where he was standing, the card on the mantelpiece was propped up, facing outwards, and his eyesight was good enough to read the thick black lettering on it, some handwritten, some printed:

Elsie invites Louis to
the Midsummer Costume Ball
Pencradoc
Friday, 21st June 1907
I shall collect you, never fear!
Please produce this in order to board the carriage

Then, as he stared at the figure drawing furiously on the *chaise longue*, she faded into nothingness to be replaced by Sybill –

sitting in the same position, her bare feet up on another chair, looking out of the window.

She turned, seemingly sensing that he was facing her, and grinned. 'I've got the spot she drew it in, I think. It matches perfectly. Did you get a magnifier?'

It was all Coren could do to keep his face impassive and nod. 'Yes. I've got one.' He held it up and she clapped.

'Great. Let's see what the card says.'

Coren knew that whatever he saw or didn't see through that magnifier, that he would be able to tell Sybill word for word what was printed on that paper.

And it probably raised more questions than it answered.

Because it looked very much like that by Christmas 1907, Lady Elsie Pencradoc was still hanging onto memories from Louis Ashby and a Pencradoc midsummer ball – and that she was also expecting a baby.

1911

Elsie had slipped out of Pencradoc almost before the sun rose. Being here and knowing that she and Louis had been in the same room meant that her dreams were too vivid and too intense for her to fully settle into sleep. Every time she closed her eyes, she saw his face; saw that almost defeated look in his eyes, and she knew she was to blame.

Was what she'd done so very wrong, really?

Don't be silly, Elsie. You had no other choice. You had to protect him. You couldn't let it spoil his future. You couldn't trap him. Your families needed to be spared it all …

And thus her mind went around in circles until she couldn't bear it any longer. She slipped out of bed and, dispensing with the idea of clothing, she threw her cloak around her shoulders and padded barefoot through the house and out of the side door.

Running across the cool, dewy lawns, she headed towards the old rose garden and wove her way through the sleepy blooms to the Wilderness Gardens, taking care to stay on the grassy pathways and relishing the feel of the earth beneath her feet. She headed to the waterfall and followed the river to the little wooden footbridge. Hurrying across that, she found herself in a less formal landscape, and it wasn't long before she was on Bodmin Moor itself, out of sight of Pencradoc and away from real life.

Elsie slowed down and took her cloak off. The fresh chill of the early morning air was still there but it held the promise of a glorious day, and she raised her face to the east, closing her eyes and letting the magic of the sunrise fill her being. If she could ever capture this feeling in a painting, she would be happy …

Then she opened her eyes again and wondered if she ever really *would* be happy, or if there was always going to be that feeling of something – or someone – missing.

But she didn't have time to contemplate that for too long, because a figure was coming over the hill. Her heart began to pound – all she could think of at first was that she was alone, in her nightgown, in the middle of moorland, and not a soul knew where she was …

Then she caught her breath as he came nearer, and her heart began to pound *differently* – because the person she saw now, the person who had pulled up short and stopped for a split-second, then had suddenly begun to run towards her was no threat. No threat at all …

Before she was aware she was doing it, Elsie began to run as well, arrow-straight, towards the figure, her eyes fixed on him, her hair flying out behind her, the hem of her nightgown damp and muddy.

'Louis! *Louis* …'

'Elsie. It's you. It's *you*.' They met somewhere in the middle, and his arms were around her waist and hers were around his neck and their lips were on one another's, kissing as if they'd been starved of contact for a thousand years.

She was wrong. He *was* a threat. He was the biggest threat to her peace of mind she could ever have imagined. And, as she felt herself pulling him down towards the ground and he didn't resist, and then she found herself in his arms, lying next to him, lying beneath him, their limbs entwined and the world spinning out of control, it was too late. It was too late again …

Afterwards, she withdrew completely into herself; Louis could tell.

She regretted it. He could tell that as well, and his stomach lurched unpleasantly. If, for a brief moment, he had thought that Margaret and Fabian were ghosts, insubstantial beings who drifted around them hoping in vain to win their hearts, then he was very, very wrong.

They lay awkwardly, side by side, both staring up into the sky. His arm was still around her soft body, but then she suddenly stiffened and rolled away from him. She sat up and grabbed her cloak from the heap it had landed in, then threw it around herself. She began shivering, but there were no tears; just a dreadful stony silence where she looked into the far distance – looked anywhere but at him.

Her face, so recently flushed and rosy and damp with perspiration with her dark curls sticking to her skin, was white and pinched, and she eased herself away from him a few more inches.

'Elsie. What the hell was that? Because from where I'm looking, I'm damn well confused.'

'That was goodbye.' Her voice was cold, removed, emotionless. 'I needed to finish it, Louis. I needed to get you out of my system. And I have done. I'm hoping we can both forget about it now. Just – move on. You can marry Margaret. No regrets. No unfinished business. End of.'

'What? So you can marry Fabian? You've realised that I'm not that regrettable then?'

'Forgettable, I'd say.' Her mouth twisted unpleasantly. 'Not regrettable. At all. No regrets for finishing it at least. Goodbye, Louis.' She stood up and prepared to walk away, but he couldn't let her go like that – he just couldn't. Even though the message that she spoke was clear as day, the messages her body had given him were quite different.

'Elsie! Wait.' He scrambled to his feet and took hold of her hand. 'Are you going to the ball tonight? Will I see you there?'

There was a beat. 'Yes. I'm going.'

'We need to talk, Elsie. We can't just leave it like this.'

'We can, Louis. We have to.'

'Elsie—'

'No! Just – no.' Elsie shook him off. 'No, Louis. I'll smile and be polite and everything like that so as not to spoil it for Pearl and Ernie if I see you there. But please. Don't seek me out. Just don't.' And with that, she ran away from him, her hair flying loose, her cloak billowing out behind her.

Louis could do nothing but watch her go and pray that tonight would come quickly. And if she wouldn't seek him out, God help him, he *would* seek her out.

Chapter Ten

Present Day

Coren came over to her, clutching the magnifier, his brow still furrowed. 'This might help. Can I have a look, please?'

'Sure.' Sybill held up the picture and he took it from her, spreading it out on the desk. She stayed in the chair, looking out at the view from the window, and imagined what it must have been like to wake up to that every day. Currently, she lived in a flat about ten minutes' drive from Wheal Mount. It was a nice enough flat, but it was quite central to the town, which was fine as she didn't have to go far for milk or bread. But not fine in the fact that she had a scrubby bit of garden out the back that was barely big enough to put a bistro set in, and the front of her home looked out onto shop fronts. It would be lovely, she thought, to be able to throw the window open and breathe in fresh air instead of car fumes. But it was *fine*, of course. She'd just sit here for a few more minutes and let her imagination take over ...

There, for instance, would have been the bed. And there, quite clearly, would have been the fireplace.

Over there, there would have been a packing trunk, because, after all, she was just visiting, and she couldn't wait to get back to London ...

'Got it.' Coren's voice sounded a little strange, and it startled her out of her reverie.

'Oh! Okay. What does it say?' She made to get up, but he indicated she should stay there, and he didn't come any closer. In fact, he took a step backwards, then stood behind Matt's desk, his palms resting either side of the picture that was laid out on it, just like he was a bloody teacher.

Great. He'd obviously retreated into himself again. She could tell by his face.

'It's an invitation, just like we thought. The Pencradoc Midsummer Ball in 1907. And it seems as if it's actually Louis' invite, but for some reason Elsie has it here. You're right. It's definitely her.' He read out the words on the invitation, and Sybill felt her eyebrows disappear up into her fringe. It wasn't all to do with the information; part of it was to do with the staccato way he delivered it.

She made an effort to keep her response light. 'Wow. So, it's probably Christmas because we've got the decorations on the fireplace and in the windowsill and things, but she's got the invite there from six months ago. Or even longer.'

'So would Elsie have been married and expecting a baby at that point? Just to be sure?' He was still behind the desk, looking quite furious for some reason. 'Or would she still have been Elsie Pencradoc?' He just sounded downright blunt now.

'I'll have to check the records.' She couldn't help it, she spoke sharply. The records weren't uppermost in her mind right at that moment. Because damn him, if he was going to growl at her across the length of the room rather than come over to see her – she would go over to see him. She stood up, stuffed her feet back into her shoes and stalked over to the desk.

He pulled back, glaring at her, and deliberately she mirrored his position, leaning forwards, glaring back up at him, palms flat against the desk. 'So, would you mind telling me exactly what's going on, Coren?'

'What? Elsie drew a picture at Christmas. She spent a lot of time on it. And we've found it again.'

'Bog off, Coren. You know that's not what I mean.' She slammed her hands on the desk. 'What's going on with you? With *us*? I thought we were okay. I thought today we were okay, and the stuff that happened at the weekend had just ... happened ... and we were done with it. We were holding hands earlier, for God's sake. Then you peer into a bloody magnifier and suddenly it's like you can't wait to get rid of me again. What the hell have I done, Coren? What the *hell*?'

He stared at her for a moment then leaned in again, his face close to hers. Despite the anger in his eyes, she got a little jolt of electricity from him being so near.

'Nothing. You haven't done anything. It's this bloody place. It's here. It's bloody Pencradoc that's done it.'

Now, that wasn't an answer she'd been expecting and she stood up, confused and mutinous. '*What*? What's Pencradoc got to do with the way you blow hot and cold and, oh, I don't know, the way I think we're finally going to stop tiptoeing around each other and act like adults and try not to deny what's clearly going on under the surface, and then you go all weird on me again? What has *Pencradoc* ever done except given us a common ground, Coren?'

He stared at her silently. She could see the pulse in his temple as he fought to control his temper.

'You want to know what Pencradoc's done? Well. Come with me, and I'll show you what it did.'

And with that, he grabbed her hand and stormed out of the room, leaving the sketchbooks lying there, before slamming the door behind him.

He forced himself to let go of her hand almost as soon as they were out of the room. He couldn't – and wouldn't – force *her* to do anything, and he certainly didn't want to be seen hauling Sybill Helyer, Manager of Wheal Mount Arts Centre, through Pencradoc Arts Centre, spitting and hissing like a cat.

'Where are we going, Coren?' Sybill caught up with him and matched his strides, still angry, her eyes flashing with temper as she stormed along beside him.

God, she was gorgeous.

But he couldn't let himself think that. He needed to blank out his feelings and take her to one specific part of the grounds; a part he detested and avoided when at all possible.

'To the grounds.' His response was short. 'Over the bridge from the waterfall.'

They stomped through the house, out into the gardens, and along to the waterfall. Taking a little-used route through the Wilderness Gardens, Coren practically vaulted a locked gate, followed closely by Sybill who scrambled over the accompanying stile, cursing as she did so.

Soon, they stopped in a field. There was a blackened, burned part of the ground before them, no trees or bushes or greenery anywhere near it, and, to his mind, an atmosphere hung heavy over the spot.

'What's this?' Sybill stopped and turned around, scowling. 'It's not the prettiest part of the estate, but it's not exactly clear why we're here.'

'It's where I set fire to a fucking priceless work of art.' He spun around and faced her. 'Ellory. The Duke before Jago. Elsie's father. I'm sure you know the family history. I turned his portrait into a bloody bonfire.'

He stared at her, and there was a challenge in her eyes as she glared back at him; a challenge he felt was matched by the look in his own.

'I'm well aware of the family history, thanks. But that doesn't explain why we're here.' Her voice was icy. 'And it doesn't explain why you've flipped out or why you keep pushing me away. What are you scared of?'

'Ellory.' In his mind, the answer was simple. Ellory had invaded his mind in ways he didn't want to think about. He'd gone for several years or so without being bothered by him again; without seeing or experiencing any of the weird things Pencradoc was capable of making him feel. And now he'd let Sybill in, now he'd allowed himself to relent a little and get closer to her, he was seeing bloody ghosts again.

It would be a hell of a challenge to explain that to her. But he knew he had to try. It wasn't fair on either of them, and he actually hated himself right now, which was not a great situation to be in.

'*Ellory*? Coren, he died years ago. What on earth are you scared of?'

He blew out a breath, trying to gather his thoughts; there was nothing for it. 'When we inherited Pencradoc, all sorts of strange things happened. Like what happened at the Lacy. Ellory just seemed to be infecting the place. He didn't seem like a very nice person, and his – I don't know – personality, maybe, came through in me.' Yes, that seemed like a reasonable explanation; he could blame it on genetics. 'It seemed like all the worst parts of my personality were sort of amplified in the way I behaved. Ellory had been a bully to Jago, he'd been a despicable husband ... and I started to treat Kit like shit. Nothing, not even my family, was as important as Pencradoc, and I lost sight of everything that meant something to me. I just don't ... I just ...' He wasn't sure how to continue. He turned away from Sybill and shoved his hands through his hair in frustration. 'I just don't want to let him in again and hurt you.' He swung back around to face her and shook his head. 'So, there was a portrait of him in the hallway, where Duchess Rose is now. When I realised he was hanging around, I destroyed it. And that patch there, that burned bit, was where I did it. And that was ages ago, so you tell me why nature hasn't reclaimed it. Whatever evil was in that portrait seeped out and was incinerated. But every time I look over here, I remember what it was like. And I *really* don't want to hurt you.'

'But why do you think that you would hurt me? Ellory's got nothing to do with me and you?' Sybill looked, quite rightly, confused. And she still sounded angry.

'I know. I *know* that should be the case. But, when you were sitting in that bedroom earlier, it wasn't you. I got that magnifying glass out and turned around, and it wasn't *you* there. It was Elsie. Elsie, sitting in her bedroom, in exactly the same space you were. I could see her bedroom, and I could even read that damn invitation on the mantelpiece. I saw the Christmas cards on her bed – and yes, it was Christmas 1907, and whoever wrote that top card out addressed her as Lady Elsie Pencradoc. Which is why I asked if she was married by then. Because she might not have been married, but she was sure as hell pregnant.'

Sybill just stared at him, speechless. 'And you know it was definitely 1907? You saw the invitation? You read it without looking at the picture?'

'Oh no.' He laughed, bitterly. 'I saw it through the magnifier as well. And it was exactly as I'd seen it in the room.'

Sybill shook her head. 'Coren. I don't know what to say. It all sounds ... well. Stupid. Yes. That's exactly it.' She laughed mirthlessly and shook her head. 'No.' She held her hand up. 'Before you say anything, I'm not denying that you experienced some weird things. I know I did at the Lacy. I did in Elsie's room. That's not the issue. Our minds do play tricks on us, things happen. I've always believed that. But I would never have thought you would have let whatever happened in the past spoil your chances for something that could be ... that could be ... well—' She suddenly started sobbing noisily '—that could be good for both of us.' She folded her arms and shook her head again. 'Do you know why I've finally decided to go ahead with my divorce? Because of *you*, Coren. Because of you. It's not healthy living in the past. You have to let it go. Ellory is dead, and you're a different person to the person you were all those years ago. We all are. And I for one wanted to move forwards. I'm sick and tired of being tethered to the past. I'll never forget Lucia and what I had with Marco in the beginning, but I'm not going to let it dictate the rest of my life. You should think about that, Coren. Just think about it.'

And with that, she turned away and ran back across the field, clambering over the stile. As she hurtled along the pathway and disappeared into the Wilderness Gardens, Coren suddenly found himself galvanised into action and set off after her.

'Sybill! Wait!'

But she didn't stop. She'd had too much of a head start, and he'd never been the fastest of runners. Stamina was more his thing. Give him the 1200 metres race on a school sports day and he'd be happy – the 100 metre sprint: not so happy.

A bad metaphor for my relationship with Sybill, he thought ironically.

Before he could catch up with her, she had run right around to the staff car park and then he heard a car starting up. A few seconds later, her little Golf raced out of the car park, the summer dust leaving a trail behind her as she sped along the lane, back towards Wheal Mount.

Coren stopped and watched her go, helpless to do anything about it. Then he bent down and picked up the biggest stone he could find and hurled it as far as he could, accompanied by a collection of curses.

It didn't make him feel much better, to be honest.

1911

Elsie reached Pencradoc out of breath and sobbing. Never in her life had she felt so horrible and lied so terribly to someone's face. Of course Louis wasn't "forgettable". Or "regrettable". Or anything like that at all. He was Louis. And she loved him. But she had to let him go, make him believe she didn't want him and, yes, make him hate her.

As she ran back across the footbridge and towards the house, she saw a figure sitting on the riverbank looking at the Mill House. The sight brought her up short, and she bent double, her hands on her knees, her head raised, staring at the man.

It was Fabian, unshaven and wreathed in cigarette smoke, a roll-up in his mouth. He was clutching a sketchbook, seemingly intent on capturing something in it. Elsie stood up and took a few deep breaths. Rubbing her face to try and hide any evidence of her emotions, she walked towards him.

'Good morning. Couldn't you sleep either?' she asked, sitting down beside him. Her voice was falsely bright, but she hoped Fabian wouldn't notice and start asking questions.

'Elsie. Good morning. No. Not really.' He half-smiled. No. He wouldn't notice her voice; he had that half-glazed expression on his face which meant the wider world around him didn't exist. 'All I could think about was the fact that Ruan Teague has seen my work – and do you know, he actually praised it! Wonderful.'

'I do know. You already told me. Don't draw the Mill House. I hate it.'

'You hate it?' He turned to face her, eyebrows raised. 'Why, pray tell?'

She shrugged. 'Bad memories. Someone was killed there when I was a child. It doesn't matter.'

'Oh.' Fabian turned the page over in his book. 'I'll stop then. Continue later. What are you doing here?'

'Like I said. Couldn't sleep. Went for a walk.' She pulled her knees up and hugged them. *Saw Louis*, she wanted to say. *Made love to Louis, then tried to break his heart*. But she didn't.

'Oh. I've been thinking as well. It wasn't all about drawing this place.' Fabian laid the book down and mirrored her position. 'I think I might go to Paris after the Slade. The École des Beaux-Arts, perhaps. Hone my craft somewhat, before I hit the salons.'

'Or hit Montmartre,' Elsie replied wryly. 'Or Les Halles.' He glanced at her, wary, and she caught his eye. 'It's all right. You can be yourself there. You should go.' She nodded, confirming it.

'Maybe. But I don't know. To be honest, my love, I want to see you happy first.'

'Fabian! Don't be so stupid. I *am* happy. How can I not be happy with everything I've got? With my life? It's wonderful, it really is. Honestly.'

'Darling. You forget that I've seen Louis now. Need I say more?'

'No. No, you don't need to.' She looked at her most dearest friend in the entire world, and he held her gaze. She was the first to look away. 'But I'd much rather you didn't say anything anyway. It's the way it has to be. That's it.'

'Elsie. You're a stubborn, annoying woman. I'm saying that, then I'm not revisiting it again. Smoke?' He held out the stub of the cigarette. Elsie considered it briefly, then shook her head.

'No. No thank you. Not before breakfast anyway.'

'Fair enough.' Fabian popped the cigarette end into his mouth and started a new sketch. Like Elsie, he didn't do well without a pencil in his hand if he was deep in thought about something.

Elsie looked at his bowed head and his furrowed brow, and a wave of affection washed over her. *Dear Fabian*. Paris was the place for him, really. Boys like him needed to be somewhere like that – not in England where his feelings were at best frowned upon, at worst illegal. They had gravitated towards one another, these two – both knowing that they were slightly broken in modern terms, and both knowing they couldn't do a thing about it.

'I met Louis.' The words came out in a tumble and Fabian's hand paused over his sketch, but he didn't look at her.

'I see.'

'Just now. On the moor.'

'Very good.'

'It wasn't. I … I made love to him.'

Now she had his attention. His head snapped around and he stared at her, his eyes half-admiring and half-shocked. 'Outside? On the moor? Just this morning?'

'Yes. Oh God!' She covered her face with her hands and spoke through her fingers. 'Then I told him he was regrettable and forgettable and to go away and get married to Miserable Creature. That's the girl who seems to have set her sights on him. Margaret Corrington. MC. She's an utter beast and *utterly* miserable. Yes, Holly and Pearl have told me *all* about her latest dramas in their letters, and it is a fine name for her, a *jolly* fine name they've created. I like it. I do. It suits her. Oh Fabian. I am hideous. I'm a hideous person.'

'Oh, darling. No, you're not. But I'm sure MC is *quite* hideous, if that makes you feel any better? But sweetness, you know, I might have done the same. The regrettable and forgettable thing.' There was a beat. 'But not with him, obviously, because then you would kill me. But Rupert Brooke ... well.'

'Fabian!' Despite herself, Elsie laughed. 'He's all wrong for you. He really is.'

'But he's very beautiful.'

'He's extraordinarily beautiful. But darling—' she leaned in towards him and said in a stage whisper ' —he also likes girls.'

'Damn it.' His protest was mild, teasing, but it made Elsie smile. 'Good girl,' he said, pulling her towards him in an affectionate hug.

She laid her head on his shoulder, grateful for the human contact, a human contact that held no expectations beyond friendship.

'I'll miss you if you go to Paris,' she told him.

'Then come with me. Bring Marigold. Leave Louis and everything else in Cornwall.'

'I can't do that to you. I can't cramp your Parisian style like that.'

'What if you're pregnant again?' His voice was soft. 'I'm assuming no precautions were taken this morning. It could happen, you know?'

'Please! I hadn't even considered that. Oh God!' She sat up, horrified. 'Oh. God.'

'I suppose if that *does* happen, I could always marry you,' Fabian said slowly. 'Save both our reputations and stay in London.'

'You're wonderful. And far too good to saddle yourself with someone like me. I'm not going to worry about that unless it happens,' she said with more conviction than she felt. 'And if it does, well.' She laughed shortly. 'I managed once, I can manage again.'

'The offer is there,' said Fabian seriously. 'There are worse things in this life than to marry one's best friend.'

'There are, darling. There are. But, please – let's not concern ourselves with that just now. Let's concentrate on getting through this hideous day, attend this ball and make polite conversation with Holly and Pearl. And then – *poof*.' She fluttered her hands in the air for effect. 'We'll disappear back to London tomorrow and forget this weekend ever happened, yes?'

'If you say so, darling. If you say so,' said Fabian. And he dropped a kiss on her forehead before turning back to his sketchbook.

Sitting in the carriage with no hope of escape was torture. Absolute torture. As they bumped along the roads to Elton Lacy, Margaret sat primly opposite him with her hands folded in her lap. Squashed next to her, was her mother. Both women had sour, put-upon expressions on their faces. It was an expression he wasn't used to seeing on Margaret, and it didn't become her. It was so strange, he found it difficult not to study her intently; he just couldn't help but notice all the little lines of spoiled discontent around her pursed lips.

Perhaps *this*, he thought with a small shockwave of horror, was the real Margaret, and the girl he had been used to seeing recently was the polished waxed fruit version.

It was an odd, uncomfortable thought, and not one he wanted to dwell on. In fact, did he really *know* her? Know the woman he was getting closer and closer to committing himself to?

He surmised that he didn't.

Margaret had thrown a small tantrum because she felt her gown exposed too much flesh around the cleavage area (it didn't) and her mother had retaliated with a lace *fichu* she had forced Margaret to stuff down the offending area of her anatomy, which Margaret felt was old-fashioned and not conducive to her Dresden shepherdess outfit.

Louis had heard a concise retelling of this story and had nodded and looked concerned where appropriate, but he really didn't care one jot about Margaret's *fichu*, or indeed lack of it.

He was also beginning to suspect that he didn't care all that much about Margaret herself. Elsie's return had certainly made him rethink that – even though a few short hours ago, he'd been ready to commit to Margaret in holy matrimony. It had definitely been a day full of about turns and indecision.

Good God.

Unfortunately, Margaret had also seemed most put out when he'd refused, very politely, to come dressed as a shepherd who was a-courting the shepherdess. Privately, he thought he may as well pull a woolly fleece around himself and go as a sheep if she wanted to lay claim to him that badly.

It was very different to the costume ball he'd attended with Elsie four years ago – they had shared a carriage, just the two of them, and they had sat right next to each other, heads together, hand in hand, as they had laughed and talked away the journey.

The ball had been at Pencradoc – but Elsie, being Elsie, had decided to travel to Ashby Court to meet Louis first. She had, she told him grandly, a burning desire to feel the excitement of travelling to a ball whilst hidden inside a carriage with the man she loved. It was the first big social occasion he had attended since his illness the previous winter, and he was very much looking forward to seeing the crowd again. He had mock-seriously showed Elsie the invitation she'd sent him, and asked if she was the person he should expect a carriage ride from. She had whipped the invitation out of his hand and, laughing, tucked it somewhere down her bodice, somewhere no lace *fichu* had ever nestled, and said she was keeping it as a memento of the day she'd dragged him back into Society.

That was the ball where she had dressed as Morgan le Fay, and he as King Arthur. Despite that, or perhaps because of it, he had decided to dress as that good king again. If he saw her, she would remember – not that they could ever forget that night, or at least *he* wouldn't forget it. His anger smouldered as he remembered what she had said about their relationship being "forgettable".

'... and I do believe she's brought a man up with her from London. Isn't that right, Louis?' Margaret's cutting voice had interrupted his thoughts.

'Excuse me? Pardon?' Upon reflection, MC's interruption might have been a good thing though, as he could feel his brows knotting together as he considered all that had passed between himself and Lady Elsie Pencradoc that day – and all the time that had passed since. Then he flushed as he realised he had just caught himself thinking of his potential future bride with Holly and Pearl's name for her: Miserable Creature.

'Elsie Pencradoc.' Margaret spoke Elsie's name as if it dripped poison. 'A man. She's supposed to have brought a man up with her. No idea who he is – I heard he was some sort of Bohemian.' Margaret's face told Louis all he needed to know about her opinion on Bohemians. His opinion of MC slipped a little more – *that* was a personal affront to Elsie; no matter what she had said or done this morning, he simply couldn't switch a lifetime of emotions off like that.

'Well what do you expect – her mother is a walking scandal.' Mrs Corrington practically bristled with disgust.

'No better than she should be. Really – all those children out of wedlock. Disgusting. Comes out of getting involved with Bohemians.'

The women nodded in tandem, suddenly united in agreement about the horror that was Elsie's family. They agreed with one another a lot, Louis suddenly realised. He had a vision of Margaret sat there twenty years from now with her own daughter, doing exactly the same thing. It was hideous. He truly felt sorry for that future child, he really did!

'The Teagues are a perfectly lovely family,' he said now, unable to stop himself defending them. He held Elsie's family in very high regard and respected Ruan Teague immensely. And Zennor was like a second mother. He'd grown up alongside Elsie and her siblings and had often been told he was one of the family.

'Unwed mother. That's all that Zennor woman is. And those children are shameful.' That was Margaret.

Louis had had enough, and something inside him snapped. *This* was the woman everyone seemed to expect him to marry? God give him strength. 'There are only a *few* that were born out of wedlock – in fact, Elsie's real father died before she was born, so she doesn't come into that category. However—' Louis began counting on his fingers '—you're quite right. Laurie, Isolde and Medora came along before the wedding. But Clem, Enyon and Arthur are perfectly legal, as they were born within wedlock. So – only three of them. Half the family.' He held his hand up, showing three fingers. 'Only *half* the family are preposterously ... well ... I won't use the word you're thinking as I find it offensive.' He shrugged, nonchalantly. 'But there you go. Only three of them.'

The women stared at him, speechless for once. Until Margaret found her voice. 'I can't believe you're defending them, Louis. I have very strong morals, and I find I can't agree to it being acceptable within our social circle. And they have that big house! Pencradoc, of all places. To raise a family like that. A family of ... *Bohemians*.' She looked at her mother for validation and got it in another series of enthusiastic nods.

'Ah well. Just as well we're heading to Elton Lacy then, isn't it? I'm sure even the Devil himself couldn't drag *you* to a party at Pencradoc.' He smiled, surprising himself at how even he'd kept his voice, and nodded to show the conversation, as far as he was concerned anyway, was closed. He did know, however, that Margaret had complained bitterly when the Teagues had held a Harvest Supper Dance the previous year, and she'd found herself lacking an invitation. In fact, he believed it was jolly sporting of Pearl and Ernie to allow him to escort MC to their party tonight, but he kept that thought to himself.

Also the thought that perhaps they hadn't banked on Mrs Corrington coming along as well. That might be an interesting situation.

Margaret flushed angrily and stared out of the window. She perhaps didn't know that he knew about the Harvest Supper complaints, and she was obviously keeping her feelings well-hidden on that one.

He knew he should really make his intentions known tonight, but he felt more like a man being dragged to a scaffold than a man preparing to propose to someone.

Dear God above. It was his turn to stare out of the window. His heart felt like stone and settled unpleasantly somewhere in his chest.

This, he thought, *might be the pattern of the rest of my sorry life. Unless I can find Elsie tonight and change my whole rotten future ...*

Chapter Eleven

Present Day

'Will you be popping up to Pencradoc any time soon? You haven't been for ages. I miss you.' Merryn's voice was cheerful, which certainly didn't match the way Sybill was feeling. She was still seething at the conversation she'd had with Coren, a couple of weeks ago now, and alternating that with throwing minor tantrums that, thank goodness, nobody else was there to witness.

'I hadn't planned to.' Even as she said that, she was looking at the Morgan le Fay outfit. She'd brought it down from the attics, and despite offering it to Coren for the exhibition, she was reluctant now to take it up for him. It would be horribly awkward this time, after all that shit he'd talked about Ellory stopping him from wanting to take it any further with her. 'I've got something here that's actually destined for you guys, but I'm too busy right now, so I was going to arrange a courier to bring it up.' The dress was currently hanging in the exhibition room with all the portraits of Elsie, as the temperature was better controlled there for old fabric and works of art.

'Oh, no need for that. I've got something for you, so I'll drop it in on my way up. I just thought I'd check what your plans were. But if I know you're around, I'll call in later.'

'Okay. What time?'

'Half an hour or so. See you then.'

'All right. See you then, Merryn. I'll have the kettle on.'

'Excellent.' There was a smile in Merryn's voice as they said their farewells and disconnected the call.

True to her word, Merryn turned up, swinging her car into the private car park around the back of Wheal Mount and coming in via the staff entrance. She had a big smile on her face, and despite the situation with Coren that was playing on her mind, Sybill was pleased to see her. She was still horribly envious, of course, that Merryn was going to have a baby, but she was trying to tell herself that she couldn't blame her and Kit for that – and, to be fair, she had never told them about Lucia, so why would Merryn feel the need to keep things quiet?

She wouldn't.

So, because Sybill knew she hadn't exactly been the best friend to Merryn recently, she greeted her warmly and hugged her, tucking her arm into hers as she led her into the office. 'I love your dress,' she told her.

'This?' Merryn looked down at her pretty patchwork pinafore. She'd teamed it with bare legs, unicorn-patterned trainers and a flowing, rainbow-coloured silky scarf. 'I made it.' She flushed, seemingly embarrassed to admit it, but Sybill was impressed.

'Really? Gosh, you're so clever.'

'I wanted something colourful that made me feel good about myself.' She pulled a face. 'I don't feel that good about myself right now, so this helps.'

'But you're gorgeous!'

'Hmmm. Kit says so. But I feel like an elephant, my spatial awareness has gone AWOL and I can't bend over if I drop anything. But!' She brightened up again. 'I know how lucky I am. We tried a long time, we had some upsets on the way, and now it's happened, so I'm determined to enjoy it all.'

'Did you?' Sybill was surprised. 'I never knew.'

'It's not something we shared.' Merryn sat down awkwardly. She seemed a little uncomfortable today, and Sybill understood how that might feel. 'We were *this* close to seeking help, but then it happened, and everything went along as it should do, so we finally breathed a sigh of relief – and that's where we are. It was meant to be, I think.' She smiled again. 'Someone once told me that things happen when they're supposed to, so—' she patted her tummy '—this one will make its mark in the world, right when it's meant to.'

'How lovely.' Sybill went over to a small side table and flicked the kettle back on to boil. She paused for a second, then it just came out. 'I was pregnant once. I got to twenty-four weeks, and she was "born sleeping", as they say.'

'Oh my God! Sybill!' Merryn began to struggle out of the seat to come over to her, but Sybill waved her away.

'It's all right. It was a long time ago. Me and Lucia's father – we aren't together any more. Haven't been for a long, long time. None of it was meant to be. But I still miss her and I still think of her.'

'Oh, you're bound to.'

Sybill carried the mugs over to Merryn, and was sad to see her friend's pretty face crumpled and teary at Sybill's revelation. 'Honestly.' She sat down on the edge of her desk facing Merryn and wrapped her hands around her own mug. 'They don't know what caused it, but I don't think she was ever meant to be in this world. These things happen.'

'I don't know what to say.' Merryn shook her head. 'And here's me moaning about feeling fat. I feel awful now.'

'Don't. Don't feel awful. I'm sure at some point, I'll be able to moan back at you. I hope so anyway ...'

'You and Coren just need to sort yourselves out.' Merryn scowled, her sweet face looking angry now, and Sybill hid a smile behind her mug.

'Me and Coren. Ha. Well. It's not going great so far. Anyway. What is it you wanted to bring me?'

'Oh! He's *such* a stupid person! Anyway. Yes. These.' Merryn put her mug down and dived into her spacious bag. 'Two sketchbooks and a picture. Here. Everything was piled up in Matt's classroom. One of the cleaning staff found it all and left everything on my desk at Pencradoc with a note. I asked Coren if he knew anything about anyone bringing sketchbooks into that room and he said you'd been. I asked if he wanted to give them back to you, and you know—' here Merryn's face ran through a gamut of emotions – incredulity, anger, disbelief, then realisation '—you know, the idiot said no. God! Now I know why. You've had a tiff and you're both bloody stubborn. Is *that* why you were going to courier something up to us?'

'Maybe.' Sybill's eyes slid away from her friend's.

'Honestly. You're as bad as each other. What if I refuse to take it back up with me? Hmm? What if?'

'But you won't. Because it's so lovely that once you see it, you'll go *oooooooh*, and you'll want to spend some time with it. In the car. When you take it back up to Pencradoc. I mean—' Suddenly she stopped as her eyes settled on the sketchbooks. On top of them was the folded picture they'd looked at so closely in the classroom. She picked it up, meaning to tuck it back into the pocket in the book but, as she opened the sketchbook, there was a strange lumpy thing in there instead. She peered inside the folded cover, and, curled up into a little "S" shape, was a locket on the chain. Next to that was what looked like a pressed flower, but then she realised it was more of a slightly squashed, fresh flower – a marigold, if she wasn't mistaken. But, the locket was what concerned her the most. 'Hang on. There's a locket in here.' She pulled it out, and her stomach turned over. 'It's the same one we found on Little Elsie. I gave it to Coren because I figured it was lost property.'

'Oh! I wonder how that got there? Maybe it was stuck in a drawer and slipped in. I'll take it back then.'

'Thank you. It looks like someone put a flower in there too. Probably your cleaners. Anyway…' Sybill looked at the locket, knowing what was inside it. Someone was missing a picture of their family members, and she hoped it would find its way home eventually. 'Right. Okay.' She was definitely shaken a little bit but didn't want to let Merryn see. 'When you've finished that tea, we'll go and head into the exhibition space for you to see what I was going to courier. You can see the pictures as well. You might be able to help with one in particular. We don't have a name for the artist.'

'My favourite sort of mystery. Let's get going.' Merryn eased herself out of the chair, dropped the locket back into her bag, and they headed off towards the portraiture room.

Meanwhile, at Pencradoc, Coren was puzzling over Merryn's job description. He wasn't quite sure what attributes he would want in a temporary employee – a simple "please be like Merryn" would be perfect, but he didn't think that would translate too well in HR terms.

Kit wasn't at Pencradoc today, so he had nobody else to check with really. As they all said, he didn't "people" that well, but surely, given his history in business, he was pretty astute with the hiring and firing of employees. And that was true, but he'd always had the back-up of an HR team to do stuff like this, and, well, he'd never really had an employee as special as Merryn. He was wise enough to know that if it hadn't been for her, they would never have managed to get this place off the ground. And he would never have had the chance to meet Sybill.

Scowling, he pushed the paperwork away. Perhaps he'd move on to the wedding stuff again – then he finally acknowledged that everything was leading back to Sybill today, whichever way he looked.

Part of him desperately wanted to see her and speak to her, and part of him was still cringing every time he thought of the way they'd left things. When Merryn had offered to drop the sketchbooks off at Wheal Mount for him on her way into work, he'd had no hesitation in agreeing, but now he felt grumpy. That would have been a damn fine excuse to see Sybill again. Instead of being with her, he was sitting in his office and feeling at odds with the world.

His gaze roved across the room and settled on a folder. He knew that inside that folder was the photograph Sybill had brought across of Elsie and her mystery man all dressed up in fancy dress, along with the invitation to the Midsummer Costume Ball and the letter from Elton Lacy.

He got up and wandered over, opening the folder and spreading the papers out. *1911*. Three and a half years after the likely date of that intricate piece of artwork he'd seen in Matt's classroom – well, Elsie's old bedroom, it seemed. He picked up the photograph and studied it. So, if that had been Elsie in the 1907 piece, and she'd had a child in the early part of 1908, was this chap the father? Was this the great love of her life?

Something told him it wasn't. He put the picture down again and drummed his fingers on the tabletop. There was just something about the body language – they were obviously close. But they gave the impression of being more like friends than lovers. It was frustrating in the extreme – and, to be fair, he didn't quite know why he was so twitchy about it. Then he realised.

It came to him in a flash; so much so, that he felt a little light-headed and hung onto the edge of the desk for a moment until he felt more like himself.

This was not her husband. He knew this because, as he'd told Sybill, Aunt Loveday had often sat him and Kit down with the family albums and gone through, picture by picture, to make sure they understood their heritage and their family. Even then, when he and Kit were teenagers, Loveday must have already decided that they were going to be the ones who inherited Pencradoc, and it would be up to them to continue to love it and care for it as all the past members of their family had done. It was as good as their duty to understand and respect their ancestors, and to know a little about them and the history they'd brought to Pencradoc.

He knew this wasn't Elsie's husband, because he'd seen her wedding photograph. And if this was 1911, and she'd been married earlier than that, as they'd both surmised by the fact Elsie appeared to be pregnant in the impossibly detailed picture, then why was she still Lady Elsie Pencradoc on her 1907 Christmas cards, and who was this dark-haired man she was posing with? Her husband had been fair – he'd had, more or less, Coren's colouring. And he knew where he'd seen a recent picture of that man as well – in that damn locket that had been around Little Elsie's neck.

He knew now, without a doubt, that the man in that locket was a younger Louis Ashby.

1911

'Will I do?' Elsie appeared at Fabian's door dressed in her costume ball outfit. She indicated the dress and raised her chin defiantly, as she silently dared Fabian to disagree.

'Elsie! Should you really be here in my bedroom?'

Fabian was laughing at her, and she shrugged. 'I always like to visit my friends before we go to a ball. I like to see what they're wearing and to offer suggestions for improvements. And share a glass of champagne first – want one?' She brandished a bottle she had brought with her along with two glasses. 'Anyway, aesthetics are *so* important.' She rolled her eyes to heaven to emphasise the word "so". 'Yet you, my darling, could probably offer me advice. You look delightful.' She breezed in and he held the door open for her, mock-regally.

'Delightful? I see.' Fabian grinned. He was the image of an eighteenth-century dandy, complete with smart suit and highly polished boots. 'It was this or Lord Byron. But then I'd have to limp a bit. Club foot and all that.' He limped across the room to join her, clearly to make her laugh, and she did.

'To be fair, that outfit would work wonderfully either way.' Elsie nodded thoughtfully, satisfied that he had entered into the spirit of things. 'I like it. I don't need to improve you much at all.'

'I am perfection. That's good to know. But you – what are

you? That – whatever it is – wasn't what you told me you'd be going as.' He indicated her outfit – black dress, black cloak, wild hair. Basically, Elsie on a particularly "Elsie" sort of day. The dress was medieval in style, off-the-shoulder with long sweeping sleeves made of black lace and a corseted black bodice. She was using a jet necklace as a sort of crown which rested across her forehead, and had a black velvet band around her neck. The cloak was black velvet, trimmed with more jet and sparkling crystals, and there was an ornate gold fastening at her throat with the locket she always wore dangling into her ample cleavage.

'I'm a witch.'

'I see. You were going to be Queen Victoria, were you not?'

'I was. Not any more. Gone off the idea of a crinoline. Too awkward to move in.'

'I see.'

She put the glasses and the bottle down on the dressing table and indicated that Fabian should open the champagne. 'So, the carriage is coming in around twenty minutes. We should have a glass of this, then go downstairs and wait. I've asked Teague to take a photograph as well. I think it's important to record these momentous events, don't you?'

Fabian opened the champagne and poured them each a glass. He handed Elsie hers and they raised the glasses to one another mock-seriously before they took a drink. 'What's so momentous about this day that you need to record it? It's just a ball – I'm sure you've been to hundreds.'

Elsie took a deep, steadying breath. 'It's the first day of the rest of my life,' she said quietly. 'The day I've finally banished Louis from it.'

'We both know that's a lie,' said Fabian, smiling gently at her. 'You could never do that.'

Elsie dropped her gaze. *He was right, of course.* 'Well. Whatever. But it's a ball and we're both stunning so—'

'So, why not?' Fabian took her hand and kissed it. 'So, after our champagne, and after our photograph, let's go and knock 'em dead.'

Margaret stood stiffly beside Louis once they were in the ballroom of Elton Lacy. Her mother sat on one of the chairs arranged around the side of the room and settled herself to gossip with another chaperone.

'I think you should probably ask me to dance, Louis.' She cast a glance up at him, then focused again on the guests who all appeared to be having quite a good time. 'Perhaps after this little exhibition is finished, though.' She pressed her lips together disapprovingly as a young man and a younger woman held court in the middle of the floor, dancing in a way Louis had never seen before. They were laughing and the little crowd around them were nothing less than encouraging. She was dressed as a Parisian showgirl; he was dressed as a Wild West outlaw.

'Ah, that must be Pearl's brother and sister, Sam and Viola.' Louis smiled across at them. 'Pearl did say that they were coming – they've been in Paris and saw some interesting dancing, I believe. Ragtime, I think they called it. Rather progressive. And it looks quite fun. I think that one must be the Bunny Hug.' The pair were hugging one another, cheek to cheek, while their bottom halves were much further apart as they stomped and twirled to a fast piano tune, played on a shiny black Steinway by a laughing Pearl, who looked very much like Nell Gwynne this evening.

'I think it's appalling.'

Inside, Louis was screaming, *well you don't have to do it, do you?* But outwardly he simply shrugged and said, 'I don't think they're doing any harm.'

'That sort of exhibitionism is why I prefer to stay away from this sort of crowd. But never mind. We all must make sacrifices to assure our place in Society.'

Ah. So that was why she'd decided to come here – it was a way to get in with his "set".

He also knew that, had Elsie been beside him, she – or rather the old Elsie, not that strange creature he'd met this morning on the moor – would have tugged at his arm, her eyes sparkling with mischief, and suggested they give it a go.

'Oh dear. The evening just became *much* worse,' moaned Margaret, suddenly clutching Louis' arm. 'Look who just came in. Shocking. That's not an outfit suitable for this occasion, is it? She looks like she's in mourning.'

But even before he turned to see who Margaret had so scathingly referred to, he knew, he just *knew* who had walked in. The atmosphere shifted for him, and her very essence stole around him as the world seemed to slow down and shrink; a world just big enough for the two of them ...

He turned to face the door, and, before it seemed she'd even scanned the room to see who else was there, her eyes gravitated to his, and they stared at one another for what felt like a lifetime. In reality, it could only have been for a matter of seconds, but those few seconds were enough for Louis to read something in her eyes – something desperate that was still left unsaid between them. But as a slow flush coloured her cheeks and he took an involuntary step towards her, he felt the pressure of Margaret's hand on his arm and he was restrained.

'Isn't it a dreadful outfit for a party?' hissed Margaret.

'No. It's perfect.' There was a beat. 'She's Morgan le Fay.'

Chapter Twelve

Present Day

'Oh my word! That *dress*!' Merryn was suitably impressed with Elsie's Morgan le Fay outfit. The light from the chandeliers in the exhibition room, along with the sunlight dappling the wall, made it twinkle and almost breathe, so beautiful and delicate it was. 'It's like gossamer.'

'It's a bit sturdier than that, I think.' Sybill ran her hand over the old lace lovingly. 'I know I shouldn't really be touching it, but, well …'

'Sometimes you just can't help it, can you?' Merryn grinned and stood well back from the dress, her hands shoved in her large patchwork pockets, almost as if she was resisting the temptation herself. 'What's the story behind it?'

'I think it's the dress Elsie wore to the Elton Lacy Midsummer Costume Ball in 1911. I … I, um, found it after I'd discovered the photograph and everything in the archives here.'

'Oh yes – Coren said you'd taken some things up to Pencradoc. I need to have a look at them properly myself, but I got caught up in something for the art dealers so haven't managed yet.' Merryn was still a consultant for her old employers in London and occasionally she worked on a project or two for them. Sybill sometimes wondered how she did it all but had long ago come to the conclusion that Merryn was indeed Superwoman. 'Actually—' Merryn's eyes twinkled with mischief as she got her phone out ' —I'm going to text him right now to ask him to send me a copy of that photo. Then we can compare it against the frock, and we'll know for sure. Then, if you trust me with it, I can take it up to Pencradoc today. I had a good look at what we have, and the tailor's dummy from Aunt Loveday's sewing room will be perfect to display this dress on. Don't worry – it's not going to fit me right now, so there's no danger I'll run away with it and wear it. Can you even *imagine* having a waist that tiny? Elsie must have been well-corseted to get into that. Plus, Coren will be so happy that I'm here with you, he'll call me right back and demand to speak to you.'

'Oh ha ha.' Sybill rolled her eyes. 'I doubt it. And yes. Her waist must have been so small.' She stroked the dress, then made a great effort to walk away from it.

'He *should* call. Otherwise he's even more stupid than I give him credit for.' Merryn finished her text and pressed send, then looked at the pictures hanging up. Sybill could tell where Merryn's heart lay – her eyes widened even more at the sight of all the portraits than they had done at the dress, if that was even possible. 'So, which is the picture you're having problems with?' She wandered off towards the portraits and Sybill followed her.

'This one.' She pointed at it. 'It's actually my favourite one, so I'm quite annoyed I don't know who did it.'

'Ahhh – yes. I see it.' Merryn studied it a bit more closely and leaned into it. 'I know why you like it though – it looks like you.' She smiled and pointed to the girl on the canvas. 'If your hair was curly, and you looked really super snooty one day, that would be you.'

'My hair *is* curly. But I'm not sure I like the super snooty reference!' Despite her teasing, her stomach somersaulted. *Was* that why she liked it? Why she felt drawn to it? 'I thought it was more her attitude that I needed to channel. She just looks – well – like she doesn't give a damn.'

'And isn't she fabulous? Yes. That's an early portrait of Elsie all right. I like the style. It's similar to James Tissot, but we're looking at a contemporary of Elsie's. Hmm. I wonder ...' Merryn tapped her fingertips on her chin thoughtfully. 'His style is a bit untrained here, but we're talking a few years before he—' Her words were interrupted by an alert on her phone. 'Oh! Coren sent an email. That was quick.' She flicked open the screen and studied the message. 'Oh my goodness. Yes!' She punched the air, and Sybill took a step back in astonishment. Merryn turned to her, her eyes sparkling and brandished the phone. 'That dress over there, it *does* look very much like the one in this picture. And this portrait here.' She waved the phone at the picture. 'I'm pretty sure now who it is. Fabian Austen. He was a friend of Elsie's at Slade. He was mentored, sort of, by Teague, and I'm certain he's this guy – the chap in the photograph who escorted her to the ball. He's a few years younger here, but I've seen plenty of photos of him from the war, so I'm confident it's him.'

'Fabian Austen? The war artist?'

'The very same.' Merryn smiled. 'Oh, that's made my day, that has. I was at an auction a couple of years ago, and some of his Paris Portraits were going for sale. He was famous, as you say, for his World War One art, but then after the war he picked up his portraiture again and was hugely successful in Paris. He did a very early series for the Teague family, some of which are in the National Portrait Gallery, I believe. Most of them went to the homes of the family as they moved away from Cornwall. I did a bit of research when we were setting up Pencradoc for visitors to see if we could get the London ones on loan, but I had no luck. We'd just started out, so I guess we needed to prove our worth first.' She shrugged. 'Not to worry. I haven't forgotten about it. It's all on my list.'

Sybill felt faint. 'Why on earth did I not know any of that about Fabian Austen and his work for the Teagues? I only knew about the war stuff!'

'Because it's *my* job to know snippets like that about the Teagues, not yours.' Merryn smiled, and of course she was right. Wheal Mount had been Alys and Jago's house, whereas Pencradoc had been Zennor and Teague's – and, much later, Elsie's. Sybill had invested most of her time into learning about Wheal Mount, and then moving on to Elsie and her immediate family where it all dovetailed into Wheal Mount's history; she'd never really delved into the wide range of friends Elsie had made at art college or the Slade until she was preparing for this very exhibition.

Suddenly, there was a faint giggle from the direction of the dress, and then a whispered comment in Sybill's ear which made her shiver: *'He did rather well for himself in the end. We all adored Jean-Luc.'*

Merryn was chatting away, happily unaware of Sybill's pounding heart and dry mouth. 'Fabian was much more famous on the continent – I think he moved there because of, well, personal circumstances, shall we say? He met someone just after the war, a French soldier, I believe, and they were lifelong partners. Montmartre and Bohemian Paris was their world. As far as I understand he loved it, and it loved him.'

'His partner—' Sybill managed to make the words sound relatively conversational. 'Who was he?'

'Jean-Luc Allard.' Merryn answered without missing a beat. 'He was a writer. One of the portraits that went to the auction was a portrait of Jean-Luc. Fabian had painted himself in the mirror behind him as if he was just doing a normal portrait, but the meaning was pretty clear to all concerned, I think. And there's lovely Fabian Austen himself in our photo. Escorting Elsie to a ball. That's absolutely brilliant, it really is.' She looked back at her phone and tapped a few more keys. She held it up to her ear until it connected, then she grinned at Sybill.

Sybill thought she might genuinely faint. *Jean-Luc*? She'd never known that name – but someone had just whispered it right into her ear.

'Oh! Hello.' Merryn was speaking now, stalking around the room, barely able to hide her excitement. 'Yes. I've got someone to speak to you. Just to let you know what we've discovered.' Then, before Sybill could think straight, Merryn shoved the phone at her and backed away.

'Merryn?' There was an odd noise on the other end of the phone, a crackling of some sort, and the voice that eventually spoke back to him was not Merryn, even though she was the one who had made the call and who he'd been speaking to only seconds before. '*Sybill*?'

'Yes. It's me. Hello, Coren.' She sounded a little stiff and formal and he didn't like it one bit, but then who could blame her after he'd dumped the Ellory story on her and brushed her off? *God*! He dropped his forehead onto the table and closed his eyes. What the hell was he doing?

He sat upright again and cleared his throat. 'It's good to hear your voice, Sybill. Really good. I mean it.'

'I'm sure you do.' There was a beat, and the unsaid comment went something like, *but not good enough to let us become any closer*. He closed his eyes again and raised his face to the ceiling, despairing of his own idiocy. He was glad Kit wasn't here today now – *so* glad. 'Anyway. Merryn made me talk to you.' And there it was – *Merryn made me*. Not "I wanted to". But really, who could blame her? 'Because we've just made a connection to Elsie, the 1911 Midsummer Costume Ball and a portrait in my exhibition.'

'Really?' That made him sit up even straighter. He glanced at the photograph which was still on his desk. 'Because of the photo I sent?'

'Yes.' Her voice was brisk, efficient, typical professional Sybill. He wanted that warmer Sybill back, the one he had come closer to knowing so recently.

Then an odd, clipped voice, which certainly wasn't Sybill's because it was male, suddenly grumbled in his ear: '*It's your own bloody fault, man!*'

He jumped and stood up, his heart thundering. He moved away from the desk, as if that would remove him from the area where the man with the grumbling voice could reach him.

The saving grace was that the voice did not sound or feel like Ellory – but it was still deeply unsettling. He forced his attention back to the call. 'Okay. Hit me with it.'

Hit me with it? What on earth? Was he now channelling some New York business mogul? He cringed again, but suddenly there was a note of amusement in Sybill's voice.

'My God, Coren. Where did *that* come from?'

Relieved to hear her sounding less formal, he smiled into his phone and relaxed a little. 'No idea. I wish I could take it back, though.'

'Me too. Well, putting your desire for brute force to one side, it was just to say that we think – what? – sorry, Merryn, we've now decided we *know* – that the chap in your photograph is Fabian Austen, the war artist, and one of Teague's sort-of pupils. We've also established that the unsigned picture I've got here of Elsie is by Austen as well. Hurrah.'

'Really? That's great news.' As he was speaking to her, he pulled open the desk drawer where he'd been keeping the locket, ready to tell Sybill what he suspected the miniatures inside to be as well. But the locket wasn't there. He frowned into the desk and rummaged around, pulling out bits of paper and oddments of stationery. Even some sort of orangey-yellow flower was buried under there, just like the garland Elsie had been wearing. God knew what that was doing there ... unless one of the flower heads had somehow snagged on him and fell in the drawer? That wasn't important though, and he focused back on the lost locket.

He knew he definitely hadn't moved it. They had initially thought it was lost property, so it really should have gone in that box, tucked away in the cupboard. But Coren had found himself reluctant to put it in there for some reason. And now ... now it had gone.

Dammit.

Slamming the drawer shut, he felt his face settle into that familiar scowl again. 'I had something else to run by you, but it'll have to wait,' he said. 'I just need to double check something first.' Yes, he needed to double check where that bloody locket was.

'Okay, no problem.' There was a beat. 'Do you need Merryn today? Does she need to be on site for anything?'

Coren thought about it. 'The only thing I was going to get her to do was look at this stupid job description. That's all I needed her for. Why?'

'Just checking. Merryn—' Sybill's voice faded a little '—Coren just wants you to look at your, and I quote, "stupid job description", today – so if you've not got anything else on, he says you can take the day off and he'll email it to you.'

Coren could hear Merryn's response. 'Really? Well, Kit's working in Marazion today. Maybe I'll head back and see if he can bunk off for a bit and we'll do something nice. Have lunch maybe. That's great. No, whatever I had to do was mainly just admin which can wait. I was going to take those things up for you, as you know, but if that can wait too…' She raised her voice. 'Thanks, Coren! Appreciated!'

'It's fine. I'll take them up myself.' Coren's heart turned over as he heard Sybill's response. 'Tammy is in, so she can cover me for a couple of hours if I tell her what needs doing. I need to see Coren anyway.' Her voice on the phone became louder again as she began to speak directly to him. 'Did you hear that? Merryn's taking the day off, and I'm heading up. I've got something for your exhibition, and something else I think I need to return. See you soon, Coren.'

'See you soon, Sybill. And …' He paused. 'Thank you. You've no idea what this means to me.'

'Hmmm. See you soon.'

'See you soon.'

And this time, when he disconnected the call, he couldn't

stop smiling and the day seemed one hundred and ten percent better already.

1911

'Are you all right, my love?' Fabian whispered in Elsie's ear, breaking whatever spell she'd been under as she stared at Louis.

'He's King Arthur,' she said, rather stupidly. What difference did that make to whether she was all right or not? 'I mean, that's what he was dressed as at the last one of these we went to. Well … hosted. It was at Pencradoc.'

'I see.' Fabian steered her away from the entrance towards a manservant holding a tray of champagne. 'Maybe you need another one of these.'

'Can't hurt.' She took one and sipped it, her gaze darting around the dance floor to see who was there and who wasn't; who she could recognise and who might be new to the set.

'And this witch outfit you're wearing?' Fabian was nothing if not persistent. 'I'd hazard a guess that you're actually Morgan le Fay. She's Arthurian, isn't she? An Arthurian witch?'

'I have no idea.'

'Quite.' Now he sounded amused. Elsie wasn't stupid, and he knew that. She flushed. Of course he knew that she knew that Morgan le Fay was Arthurian. *Damn him!*

She took another sip of champagne, turning away from Louis and the awfully frilly woman on his arm. Whoever the hell that was – and she had a horrible feeling she knew who it might be – the woman was well hidden under a ridiculous poke bonnet and an innumerable number of pink ribbons. They made an incongruous pair.

'Elsie! My goodness! You look simply perfect. Bang up to the elephant, in fact.' Elsie felt a pressure on her arm and turned to see Holly next to her. She couldn't help smiling at her old friend, despite the energy she could sense coming off Louis, fizzing, sparking almost, towards her.

'Hols! Look at you – just *look* at you.' Holly was shrouded in some sort of Greek toga, which was tied under her bust with a gold cord. It had been several months since Elsie had seen Holly, and her friend's pregnancy was extremely obvious now. 'Should you even be here? In this condition? My goodness, you can't have long to go! May I?'

'Of course.' Holly laughed and nodded, and took hold of Elsie's hand. Holly laid it on her stomach, pressing gently, and Elsie felt her heart melt a little as the baby responded.

'Oh my goodness. I'm speechless.'

'It's all very new to me. I'm not sure I like these later stages. The strange twinges, and the constant need to relieve oneself ...' Holly raised her eyebrows comically. 'Five weeks to go. And really, if I didn't wear this thing today—' she plucked at the white fabric crossly '—then my choices would be quite limited. Perhaps an Elizabethan farthingale, hitched up quite high to cover one's body? Perhaps one could emulate a Regency heroine, and drape the fabric of the frock fetchingly over one's torso? I have no idea. I'm damn sure I'm not hiding in the house for the next five weeks though. No. I will waddle my way around Society as much as I can, *whilst* I can.'

Elsie felt herself flush at the mention of Regency heroines. That was the exact style of dress she had worn that Christmas she had come home. 'You look beautiful. It suits you,' she said honestly. And indeed her friend did look glowingly happy. It was, however, another little twist of the knife. Elsie had had nobody to confide in or talk to or support her over that time apart from Lily and Edwin, to whom she would be forever grateful. She cast a glance over Holly's shoulder and caught Louis in her sights. Tears pricked at her eyes, and she blinked them away rapidly before Holly noticed, then decided to quickly change the subject.

'Oh. Excuse me,' she said. 'This is Fabian. From London. He's my escort for this evening. He's taken the opportunity to meet Teague whilst he's down here this weekend.'

'Fabian!' Holly smiled at Fabian, who bowed low and kissed her hand in the correctly dandy-ish fashion. 'How nice to meet you. Pearl's over there. Perhaps we should go and introduce you, now that she's finished her piano playing. You may see a Greek god conversing with King Charles the Second. If that's the case, it's Noel and Ernie, and we should probably say hello to them. And I should probably ask who you've come as, Elsie? You'd make a perfect illustration.'

Holly eyed Elsie thoughtfully and Elsie just smiled, adjusting her jet head dress. 'I'm a witch.' Deep down, she was thanking God that neither one of her friends had been able to attend the Pencradoc ball where she had worn this outfit last. One had been far too heavily *enceinte* with the twins, and the other had been travelling abroad.

'She's not. She's Morgan le Fay,' added Fabian helpfully.

Damn.

'Oh! But isn't Louis King Arthur?' Holly swung around to see him. 'There! There he is—'

'Yes. Yes indeed.' Elsie grabbed Holly's arm and pushed it down, just as Holly was about to point at Louis. 'Honestly, dearest, I'm just a witch.'

'You're not.' Fabian dipped his head as he muttered the phrase, and Elsie took a very large sip of champagne, draining the glass. It was a mistake. The bubbles and the alcohol went straight to her head, and she blinked again.

The room spun, just a little, and she took Fabian's arm. 'Come. Let's go with Hearl and see Polly – I mean Pearl. And Polly. *Holly*!' She shook her head and fastened herself more closely on Fabian's arm. 'Come.'

She began pulling him towards Pearl, but he was terribly slow this evening. 'More champagne, Miss le Fay?' he murmured, and she knew he was teasing. He grabbed a glass from a passing tray to tempt her though and waved it in front of her nose.

'Maybe. Maybe later.' Goodness, she'd need a bucket of

the stuff to get her through tonight if Louis kept appearing everywhere she looked. He was, it seemed, heading over to see Pearl as well. They were heading in some sort of parallel trajectory towards the hostess, and there was nothing she could do to stop it, flanked as she was between Persephone, the Greek goddess of damnable fertility, and Beau Bloody Brummell …

'Give me that.' She snatched the glass of champagne from Fabian and, much against her better judgement, drained that one too.

My goodness.

Not since her college days and her brushes with absinthe had she felt *quite* so floaty-away …

Elsie stumbled a little and Fabian pulled her upright. 'Steady on, Morgan. Maybe that was a glass too far.'

'Maybe,' she muttered and tried to focus on Pearl. And not look at Louis. And that frilly thing on his arm! It *was* Margaret. Margaret Corrington. Could the evening get any worse?

She stopped dead and refused to budge. 'She's here. What's she doing here?' Elsie demanded of Holly. 'Ah! She's the one he's supposed to marry, you know?'

'I think you've just answered your own question, darling,' said Holly, wide-eyed and apparently trying not to laugh at Elsie. 'I don't think she was officially invited, if that makes you feel better. But dear God. You're inebriated! I thought you were made of sterner stuff.'

'Perhaps she shouldn't have had two glasses of champagne within the space of fifteen minutes.' That was Fabian, and his voice seemed to come from a long way away. 'Oh God. That's my fault. We'd already had some at Pencradoc. She can normally take her alcohol a bit better than this—'

'Mmm. Champagne and Elsie don't go together that well,' commented Holly.

'Do so,' muttered Elsie. ''s lovely. Lovely champagne.'

'She matches me quite well, glass for glass with normal wine,' said Fabian. His face swum, concerned, in front of Elsie's, and she blinked, trying to wave it away from her.

'Normal wine is fine. Not champagne though.'

'Oh *ssssshhhhhh*.' Elsie flapped her hand in front of Holly's face this time. 'I won't have any more. Promise. Now. Let's see Pearl.' She stood straight up, tugged her cloak together quite neatly at the front, and began to walk forwards again.

'Come on then, old girl.' Fabian continued to escort her, and Elsie saw Pearl waving madly at them. She waved back, making sure she looked straight at Pearl, and not anywhere near Louis. Who, *oh God*, had almost made it over to Pearl too. Still. She could ignore him. She really could.

Louis kept apace with Elsie, far away at the other side of the ballroom. His long strides carried him across the room, heedless of anyone who might be in his way.

'Louis, where are we going?' Margaret was trotting alongside of him, looking cross and very flushed. 'I don't want to go and see those awful Ragtime dancers.'

'I'm going to see Pearl. And I'm going to meet her family. It's up to you if you come or not.' *And I know Elsie is heading that way, so I'm damn well doing the same.*

'But her family seem rather common, don't you think? Are they really the sort of people you feel you should be introducing me to? If you encourage them, they might think that they can do that sort of thing in *our* house on a social occasion.'

'In *our* house?' Louis stopped for a split second and stared at her, incredulous. 'Dearest Margaret. We don't share a house. I've never, if you think back, actually expressed a desire *to* share a house with you. We'd probably need to be married first, and I'm *damn* sure I've never asked you that question either!' *And I'm really* not *going to ask you that question tonight, tomorrow, or any other day, ever, at all*, he wanted to add. It was still, as it always had been, astoundingly obvious to him which one of these women he wanted to spend the rest of his life with. His mind had been quite clearly made up on that matter the moment Elsie had walked into that ballroom, and all thoughts of half-heartedly proposing to Margaret Corrington had fled from his mind. He loved Elsie. He couldn't and wouldn't exist without her. As Holly had said, it was time to fight for what he wanted. Louis' next words came out a lot more calmly than he thought they would, as he continued to walk determinedly towards Elsie Pencradoc. 'I would just simply like to see my old friend Pearl and meet her family, that's all. They've come a long way to be here tonight.'

'You're heading that way because Elsie Pencradoc is heading that way, aren't you? Look at her – with that dreadfully foppish looking man and that awful Holly Edwards. She should be lying in or something – not parading herself around like that. She's with child!'

'With child!' This time Louis did laugh, but he kept walking. 'My dear, it's hardly contagious. I don't think you'll catch it from her.'

'You know what I mean! It's … obscene! Being in public in such an obvious condition.'

'Babies are born. Women have to carry them. That's just the way it is.' His patience was wearing thin. And the physical distance between he and Elsie, *thank God*, was finally decreasing …

Chapter Thirteen

Present Day

So, here she was again, pulling up into the staff car park at Pencradoc. Sybill sighed. It seemed she was fated to spend the rest of her earthly days shuttling between the two, no matter what her head told her. One small conversation with him, and her heart had told her to jump in the car and go to him.

It must have been easier, she thought, *in the olden days, when it was literally a stomp across Bodmin Moor to see the love of your life.*

Then she battered down that thought, wondering where it had come from. She caught sight of the Morgan le Fay dress neatly packaged up again and then glanced at her handbag in the passenger footwell.

She had left the sketchbooks and the picture of a possibly pregnant Elsie at Wheal Mount, uncertain where they best fitted in. At the moment, it seemed right to keep them with Elsie's other books but, as Sybill often did, she privately reserved the right to change her mind. She had, however, brought the locket with her. That *should* be here. There was no doubt about it in her mind. She hadn't quite had the courage to open it up again; the image of the little dark-haired girl was seared into her mind and, without Coren there, she wasn't sure she wanted to look at it.

There was more now though. As she thought about it, and re-imagined the faces of the people inside smiling out at her, she focused more on the man. There was a niggle there, and she didn't quite know how to interpret it. The only way she could think to describe it was a sense of familiarity. But there was no time to dwell on it, as she looked up and saw Coren coming out of the door. He must have been waiting for her to pull up, and that thought gave her a little warm feeling in her treacherous heart.

'Hello, Coren.' She climbed out of the car and went around to the passenger side. 'I've got a couple of things for you. Here. Take this.' She opened the back door and carefully took the dress out. 'Then we can go in and you can have a look at it.'

'Sure, whatever you think.' He took the package off her and gestured that she should go in front of him. Sybill led the way into Coren's office; a route she could probably do blindfolded, if she was honest. She felt as if she knew Pencradoc as well as Wheal Mount now.

'Whatever it is, it's heavy.'

Coren laid the package down on the sofa in his room, and Sybill started unpacking it, peeling back the layers of tissue. 'It is. But it's worth it when you see it.'

Sybill saw realisation dawn on Coren's face as soon as the sequins and beads were exposed against the rich black fabric. 'Is that *really* Elsie's Morgan le Fay dress?' He looked stunned as he stared at it.

'I believe so. Like I said, it would be good to display here, and Merryn said you definitely have Aunt Loveday's tailor's dummy somewhere. So that would be great.'

'Yes. We've got that. We left Loveday's sewing room much as it was when she lived here, so that's easy to get to. I wasn't sure if it would work, but I'm sure we can try. It's probably the wrong shape.'

'Hmm. The thing with tailor's dummies is that the good ones are usually adjustable. We'll have a look and see.'

"We'll *have a look and see?" Really, Sybill?* She scolded herself. This wasn't drawing away from him. This was like finding excuses to be near him and spend more time with him.

'Great. We'll go and have a look. Come on.' Now he was smiling at her, holding his hand out, and she was helpless, eager and totally unable to formulate a justifiable reason not to ...

'Okay,' she said. And that was it.

Coren knew Aunt Loveday's sewing room had been more than just her sewing room. It had been her hideaway, a place to read or sew or simply spend time in. It held all her precious things, and it had been particularly hard to go into that room when Coren and Kit had inherited the place, when Loveday was no longer there with her welcoming smile, her bright eyes and her carefully powdered cheeks that always made Coren sneeze when he kissed her.

It was a scent, though, that he remembered well, and Loveday's room still smelled faintly of it. He immediately felt himself calm down a little when he unlocked the door and they stepped inside. He hadn't realised how wound up he'd been waiting for Sybill to turn up, until he felt the tension leave his body and his shoulders relax a little when they shut the door behind them.

'Oh, what a lovely room.' Sybill looked around her in delight. 'And this was Loveday's haven, I suspect.'

'It was. It's not generally used now, so it's only me, Kit and Merryn who come in here every so often. When Kit and I were kids, we used to come in here and poke through all the drawers and cabinets.' Coren smiled, remembering. 'That one there was full of old-fashioned soaps and bath cubes, and the one next to it had all her beads and costume jewellery in. She didn't keep anything expensive in there – but she was big on her animal brooches, so Kit used to make a farm for them, and build the walls out of cotton reels and things. I was more interested in the books. She loved detective stories and had all the Agatha Christie ones, plus a huge collection of Enid Blyton books. I was a massive Famous Five fan.' He nodded over to a bookshelf. 'They're still there. And look – that's the thing I was thinking about.

Will she do? Loveday always called her "Tilly".' The tailor's dummy was standing in the window, draped with scarves and swathes of fabric.

'She's perfect.' Sybill went over and inspected the dummy carefully. 'Yes. She's adjustable, so we can easily get the dress onto her. I think the waist should go small enough – the dummy looks old enough to have been from the early part of the twentieth century anyway so, if we're careful, we should be okay. We'll just need to make sure she's sturdy enough, but we can get that all checked over quite quickly. I'll have a go and see if I can squish her around a bit. Brilliant.' She clapped her hands in that funny little way she had, and, yet again, Coren realised how much he had missed her being at Pencradoc.

'Oh!' He suddenly remembered something. 'Photographs. This is where Loveday kept the albums I told you about.' The memory of the strange scene in Elsie's old bedroom came back to him, but he refused to acknowledge it and deliberately pushed it to the back of his mind. 'I'll get the one out that had the pictures in I, um ... recognised. The one I'm thinking of has Elsie's wedding picture in too. You might like to see that.' The image of Louis popped into his head again, and he felt himself grow hot as he remembered that he still hadn't found the locket.

'Thank you.' Sybill looked up at him and smiled cheekily. 'I'd love to see them. But first – who are these two cute little guys here?' She pointed to a school photograph of Coren and Kit, and Coren couldn't help but laugh.

'I'm not even going to dignify that with a response. Go and meddle with Tilly over there, and I'll dig some interesting photos out.'

'Spoilsport.'

But he had to acknowledge that he was very gratified to hear that note of fun creep back into her voice. He had missed it terribly.

'Elsie! How splendid to see you!' Pearl swooped down on her and embraced her. Elsie aimed a kiss at her friend's cheek and Pearl laughed. 'You look stunning. Absolutely wonderful.' She pronounced it "wunnerful", and that made Elsie smile.

'Thank you. I'm a ... *witch*! Please don't burn me at the stake.'

'Would I ever. And who's this?' Pearl looked curiously at Fabian.

'My friend. Fabian. He's good at art – an artist. A really, really *good* artist. Yes. Salons. Portraits. All good.' She nodded sagely. 'Teague likes him. He really does. Good news! Hurrah!'

'Pleased to meet you, Lady Elton.' Fabian bowed and nodded, and, despite her fuzzy head, Elsie was pleased he'd remembered Pearl's title. She'd briefed him on it earlier. She nudged him and whispered, far too loudly, 'Well done.'

'Thank you,' he whispered back, seemingly trying to fight back a smile.

'This is my brother, Samuel. And my sister, Viola.' Pearl indicated the two people who stood next to her. 'I'm so pleased they're here.'

'Wunnerful,' agreed Elsie, smiling at them. 'Lovely to meet you. I'm Lady Elsie Pencradoc. But tonight, I'm a witch.' She unfastened herself from Fabian's grasp, and curtsied deeply and theatrically to Sam and Viola.

'You're Morgan le Fay.'

Elsie was still deep in her curtsey, her head bowed, staring at the floor, when she heard *him* say that. She froze for a moment, then took a deep breath and stood upright again. Inclining her head – *oh my, the world really* was *wobbling tonight* – she greeted him.

'And you're King Arthur.' She was surprised the words sounded as conversational as they did. Well, they did to her at least. 'Surprising.'

'Not really.' His eyes locked on hers, and she found she

couldn't look away – although she wasn't entirely sure she was focusing on them properly either.

'Oh!' Pearl suddenly clapped her hands. 'King Arthur and Morgan le Fay! Of *course*! They'd go together quite well, wouldn't they?'

'They would,' Louis responded without taking his eyes from her. 'They do.'

'They don't. They can't.'

'They did before.'

His voice was quiet, stony, but she knew exactly what he meant. He didn't mean "before" as in four years ago, when they'd last attended a costume ball together. He meant "before" as in a few hours ago, when their bodies were tangled on Bodmin Moor, when real life was just a dream and anything had seemed possible ...

'No.' She shook her head. 'Not any more.'

'Louis!' The shepherdess spoke quite harshly, and Elsie looked at her in surprise. She'd almost forgotten there was anyone else in that ballroom. Again, the world had shrunk to hers and his alone. 'Come away. We can speak to *Lady Elton—*' at this she bowed and curtsied in a flurry of petticoats at Pearl '—later. When it's not quite so ... *dreadful* at this end of the room. There are people here who perhaps shouldn't be here, and they really shouldn't be encouraged to linger.' She said the next few words in a stage whisper to rival anything that Elsie had said in a similar way that evening. 'Unconventional families, you know. All those *children*. And the Bohemian types they associate with.' Here, she flicked a disgusted glance at Fabian. Elsie wanted to slap her. 'Just as we were saying earlier. In the carriage. When you were escorting me here. *Darling*.' She made her eyes wide and huge and nodded very indiscreetly towards Elsie.

'Dreadful?' Elsie stared at her and blinked. She felt the anger bubble up inside her; a burning hot rage she had never ever felt before in her life. Suddenly, her friends were flanking her, moving towards her like a protective shield. She glanced right and left, and caught Holly and Pearl looking in horror at Margaret Corrington. Their presence – and, to be fair, the champagne – gave her courage, although, in this moment, she suddenly felt as sober as a judge. 'Dreadful? You've just insinuated my family are *dreadful*? That my dear friend here, who has come all this way to escort me tonight, is too Bohemian for your tastes?' She clenched her fists, digging her nails into her palms and glaring at the woman before her. 'Why, pray tell, are my family so dreadful? Why am I so dreadful that you can't even bear for Louis to talk to me? What have me or my family ever done to you?'

Margaret was apparently taken aback and clutched Louis' arm. Louis, however, gently slid his arm out of her grip and folded his arms, staring at Elsie. 'Elsie. It's not worth it,' he said.

'Oh, but it is.' Elsie continued to look at Margaret, her fists balled. 'I'm not going to allow her to speak of my family or friends like that. And you, Louis. Why on earth are you even considering marrying her? Do you know what she said when your brother married? She said she was pleased she didn't have to marry into a family who had "only" had a title for a couple of hundred years. She wanted to be presented at Court properly, and do the Season to, and I quote, "get out of this awful old county and away from people like the Ashbys". That's what I wanted to tell you that day you came to my house. I wish I had said that now, I really wish I had!'

'I did *not* say that!' Margaret began to defend herself and looked up at Louis, shocked. 'I did not. She's lying. Like she always has done—'

'You did. You told Clara. The same day you told her Pearl was "brash" and Holly was "too liberal"! Yet here you are being all curtsey-ish to Pearl, because she has this huge house and you're lucky enough to be in it tonight. You think if you're nice to her, she'll help you get a foot up the social ladder. And

God knows what you said about me. Clara didn't tell me that one, but I can imagine it was less than complimentary.'

Margaret flushed an angry red. There was no denying it, Elsie knew. She *had* said all that and more; she couldn't get out of it. At this stage, it seemed that attack was Margaret's best form of defence. 'Whatever I said about you was absolutely true.' Her voice was cold and bitter. 'You act like a Lady, but everyone knows you're not really. You live a life of God knows what in London. You think everyone should do exactly as you ask. You have no concept of anyone else's feelings. You drift around without a care in the world and, yes, I did want to get away from here. It's because I can't stand being around people like you. You and your horrible family, with all that money and all that privilege and all that immoral behaviour that goes on behind closed doors. It's true that Zennor Teague is no better than an unwed mother. Louis is best off without you in his life, without someone so dramatic and so ... exhibitionist. And when we are married, I shall make it compulsory that he doesn't associate with you any more. That, *Lady* Elsie Pencradoc, is a foregone conclusion, and I expect him to transfer his loyalties to me – his *wife*.'

'His wife. I see.' Elsie felt something inside her finally snap. The pain and secrets and hurt from the last four years started to boil over, and she couldn't stop herself – couldn't stop herself from saying it. 'And the mother of his firstborn child, no doubt.' She nodded. She'd gone too far this time. She couldn't reel it back in.

'Elsie!' Fabian's voice was in her ear, warning her. 'Stop it. Not here, darling.'

'Yes, here. Where else would I get such a wonderful opportunity? Don't forget, I'm overly dramatic and an exhibitionist to boot.' She curtsied theatrically again and then straightened up to her full height. Elsie took a few steps towards Louis, stood right in front of him, fixing her dark eyes on his grey ones. 'Louis. We have a daughter. Her name is

Marigold Louisa Pencradoc. She lives in London. She's three years old. So, I, too, am an unwed mother. And I will be just as glad never to associate with you and your wife-to-be as she will be to banish us from your life.' Elsie turned to face the rest of the listeners who all looked completely shocked. 'And that, my friends, is the end of the show.'

She curtsied again, and, holding her head high, took hold of Fabian's arm, and walked towards the open French windows that led out into the gardens of Elton Lacy.

There was a stunned silence as Elsie's words died away in the ballroom.

Louis' head began to spin – if ever there was a bolt from the blue, Elsie had just delivered it. He felt as if a man at least ten times bigger than him had just punched him in the stomach, and all the air had *whooshed* out of his ropey old lungs. He struggled to comprehend her words for a second or two, but then a million questions flooded into his mind. The most immediate thing was to go to her, to find out if it was true, or whether it was something she had simply said in the heat of the moment, in the most truly shocking incredible "Elsie" fashion. He realised with another powerful rush of emotion that he desperately hoped it was true …

'Elsie! Wait! Please!'

He went to run after her, but Noel put his hand on his arm. 'Leave her.' Louis looked at Noel without really seeing him, wanting only to touch her, to hold her, to hear her say those words again. 'Talk to her later. Not here. Not with everyone watching.' He nodded across to Margaret, who was standing aghast.

Then Margaret seemed to galvanise herself into action and hurried towards him. 'Louis! Louis. This proves it – this just proves what I said. She's a liar and a terrible person. I absolutely *trust* that you wouldn't have … *relations* … with anyone outside of marriage. All she's done is lay someone else's mistake on you and tried to make it look as if you're at fault—'

'No. No, Margaret.' Louis turned and glanced at her, then, to his great surprise, he heard laughter. It was his own. 'It's true. I know it is. And do you know what?' He suddenly grabbed her hands and clasped them tightly. 'First of all, just to be clear, I will *never* marry you, I have never *asked* you to marry me, so I have *no* idea why you've suddenly decided to announce to all and sundry that you're my future wife. And *this* all means that Elsie's an unwed mother and I'm an unwed father. How terribly … *Bohemian*.'

'Louis!' Margaret shook herself free and looked disgusted. 'No. You wouldn't do that. You wouldn't!'

He felt his mouth twist into a strange little smile. 'But I did, Margaret. I did …'

Midsummer, 1907

Louis came downstairs, adjusting his King Arthur costume, tweaking his makeshift crown and tucking a sword from his father's armoury into his belt.

'There you are! My liege.' Elsie intoned the last two words darkly and bowed, her black dress pooling around her feet, her hood covering most of her face as well as her hair. She'd left it loose, and he could see tendrils escaping from the black velvet hood, almost touching the floor as she bent forwards.

'Stand up, Penny, you duffer!' He laughed and took hold of her hand, pulling her upright and towards him in one swift movement. 'I think I'm supposed to bow to you? Or at least kiss your hand?' He made a big production of doing both those things and Elsie chuckled.

'Perhaps. You look very good as a king. Very … kingly.'

'And you look very … witchy. Tell me again why you refused to go as Guinevere?'

'Because …' Elsie pulled a face and tugged her hood off her head, shaking her curls out in apparent annoyance. 'Guinevere isn't very loyal. She tempts Lancelot and then ends up in a convent. Can you see me in a convent, Louis?'

'Not unless you're in there stealing the communion wine.'

'How irreligious of you.' She pretended to be shocked, then laughed. 'Quite possibly true though. Anyway, I could have come as the Lady of the Lake, but I thought it would be even worse to come dressed in pondweed or a dripping wet shift than it would be to come as Morgan le Fay. So here I am. I'm so looking forward to this ball! Honestly, I've missed everyone so much. I adore London, but it does somewhat scatter a group when one lives away. It's a shame Holly and Pearl are missing out, but it's not like we haven't seen them recently, at least.'

'I still think you're slightly mad. Holding a ball, leaving the house to come all the way over here, and then go back.' He shook his head, half in admiration, half in amusement. 'Unhinged. That's what you are.'

'That's why life is never boring with me in it.'

'So, are you back at Pencradoc for good then?' He tucked her arm into his, and they made their way out of the front door, towards the waiting carriage.

'I don't know.' She screwed up her face. 'I've had an offer from Slade to go and work and study there. Terribly unseemly, a person of my standing doing paid work, isn't it? I should be filling my days with virtuous deeds and charitable activities.'

'Then don't go. Stay here.'

'But it's the opportunity of a lifetime. If I don't do it now, when I have no real commitments, who's to say I'll be able to do it in the future?' She adjusted her heavy skirts and squashed into the seat next to him.

'Very true.' He pulled her closer to him in the carriage as she knocked on the window to indicate that they could pull away from Ashby Court. 'You should do it then. It's a fantastic experience.'

'That's what I thought. I'd like to concentrate on my

photography as well – perhaps experiment with some of those very clever exposures they can do. Add photographs to my paintings – I don't know. The Slade would give me the freedom to explore all that and more.'

'Don't you want to be on the stage any more?' Louis teased, and she laughed.

'Oh, I'll *always* want that – but that's less realistic than progressing my art, isn't it?'

The conversation had continued, non-stop almost, until they reached Pencradoc, where Elsie had achieved what Louis knew she adored – a grand entrance where all heads turned to watch her.

'All the world's a stage,' he muttered in her ear, 'and all the Elsies in it players.'

'Stop paraphrasing the Master!' she hissed in amusement, then she stuck her chin in the air and made her regal progress around the ballroom, meeting and greeting and mingling, all the while closely holding onto his arm.

He'd missed Elsie, he really had. He felt dreadful that he'd missed her Christmas party, and of course they'd argued about it. She'd written him an impassioned letter about how she would never do that to him, and why was a silly little cold so prohibitive?

He'd been playing it down, of course; he really didn't want her to know quite how bad it all was. When she'd realised the extent of that "silly little cold", and the fact he'd almost died just after New Year, she'd turned up at Ashby Court crying and pleading to see him, full of apologies. She'd even clambered onto his bed with him and refused to leave until she'd wept it all out on his shoulder.

She'd gone back to her arts college in London shortly after that, and he began to recover. This ball was the first proper social occasion he'd attended since it had all happened, and he'd felt slightly nervous about it all, if he was honest. But Elsie was there, stuck to him like glue, and they spent all evening together. He had a feeling that was why she'd come to collect him; firstly, to ensure he'd turn up, and secondly, to help him through the initial meeting *en masse* of most of their friends – who were, it seemed, delighted to see him.

Shortly before sunset, they made their way – by some unspoken agreement – outside. They walked, hand in hand, through the twilight grounds of Pencradoc, the sound of Elsie's skirt dragging along the paths, his footsteps echoing weirdly through the quiet dusk. The sounds of merriment and music grew fainter as they wound their way further through the estate, across the little footbridge and out onto the wild moors beyond.

Again, he knew, and she knew, by some unspoken agreement, that the night would not end in a sedate walk.

Rather, they turned to each other, the first shafts of moonlight gilding the roundness of her cheeks, the individual curls of her hair; burgeoning starlight dappling her long eyelashes as her upturned face moved just inches from his.

'Kiss me, Louis,' she whispered. He held her face in his hands and dipped down to meet her lips. They'd kissed before at some of the parties and dinners and events they'd been to, always in a light-hearted fashion – perhaps both of them had known that there could only ever be one conclusion to the spark that had always been between them if they deepened those kisses. That spark had now become a comet, racing towards both of their hearts, and in that instant they both realised that from now on, from tonight, there would be no going back to how it had been – how it had been before that midsummer eve ...

And there hadn't been.

And now, four years later, he knew why.

Chapter Fourteen

Present Day

Tilly was a bit creaky and stubborn, but after some gentle coaxing from Sybill, she relented and allowed her waist to be pinched and her bust to be enhanced, and soon Sybill thought she looked the approximate size and shape to show off Elsie's costume to its best advantage.

Sybill had never been in this room before, and it was delightful – as Coren had explained, it was usually just himself, Kit and Merryn who had access. It was right next to Coren's apartment, and in fact the door which they'd come through led from the sewing room across a small landing to Coren's front door. It very much had a family feel to it, and Sybill could almost see the two small boys coming into this warm, comforting space when they visited their aunt.

'Here you go.' Coren was coming over to her with a photo album, bookmarks sticking out in a couple of places. 'These are the ones you'll probably find the most interesting. Again, a lot of the photos got scattered around the family. If you think about it, Elsie had six brothers and sisters, and she had several children of her own. By the time they had children and so on, we got to Loveday – obviously her aunts and uncles and cousins claimed the photos which were most meaningful to them. But we've got some family group shots, and, like I said, one of Elsie's wedding photographs. I really think you'll like that one.'

'Can't wait. May I?' Sybill gestured to a chair, one of two either side of a round table, and Coren nodded. He took the other chair and laid the book out. He opened it at a page he'd marked, and Sybill was greeted with a group shot of Elsie and all her siblings. She was, Sybill guessed, in her mid-teens, and her youngest brother was still a baby.

‘Oh look at that. A perfect family,’ she said with a smile.

‘It’s one of my favourite pictures. This girl here is Medora, the one we saw in her sketchbook. And I don’t know if you can remember the background too well in that detailed picture we found of Christmas 1907, the one where we think Elsie was pregnant, but I think this is the photo she had on display.’

‘I can’t recall all the tiny details that well, to be honest. I was more interested in who had drawn it. But I remember there was that sort of shape to it.’ She indicated the triangle composition that the children stood in – Elsie, of course, the tallest and oldest, and hence the tip of the triangle.

‘I don’t know who took it. Teague maybe. Or even Edwin Griffiths, Lily Valentine’s husband. As I understand, he was a keen photographer and that’s who Elsie learned from. She was close to the Griffiths family all her life.’

Coren turned the page to another layout, and this time it was a set of portrait photographs seemingly taken at Christmas. There was a photo of every child, a few group shots and even a couple of Zennor and Teague, but none of Elsie. ‘I think she took these as well. Note how she’s conspicuous by her absence. Something tells me she got a new camera as a Christmas gift.’

He grinned and Sybill nodded. ‘I’d make that assumption as well, but of course who knows for sure? She definitely got one for her birthday one year when she was little. We’ve got a letter she wrote when she was a child telling us that – maybe she was ready for a new one by this Christmas.’

‘Quite possibly. And *this* one is the wedding photo.’ His voice changed slightly. He cleared his throat and actually sounded a little nervous. ‘Be prepared to be amazed.’

Very carefully, he turned over the page, peeled back another layer of protective tissue paper, and there, right in front of Sybill, was Elsie and her husband on their wedding day.

And in a sudden flash of recognition, Sybill knew where she'd seen the man in the locket before.

'That's him! That's *him*!' Sybill had gone pale and was staring at the page as if she'd seen a ghost. Ironically, Coren thought that was a highly likely possibility in this place. Even now, he was doing his best not to look anywhere else in that room because he knew, he just *knew*, that Elsie and Louis were haunting the corners of it, Elsie nudging Louis proudly: '*Look – don't we look innocent? If only they knew the truth!*'

He kept his voice steady and asked the question, although he also knew what the answer would be. He just needed to hear it from Sybill. 'Who is he?'

'It's her husband. Obviously. But he's the man in that locket. The one we found on Little Elsie. And the only piece of jewellery that keeps bloody following me around. Look!' With shaking hands, she dived into her bag and brought the locket out. She put it on the table and pushed it across to him. 'Take it. Open it up. Have a look. Merryn brought it to me this morning with Elsie's sketchbooks. She said a cleaner had found the books in Matt's classroom and left them on her desk with a note. The locket was tucked inside the book.'

'It was in my desk drawer,' said Coren. 'I was looking for it before you came. I thought I knew who he was too – I don't know how it ended up in the classroom, and I don't know how it got into the book. But I can't tell you how glad I am you found it.'

'Me too. Coren ...' She looked at him with wide, disbelieving eyes. 'What if it's Elsie's?'

1911

'Oh God. Oh God. Did I really say all that out loud?' Elsie looked up at Fabian, horrified. 'Tell me I didn't really. Tell me it's a champagne-induced nightmare.'

'I can't, sweet. It was said. It can't be unsaid. Cigarette?'

He sat her down on the edge of what Pearl and Ernie called the Bathing Pool. It was a deep pond, deep enough for diving, and part of their new formal landscaping. Pearl had enthusiastically read about Arts and Crafts Gardens, whereby the gardens were set out in a series of "rooms", and had steamed ahead to make the Lacy garden a perfect example of one.

'No. Drowning. A drowning would be good. I'm a witch. I can drown.' She shimmied over and began to clamber into the pool, but Fabian dragged her back before she even got one leg in, rolling his eyes languidly and pulling her towards him again, setting her the right way around.

'A cigarette would be better. Anyway, witches can't drown. That's how people know they're witches. Because they float back to the surface unscathed.'

'Damn.' Elsie reached out and took the proffered cigarette. She took a couple of long drags on it, coughed and spluttered, because really she wasn't that used to smoking the things, then handed it back to Fabian.

Her hands were shaking, she noticed vaguely, and she had begun to feel sick. It was a combination of fear, embarrassment, exhaustion, tobacco and champagne, and the world began to tilt alarmingly now that the cool night air had hit her. 'Fabian ...' she started. Her tongue seemed too large for her mouth, his name sounded strange and her voice seemed to come from far away. Her mind was swirling, the pretty landscaped gardens were spinning, then she felt herself tip forwards. The world shrunk to a pinprick, and she grappled in vain for something to hang onto before she fell off the stone wall ... then, suddenly, all was black and she knew nothing more.

The next morning, Elsie picked unenthusiastically at her breakfast. She had vague recollections of points in the journey home – one point where she had to stop the carriage and clamber out to be violently sick, then another point where Fabian was stroking her hair while she cried and told him things would never be the same.

Somehow, she had got undressed and into bed, but this morning she felt dreadful. Her head was pounding, she still felt sick and images of the previous night kept assailing her consciousness. Her little brothers were bickering at the table, she was sandwiched between Laurie and Fabian, and her parents were sitting opposite, deep in conversation about something in the newspaper that Teague had spread out in front of him.

Everything was normal. It was all hideously normal. Yet it would never be the same again – she had told Louis everything. She had told him about Marigold, and she'd also told half the county at the same time, it seemed. She remembered swanning out of the ballroom, pretending none of it mattered, and trying to drown herself in Pearl's swanky new Bathing Pool.

Oh God.

She let her head drop slowly onto the table, so her forehead was resting by her breakfast plate, and waved away the comments from her family.

'If that's what London does to a person,' brayed Arthur, 'I'm jolly glad I don't go there often.'

'Quiet,' Elsie instructed. 'I'm tired. I'm very tired.'

'She was dancing all night,' supplied Fabian. 'She is incredibly tired.'

'So tired I'm going home after breakfast,' muttered Elsie. It was the only thing to do. Pack up and leave Pencradoc before "concerned" neighbours started calling. 'Fabian, we're leaving after breakfast.'

'Oh, Elsie.' That was Teague, trying not to laugh. 'I think you can probably wait until after lunch. I wanted to speak to Fabian about something. I think I've got him a commission, but we need to firm up some details.'

'Really? Thank you! Thank you, sir!' Fabian was delighted. Elsie could hear it in his voice, even though her eyes were closed. She knew if she opened them, she'd only be focused on the white tablecloth. In fact, she realised now that a toast crumb was sticking uncomfortably to her forehead. She really needed to sit up. And pack. *Yes. Pack*. And refuse all visitors.

'Well done, old chap,' she muttered and groped around for Fabian's knee. She found it, squeezed it and patted it. 'Good show. A commission. I'm still leaving. I shall be in my room. Ready to go as soon as you've firmed up those details.' She sat up with a great effort and rubbed her forehead, no doubt leaving a shiny, buttery mark. 'And I don't want to see anyone. Especially not Louis. If he comes here. Which he might. Excuse me.' She pushed the chair away from the table and held her head high as she walked out of the room.

At that very moment, Louis was riding across the moor to Pencradoc just as fast as his horse could carry him. He'd ended up running out of the ballroom last night, outpacing a furious Margaret, shaking off Noel – and Ernie, as well, who had entered the fray – trying desperately to find Elsie.

As he wove his way around the landscaped gardens, seeing nothing but hedges and plants and dim pathways before him, he had become more and more agitated. Finally, he stood there, in the middle of what he guessed was some sort of apothecary's garden judging by the scents of lavender and herbs that surrounded him, and raked his hands through his hair, cursing his lungs and struggling to catch his breath.

Where was she? And more to the point, that man she was with – Fabian – he'd simply walked outside with her without seemingly being stunned by the revelations at all. Did he already know?

The anger rose within Louis. Was he, that man, raising *his* child? Taking on *his* little girl? Looking after Elsie the way *he* should have done for the last four years?

He cursed loudly again and stared around at the darkening evening. He heard voices, a splash, far away on the other side of the gardens, carried across the space in the muted twilight. He tried to run again but found it impossible, and he was forced to stop, coughing harshly and intermittently swearing.

Dammit. It was her; he knew it was. Slowly, he continued to walk towards the voices, not even sure what he would say to her. Then the talking stopped suddenly. There was silence, and then footsteps hurrying away, laboured almost, a strange sounding rhythm to them.

He reached the Bathing Pool – the only place he thought the splashes might have come from. All there was to hint that there had been anyone there recently was a half-smoked cigarette and the jet necklace Elsie had been wearing around her head as a crown.

The necklace was in his pocket now, as he made his way over the moors. He'd wanted to come earlier, wanted to knock at the door of Pencradoc at sunrise and demand to see her. As it was, he had been storming around Bodmin Moor at that time, retracing the steps he and Elsie had taken on both occasions they had made love out there. If he was hoping to see her, to talk to her, to make things right, he was disappointed.

The only good thing, he thought wryly as he dismounted the horse outside the Pencradoc stables with a word or two to the stable boy, was that he was no longer committed to Margaret Corrington. They'd had a very awkward, very loud conversation back in the ballroom in front of *many* guests, adding a little more entertainment to the evening.

Pearl's brother and sister had, God bless them, diverted attention by doing an even more outrageous Ragtime dance, leaving him and Margaret to a relative amount of privacy.

Another reason he'd wanted to come at the crack of dawn was to head the Corringtons off at the pass – he had a dreadful suspicion that they too would be wanting to call at

Pencradoc this morning. The idea gave him a burst of speed, and he jogged to the door before banging on it very loudly and very continuously until someone opened it for him.

As was usually the case at Pencradoc, proprieties were seldom observed, and Enyon opened the door, a mug of tea in his hand. 'Oh – good morning, Louis.' The boy grinned at him. There was a gap between his front teeth, seemingly designed to endear him to anyone he flashed that grin at. Louis smiled back before he'd really had time to consider the significance of his visit. 'Do you want to see El? She's upstairs – packing. She's in a sorry state this morning!' The boy laughed, unconcerned. At seventeen, or thereabouts, he probably recognised all too well the sorry state one could be in the morning after revels.

'Yes, please. She, um, left this at the party.' He presented the jet necklace. 'I just didn't want her to leave without it.'

'Oh! Of course.' Enyon stepped back, beckoning Louis to come in. 'I'll nip up and get her, shall I? Do you just want to wait here?'

'She's in her bedroom, is she?' Louis thought quickly. He knew what Elsie was like, and the Elsie of old would have—yes. *Yes*. He knew *exactly* what her next move would have been. 'I'll tell you what. It's a beautiful morning, so you go and tell her I'm downstairs. I'll just pop back outside for a second first.' He tapped his head and winked. 'I too am feeling a little worse for wear. I would appreciate a breath of fresh air.'

Enyon guffawed and nodded. 'Will do. Wizard! Won't be a moment.' He turned and ran up the grand staircase, two at a time.

Louis watched the boy disappear, then turned on his heel and walked back outside.

Chapter Fifteen

Present Day

It was a weird thing to think, that the locket might have been Elsie's – yet also eminently sensible within the walls of Pencradoc, in this lovely, cosy room that had once belonged to Loveday.

Part of Sybill's unconscious mind had already installed Elsie in here, a similar jumble of things lying around her as she grew up and eventually came to own the place. What if this had been her sanctuary too, a place to escape from the world when she tired of her exciting life in London and needed to recharge and regroup for a little while? She didn't think that was far from the truth and could almost swear she heard a voice: '*Very true. Well* done!'

She shuddered and blinked, trying to focus instead on the locket. 'Do you want to open it, Coren? And check?' Her mouth was dry, her heart thumping, and she looked up at him.

'Yes. Yes, I will.' He took the locket and opened it, carefully keeping the contents away from Sybill's view.

But, surprising herself, she laid her hand on his arm. 'No. It's okay. I want to see them again.'

'All right.' His voice was tender, and he laid the locket open on the table between them.

Now that she had the wedding photograph and the locket side by side, the likeness was obvious. The wedding picture was a profile shot of Louis and Elsie, both looking away from the camera to their right. Louis was behind Elsie, and they both appeared very serious. It was a beautiful photograph, and Sybill found it hard to breathe looking at it.

And even though Louis was in profile, his hair neatly parted, wearing a white cravat and a smart dark suit, it was clearly him in the locket – a smiling, much less formal depiction of him.

In the wedding photograph, Elsie's hair was up, a circlet of flowers decorating the short veil which fell from the back of her head. Her dress was white, but a huge bouquet and an enormous amount of tulle covered most of the detail.

Sybill was entranced. 'She's absolutely beautiful. I literally can't think of another word to describe her.' Sybill leaned a little closer and peered at the head dress. 'Oh. It's not flowers – it's holly and mistletoe.'

Coren peered in as well. 'Hey, you're right. I wonder if it was a Christmas wedding? Loveday always told me it was a midsummer one. She used to go on about traditions, and how the family had always married around about that time, and apparently Elsie used to wax lyrical about midsummer, so I guess she just went with it.'

'So Loveday actually knew Elsie? I realised they were related but wasn't sure how far apart the generations were.'

'Yes. Elsie was Loveday's grandmother. She was the daughter of Elsie's youngest child. I think Loveday's Mum was barely twenty when she had her, but I guess that was normal for those days. Kit and I are descended from Elsie's youngest son. We squeezed another generation in somehow, but always thought of Loveday as our great aunt.'

'I wish I'd met her.' Sybill returned her gaze to the photograph. 'At least we know who this chap is now. I'm going to go way out on a limb here as well.' She hovered her fingertip above the little girl, who still looked so heartbreakingly familiar to her. 'This is probably one of their children.'

'I'd say you were correct. Shall we do some digging? See who we think it might be?' He put his hand gently on top of hers. 'Only if you want to.'

Sybill nodded. 'Actually. I want to. I know she can't

possibly be Lucia, but she looks just like the little girl I keep dreaming about …' her voice trailed off, and she suddenly got a huge dose of that weird, sick-to-the-stomach feeling she'd been trying to ignore so far whilst sitting in this room. 'Or maybe—' she really had to think about what she wanted to say here '—it's not my daughter, but Elsie's I'm dreaming about.'

Coren didn't quite know how to respond to Sybill. All he could do was nod. Knowing what he knew about Pencradoc, it was highly likely that Elsie's memories *were* invading Sybill's dreams. He wasn't sure how he could justify that to anyone who didn't have experience of Pencradoc and its strange otherworldly history, but it didn't sound too stupid to him.

He recalled something Merryn had said a while ago – about how Pencradoc only showed its ghosts to those who needed to know about them when the time was exactly right and everything was in its place for those who needed their guidance. He wondered if, by any stretch of the imagination, the time was right for him and Sybill. Because, he had to admit, when he looked at that coloured picture in the locket of Louis as a young man today, he saw more of himself in there than he had ever noticed before in the rather formal wedding photograph. The Louis he saw before him was definitely someone he wanted to relate to more than the spectre of Ellory tarnishing the rest of his life.

He shivered. Perhaps it was *Louis* he saw more of in the mirror, rather than Ellory, despite the similar colours of their hair and eyes. Louis was the one he felt more strongly around him today, and he wanted it to stay like that.

Pushing the thought out of his mind, he took a deep breath. 'Okay.' Instinctively, he put his arms around Sybill and held her closely for a moment. 'You sit tight, and I'll nip across to my flat and get my laptop. Let's dig.'

'Elsie! El! Louis is here.' Enyon's voice bellowed through the closed door, accompanied by him pounding on it.

It did Elsie's headache no good at all.

'Tell him to go away. It's far too early!' she shouted back.

'Tell him yourself. I'm not your servant,' hollered the boy. She heard his footsteps running away back down the corridor and cursed under her breath. *Dammit*. Did she leave Louis standing on the doorstep, just waiting for one of her other brothers to find him – or worse – one of her parents? What if he tried to speak to them about it all?

But no. She didn't think he would, really. She knew he'd say nothing to them until he'd spoken to her. *But*, she thought, eyeing up the window, *he doesn't have to speak to me right now, does he?*

Before she could think about it any further, she threw the window open, hitched up her skirt and clambered out. It was a route she had taken many a time. A tree grew close enough by for her to reach across, grab a branch and shimmy her way down the old trunk. From there, she could drop onto the roof of the orangery, and shin her way down the drainpipe onto solid ground at the back of the house.

It was just as she dropped onto the flagstones that she heard his voice. 'Elsie Pencradoc. Fancy meeting you here.'

Her stomach churned, and she turned to face him.

'Trapped by your own web,' he said, nodding up at her bedroom window. 'How many times have you told me about that escape route?'

'Too many.' She folded her arms defensively. 'Look, I don't know what you're here about. I can't remember much about last night. I had rather too much champagne, sooooo …'

'Don't lie to me, Elsie.' His voice was harsh and she jumped, not used to that tone from him at all. 'You know exactly what was said. I came to find you in the garden afterwards. I heard you by the pool, but you'd gone by the time I got there. You left this.' He handed her the jet necklace, and she hesitated before taking it. For want of anything else to do, she placed it in the same position as it had been the previous evening, and fastened it at the back of her head, wearing it like a little, defiant crown.

'It must have slipped off. I ... um ... fell over.'

'Fell over. Really?'

He folded his arms at that point, and she took a step backwards, then threw her hands out in the air angrily. 'All right. I fainted. I'd drunk too much champagne, saw too much of bloody Margaret Corrington. Saw too much of *you*. Said too much. It's bound to be a bad combination ...' Then she gave up and sobbed, surprising even herself. 'Fabian brought me home. I don't remember much at all after that.' She covered her face with her hands and closed her eyes. 'I need to go back to London. Go away, Louis. I don't want to see you again. I need to be away from here. Then they can talk about me all they want.'

His arms came around her and pulled her towards him, and she pressed her face into his chest, smelled the morning air and a faint scent of leather on his clothing as he held her close. It felt *right*. It felt horribly right, as if she shouldn't ever be anywhere else – but could she really do that to him? Really pick up where they'd left off as if nothing had ever happened and Marigold didn't exist?

'It's not fair on you, Louis,' she muttered into his chest, even as her hands crept away from her face and scrunched up handfuls of his shirt fabric. 'It's not *fair*. And that's why I can't be with you any more.'

'What on earth do you mean, "it's not fair". What's not fair?' Louis was confused, but Elsie just shook her head against his chest and he laid his chin on the top of her hair, feeling the scratchy jet beads, the soft curls pressing against his skin, as he moved his face and nuzzled her curls gently.

'This. Me. Us. Marigold.' She took a deep breath and pulled away, looking up at him with pain in her eyes. 'Can we go somewhere else? To the waterfall, or the rose garden? Just somewhere away from here.' She laughed shortly. 'Away from my brothers and my parents.'

'And Fabian?' Louis couldn't resist, and she seemed to stiffen at the man's name.

'Fabian. Ha. He knows it all anyway.'

Louis felt the anger creep through his body again and moved his hands so hers were in his. 'Come. Yes. We'll go to the waterfall. Or the moors. Let's go to the moors – I think it's the best place to discuss it all really, isn't it?'

'The moors. Yes. All right.' She took a deep breath and he braced himself for her removing her hands from his. But, to his surprise, she didn't.

So, taking the opportunity, and appreciating just how precious these next few minutes would be, they walked hand in hand towards the little footbridge and the moors beyond.

Once they were out of sight of Pencradoc, Louis turned her to face him. 'Now, tell me. Tell me about my daughter and why you think I should have no access to either one of you. Tell me why you think that's a good thing, and tell me how, for God's sake, you've kept this a secret for exactly four years! I'm right, aren't I? It was the midsummer costume ball at Pencradoc.'

'It was.' Elsie nodded and tried to pull her hand away. He held tight though, and she ended up wiping her face and her nose with the back of the other hand. 'It was the midsummer ball. Blame the champagne. That's what I'm doing.' She laughed bitterly. 'Because, despite what I'm saying, I don't really want to blame either of us. And I can't blame Marigold for existing.'

'Have you ... have you got a picture of her?' Louis' heart began to thump. Then it made sense – the pictures of the toddler at Brunswick Square. That had been her, hadn't it?

That was why she looked familiar – part of him, part of Elsie. And Elsie's was a face he knew almost better than his own.

'Stupid question to ask an artist. Yes. Here she is.' Elsie fished around inside her bodice and pulled out a locket. 'May I?' She nodded towards her hand, still clamped in his. 'But difficult with one hand.'

'Oh! Of course.' He let go of her hand and hoped to God she didn't decide to bolt. He'd never catch her. But she didn't. She bent her head and unclasped the chain from behind her neck, then opened the locket and handed it to him. Her hands were shaking and he could tell she had tensed up. 'You might not want to believe me, but she's definitely yours,' she said defensively, folding her arms again.

Louis looked at the little girl who smiled out at him, then caught his breath as he saw what was on the other side of the locket. Himself. A tiny portrait of Louis, right next to a miniature watercolour of Marigold.

He looked up at Elsie. 'We're both in here. Yet you say you want nothing to do with me?' He was utterly thrown and felt his voice harden. 'Does Fabian know I'm in the locket? Does he know *that* part of everything?'

'Fabian?' Elsie looked confused. 'What the hell has it got to do with Fabian who the hell I damn well keep in my locket?'

'I would have thought your future husband might like to know, Elsie. Do you still love me? *Do* you?' He took one last look at the little dark-haired, grey-eyed girl in the picture and closed the locket, thrusting it back at Elsie angrily. She glared at him while she fastened it back around her neck, and he glowered back. 'And if so, what the hell are you marrying him for?' He took hold of her upper shoulders. 'We're a family. A ready-made family – can't you see it? I love you, Elsie. I always have and I always will, and I'm damn well not going to let you go without a fight.'

'Marrying Fabian?' She looked at him and then, to his astonishment, burst out laughing. 'God no. He's ... not the marrying kind. Really. Believe me. I love him dearly, but he's no more to me than a terribly wonderful friend. He feels the same about me. He'd *never* want to marry me! Well – he did suggest it, but it would have been a huge mistake.' She flushed and a mixture of emotions ran across her face too quickly for Louis to read. 'He's going to Paris, and he's going to live over there and do wonderful things where he can be *himself*.'

'But you brought him here? He spoke to Teague? I heard what he said – what you both said. About loving one another ...' Louis let his voice trail off. 'Oh God. He spoke to Teague.' He raked his hands through his hair, the pieces clicking together. 'It was about portraits, wasn't it? About working. In Paris, or wherever. I saw the picture he had of you ... and heard what he said ...'

'The picture of me was to prove himself. To get Teague on his side when he saw what a good job he'd done of me. No. Nothing like that has ever gone on between us. He really doesn't think of girls like ... *that*.' Elsie's breath suddenly caught on a sob. 'And it's you, Louis. It's always been you. But when I found out I was having Marigold, I knew I had to get away. My reputation around here is hideous anyway – people like the Corringtons hate me and my family. We're not conventional and I do everything I'm not supposed to. That's why Pearl and Holly are so close to me. We are three of a kind, actually.' She laughed shortly. 'Pearl is probably the most conventional out of the lot of us. Despite being American. Then she presents her brother and sister like that at the ball, and I realise she's just as bad as we are. I couldn't tar you with the same brush. If anyone found out what we'd done, and what the consequences were, your reputation would have been mud too.

'Your poor parents would have had to listen to the whispers and see the fingers pointing and see how people avoided them. And it would all have been due to your association with me – I'm wild, Louis. One of my role models as a child was a scandalous stage actress, and we all know I'm hardly traditional. I know they'll all just say it was a matter of time before I was caught out and had a baby. I personally don't care what they say about me. But I cared about what they'd say about you. I didn't want your future spoiled as well. But you know something?' She half smiled and shook her head, turning away from him and looking over the moors into the far distance. 'You've been the only one, Louis. There's never been anyone else, despite what they all think.'

'Oh, Elsie.' Louis didn't know what to say. 'Do your family know? Your friends – apart from Fabian, that is?' He felt himself flush. How wrong could a person be about a situation they'd simply walked into?

'No. Nobody in Cornwall knows. Lily and Edwin are the only other people who know the full story. They look after Marigold a lot of the time. They've been wonderful – I trust them implicitly, and they've looked after *both* of us, to be honest.'

'But you came back that Christmas – Laurie said you were at home and I was coming to see you, but then when I got here, you'd gone.' He stared at her, shaking his head. 'You ran away when you found out for sure, didn't you? That's why you left that September for London. Then at Christmas, you didn't stay long enough for anyone to realise.'

Elsie shrugged. 'One of the benefits of having a large noisy family and Christmas happening. There's too much else going on for anyone to take too much notice of barmy old Elsie. And if she can hide her mistake under a dress that's a century out of date, so be it. It's not unusual for Elsie to do something out-of-the-ordinary and eccentric, is it?'

'No. No, it's not. But Elsie. This is seriously the most ridiculous thing you've actually ever done.' He shook his head and she flinched, as if she was expecting him to scold her or lose his temper. She scowled and opened her mouth, probably to defend her actions some more, but Louis placed his fingertips over her lips and shook his head, silencing her. 'No. Listen to me. If you ever thought that I cared a damn fig for what people around here think of me or you or anybody I care for, you have another think coming. I can't think of anything worse than being stuck with someone like Margaret Corrington, especially now I know there's not just you to consider. That's why I came to see you all those weeks ago in London – do you really think I had business up there? Did I, hell. I needed to try and change your mind about us, but I went about it all the wrong way.

'What would it have taken, Elsie, to make you tell me then – to tell me about Marigold – our daughter, for God's sake? My *daughter*. Who I've never met. Who I want to meet. Who I want in my life with her mother.' His emotions were churning. There was anger; anger at the fact Elsie had hidden all this from him – but strangely not anger at her. Anger at himself for not trying harder to find out, not trying harder to win her, not trying harder to get his soulmate, his lover, his best friend back in his life. There was love for them both, an overwhelming love that he had thought himself incapable of after she'd left. And hope. He still held out hope. 'Elsie. Why the hell did I let you go?'

She shook her head, her dark eyes unfathomable. 'You didn't let me go. I *chose* to go. You couldn't have stopped me. Nothing you said or did at that time would have changed my mind. I was pregnant. I was barely twenty. I had the perfect excuse to go and start the new life that people half-expected me to do anyway. I charmed my way into the Slade – had a sort of offer there anyway – but said there were a few things I needed to get in order first before I could commit. I told everyone at home I was starting in September. But I didn't. I had Marigold that March and began at the Slade after Easter, at the end of April. With Ruan Teague in my family, they were keen to give me what I wanted and were happy to wait a few months for me to be ready. Nepotism at its very best, eh?'

'I suppose so.' There was no denying it, it certainly looked that way. Ruan Teague was incredibly successful, and if anyone thought they could forge a link with him, they'd be stupid not to try it. Louis felt himself grow warm again. It wasn't surprising Fabian had been coming to see him, and that he'd looked so nervous in the room that day. *Poor old chap*.

'But Elsie.' He had to ask, he had to try. 'Could I stop you now?' Louis searched for her hand and took it, feeling the warmth of her skin on his; the long, delicate fingers that created magic out of pen and ink. 'Could I stop you going back to London and try to persuade you to stay here. To bring Marigold here, and for us to be together properly?'

But Elsie shook her head. 'No, Louis. I can't. I have commitments in London. I have my work at the Slade. I have my house. I have Marigold to consider. I can't uproot her, bring her here and subject *her* to all the gossip. I ran away to protect you, but now I can see it's to protect her as well.' Her eyes filled with tears and she dashed them away angrily, seemingly not wanting to show him any weakness. Louis felt his world crashing down around him. It was rejection all over again ... but then she spoke, and he realised that, perhaps, hope was still glimmering on the horizon.

'You can come to London though.' Elsie sniffed and looked away again, appearing embarrassed to be making the offer. 'You can move into Brunswick Square. You can come and live there. Try to make a life with us, the three of us. Just for a little while. I've committed to two more years at Slade. If your father is better now and he can spare you, you can come with me. It might not work out. You might wish to leave us and come back here. But I can't come back to Pencradoc, and I won't come to back to Pencradoc. Not yet, at any rate.'

Louis was ready to promise anything to her; just to have her back in his life, and the prospect of being with her, in whatever way she was ready to offer, made it feel as if a huge weight had suddenly been lifted from his heart. 'Elsie.' He stared at her and shook his head in wonderment. 'Can I quite confirm the fact that you have just asked me to come and live with you, in an unmarried state, in your house in London? How terribly Bohemian.'

She looked back at him quickly, and there was, after a second, a definite twitch of amusement lifting the corner of her lips. 'Yes. I think that's exactly what I did just offer. Oh my. That *is* terrible, isn't it? Put like that.'

'Yes.' But he smiled and shook his head at the same time as he confirmed that comment. 'But do you know what? To live in sin with you would be better than being married ten times over to Margaret Corrington.'

'That's good. That's very good.' She nodded and took a step towards him. 'Louis – yesterday. On the moor. What if – what if it happens again? What if I get pregnant again? I never thought ...'

'Shhhh.' He took her in his arms and held her close, then looked down at her and kissed her. 'If it does, we'll be living together anyway, won't we? It shouldn't matter to anyone else at all. Elsie – maybe something of a more immediate concern though. We need to tell your parents before anyone else does.'

Chapter Sixteen

Present Day

They dug. They truly dug, and Sybill found herself entirely intrigued about the family history.

'So, Elsie always maintained she was married at midsummer, yes?'

'No – not Elsie, I don't think. Loveday did. That's what she always told us.'

'It certainly didn't seem like a summer head-dress to me – or a summer bouquet. But yes, if we go by that Christmas picture we found where she looks pregnant, we'd expect her to be married in summer 1907, don't you think? Or even earlier.'

'I think that would be the traditional assumption.' Coren flashed a quick smile at her. 'But this is Elsie we're talking about. I don't think she came from the most traditional background, so ...'

Sybill bit back a smile. 'So you're saying she created a bit of pre-marital scandal?'

'I'm not saying that at all. Louis came from a fine, upstanding family. It would be difficult to think that he was anything other than that. Loveday used to say I was like him – he was her grandfather, after all, so she knew him as an elderly gentleman. She said he was quite quiet and very deep and was a good match for Elsie, who was a bit of a free spirit all her life. He was her one great love, as Loveday kept telling us – every time we saw this wedding picture, in fact.'

'So, perhaps she wasn't married to Louis in 1907 then. Maybe she had another husband? Another partner? One that – I don't know – she divorced? Or just didn't stay with.'

'What, like she might have had a fling with that Fabian guy from the photograph?'

'No! No. Not like him at all. He moved to Paris and fell in love with a chap called Jean-Luc. No matter how wonderful Elsie was, do you think she could have persuaded him to forget who he was for one brief moment in time, and got him to make a baby with her?'

Another smile twitched at the corners of Coren's lips, and she thought how much younger and relaxed he looked when he smiled; sometimes, when she caught him off-guard, he looked deep in thought and quite stand-offish. She loved him either way – but, if she was honest, she preferred him this way; quirking a little secret smile, just for her. But she felt herself grow hot with embarrassment as she admitted all this to herself and tried to re-focus her concentration on what he was saying instead.

'You're supposed to be the art expert, aren't you?' he asked her, and she frowned, not understanding.

'I think you got me mixed up with your sister-in-law, Coren. That would be Merryn.'

'Whatever. You're more of an expert than me, but even I've heard of the Bloomsbury Group. Duncan Grant and Vanessa Bell? Didn't they have a brief affair, despite the fact he had a few male lovers, and then she had a baby to him?'

'Ah.' It was a thought but, try as she might, she couldn't put Elsie in that position. There was a splutter of laughter close by her shoulder, and she jumped. Coren was clearly oblivious to the laughter as he continued to throw suggestions out there.

'No,' she said, 'I don't think that happened.'

'Okay. Well if that's really not the case—'

'It really wasn't.' She was too quick to deny it, and he looked at her curiously. 'It wasn't.' She shook her head. 'Believe me. It so wasn't.'

Understanding dawned, and he stiffened a bit and retreated into stand-offish Coren. 'Ah. Okay.' He looked back at the computer screen, drawing his eyebrows together. 'If you think that.'

Sybill felt herself flush again. 'It just wasn't,' she added helplessly, inwardly cursing herself.

'No matter. Let's keep looking.' Coren clicked around on a few links and added some extra information to the search engine in the genealogy site he was engrossed in.

Sybill blew out a steadying breath. No. Fabian definitely hadn't been the mysterious man in Elsie's past. But she couldn't pursue the idea without bringing ghosts into the mix, so she kept quiet and tried to read the screen over Coren's shoulder.

'I'd guess that she was married in the parish church here at Pencradoc? The one Duchess Rose is buried in.' Coren clicked around on the screen. 'But I can't find any records of her getting married here at all. When I put a wider range of dates in, there are some of her children being baptised though – Christopher Teague Ashby in July 1912. That's her eldest son. Kit was named after Christopher, and I was named after her youngest, Laurence Coren Ashby. Here's his details.' He indicated the screen, smiling as the name came up. 'Laurence was named after her favourite brother who went off to fight in World War One. Then she had three daughters as well. Emily Christabel was one of them – the middle one.' He looked at Sybill and raised his eyebrows in amusement. 'Bit of a suffragette vibe there. Then this one is her youngest, born after the end of the war – Loveday's Mum. She just always said she was called "Jinny", and she was born abroad. But look – that's her full record. Ginevra Fabia. I never knew that! That's a whole lot of name for a baby girl.'

'It is, but it's the Italian form of Guinevere, so it makes sense. And Fabia. Well.' She smiled. 'I suspect I know where that comes from. I guess I know who she was visiting when she had the baby. They'd probably done Italy and ended up in Paris to see Fabian and Jean-Luc.'

'True.' Coren tapped a few more things in but shook his head. 'I can't find Elsie's wedding, though – and I can't find the baptism of her oldest child. Looking at the dates, they all seem to be about a year apart, except little Jinny, who I guess was a bit of a surprise, so I'd expect the eldest girl to have been born about 1911.'

'And what was her name?'

'Marigold.'

'That's pretty. And you can't find her? Not under Mary, or Marie or anything, just in case we've got it wrong and Marigold was a nickname?'

'Nope. She's not there.' Coren sat back in the chair and frowned again. 'Weird.'

'Hang on.' Sybill suddenly had another flash of inspiration. 'Elsie lived in Bloomsbury, didn't she, before she was married? That's how she knew all those artists and worked at the Slade.'

'She lived in Bloomsbury after she was married too,' Coren agreed. 'Loveday took us to London on the train once for a trip, and she dragged us to Brunswick Square and said we had family history there and wasn't it a shame that the house had been pulled down, because Elsie always told Loveday it was "rather a grand affair". Apparently, she'd only come back to Cornwall because of the Second World War and because it was safest for her family. She'd go back any time she could because she said her heart was in Bloomsbury and her little family had originally bloomed there and—' He stopped suddenly. 'Bloomsbury. *Bloom*. Marigold. I wonder ...'

'Yes! Good idea.' An image of the orangey-yellow flower she had found in the sketchbook jumped into her mind, and she felt the excitement bubble a little more. 'Let's have a look at Bloomsbury for her wedding, just in case. Perhaps she just decided to get married there, where she lived, and Marigold was christened there.' She grinned at him. 'It's worth a try. And I've got a good feeling we've just taken a turning onto the correct path.'

Of course. It was so obvious, when he thought about it. *Bloomsbury!* Where else would someone like Elsie choose to get married – and if she lived there, then, traditionally, the place of marriage would be her home parish anyway, wouldn't it?

But there was that word again – *tradition*. There was no guarantee that he would find anything, but he shrugged his shoulders, cleared the search box and started again …

And there it was. St George's Church, Bloomsbury. The marriage in December 1911 of Lady Elsie Alexandra Teague Pencradoc and Mr Louis William Ashby.

'We've got her.' He pointed at the date and looked at Sybill. 'That was *so* not a summer wedding. And it was *so* not 1907.'

'December 1911?' Sybill looked at him in surprise, then he saw the edges of her lips twitch into a smile. 'And when was Christopher christened?'

'July 1912. Do we need to do the maths?'

'I don't think so. Wow. Elsie really did live a Bohemian life. She must have scandalised everyone.'

'It's making me think,' said Coren slowly, 'that we need to look for Marigold's baptism before December 1911 …'

'Yes.' Sybill made her eyes go wide and nodded. 'How about – say – the first quarter of 1908?'

'That might work. You've done your maths for *that* one, I see.'

'Only a thought. If she was pregnant at Christmas 1907, she was far enough along for it to be quite noticeable in that picture when she was reclining, shall we say, but not far enough along that it couldn't be disguised by a clever frock when she was standing up – if that dress she drew her sister in is anything to go by. I don't know.' Sybill shrugged. 'Also, why keep a midsummer ball invitation like that – unless it was a bloody good ball. That's all I'm saying.'

'A bloody good ball that had a consequence nobody anticipated?'

'Exactly.'

'Okay. Let's go back a bit further.' Coren typed in the

information and saw the evidence pop up on the screen, almost at the same time as Sybill let out a shout of delighted laughter.

'Marigold *Louisa* Pencradoc.' She raised her eyebrows meaningfully. 'Not much to imply that it *wasn't* Louis' child, eh?'

'Not much at all.' Coren whistled through his teeth and sat back. 'But she's Marigold Pencradoc – not Ashby. And she was baptised at the beginning of April 1908.' He clicked onto the image search facility and saw the loopy writing of the cleric, revealing a little more information. 'And look at the godparents.'

Sybill leaned forwards, her hair tickling his skin as she peered at the screen and tried to decipher the writing. 'Lily and Edwin Griffiths. That's Lily Valentine!' She stared at Coren. 'My God. So they were in on it?'

'Apparently so. But look there.' He pointed to the box reserved for the baby's father's name.

'The father's name ... it's blank. Oh my.' Sybill shook her head. 'So she didn't put his name down. Do you think Marigold *was* Louis' then?'

Coren nodded. He had the most definite feeling that she was. He couldn't explain it, but there was a pull towards that document that he couldn't describe. He knew in his heart that Marigold was the result of one incredible midsummer adventure, and the pictures in the locket proved that the little girl – it was Marigold, he'd bet his life on it – was far too similar to Louis to be anybody else's.

A warm sense of relief and love and belonging swept over him, and he looked across at the locket, and recalled that odd little flower he'd found in his desk. 'It's them.' He nodded over. 'It's Marigold and Louis. Who else could it possibly be?'

'And who else could that locket possibly belong to, except Elsie?' Sybill's voice was almost a whisper.

'Nobody else.'

They sat in silence for a moment, taking it all in, piecing the puzzle together, looking at the evidence on the screen.

Elsie had been to a ball in June. She'd given birth to a daughter in the spring, hiding the identity of the child's father for whatever reason. Then, in 1911, at another ball – the ball they were concentrating on for the exhibition – something else had happened between Elsie and Louis, and that had resulted in a winter wedding and a summer baby.

'Wow.' Coren couldn't think of anything else to say.

'I'm glad we found out,' said Sybill. 'A lot of what's happened makes sense now.'

'You're right. It does.'

'Yes. And, I think—' But Coren didn't know what she thought because, at that moment, Sybill's phone rang. She glanced at the number and the colour drained from her face. 'I have to take this,' she said, picking it up, leaving the room and closing the door behind her.

Coren waited for her, understanding it was something important. But he didn't know quite how important it was until she walked back into the room and stood there, pale as a ghost herself.

'Everything okay?' he asked.

She nodded, mechanically. 'Yes. Yes, I think so.' She paused, then looked straight at him, her eyes full of emotion. 'That was my solicitor. My divorce has been finalised.'

1911

Elsie's stomach churned at Louis' comment. *Yes*. She knew she needed to tell her parents, but it wasn't going to be the easiest thing in the world to do.

'We? *We* need to tell them?' She was playing for time and she knew it. 'It's my mess. I got myself into it. It should be me who does it.' She pulled away from him. 'I shouldn't have to drag you into it. You've only just found out. You're not party to any of my previous decisions.'

'I was. I was there when we decided to make love after the ball. And Elsie, I should have been part of everything afterwards. What did you think I'd do? Seriously?'

His voice was mild but firm, and she dipped her head. 'I don't know. But whatever you suggested, I would have done the opposite. I'm capricious like that.'

'I would have suggested marrying you.'

'I know.' She met his eyes and looked at him steadily. Louis was the first to look away.

'Why?' he asked quietly. 'Why not?'

'Reputation.' She shrugged. 'They'd all say I'd trapped you. We've been through all of this. In fact, I wouldn't have married anyone. Ever. I swore off men. How awkward would it have been to introduce Marigold to a potential suitor? Tell them she was the product of one wonderful and wild midsummer night with the only man I'd ever loved, and then watch them run for the hills because they knew they'd never match up to you, and that I'd only ever be settling for second best while they raised another man's child? Not very independent, is it? Marigold and I ... we come as a package. I could never have let anyone else in if they weren't you. And you now know why I couldn't let *you* in.' She gazed at him for a moment more, and her hand found her locket. She made a decision. It had to be done. He was right. If she didn't tell them, someone else would. 'I need to talk to my parents.'

'I'm coming with you.'

'Are you?'

'Yes.'

She nodded. Then her shoulders slumped. 'Yes. Actually. Thank you.' She nodded again, knowing she had to do it and grateful he was going to be there beside her.

Tentatively, she held out her hand and he took it. He raised it to his lips and kissed it, then drew her close to him and they turned and started walking back to Pencradoc.

They were almost at the front door of the house when Elsie

saw a carriage pull up with two figures inside. Her stomach turned over at the thought that it had already started – people were already piling into Pencradoc to find out what was happening.

'Oh God, Louis – we need to get there before they do.'

'Who?' Louis paused, then raised his hand in greeting. 'It's all right. It's Holly and Pearl. I think you're quite safe for now.'

'Thank goodness for that.' Elsie's legs felt weak, and she leaned against Louis. 'What we're doing now, it's the right thing to do. People will be swarming all over Pencradoc – absolutely *swarming*.' From somewhere, she found some extra strength and she stood up straight, put her chin in the air and picked up the pace as her friends got out of the carriage and started hurrying towards her, their faces full of concern, their arms outstretched to embrace her, casting slightly astonished glances at Louis before focusing back on her again.

'Holly! Pearl!' She waved at them, forcing herself to look cheerful, and the women stopped, momentarily stunned.

'Elsie. Louis. We ... we ...' began Holly. She looked at Pearl and dropped her arms to her side, before bringing them back up to rest protectively on the mound of her stomach. 'We wanted to see you. To see if you were all right.'

'Thank you. Thank you for coming to see me.' Elsie smiled, but she could feel it wavering. 'I'm sorry I created such a diversion yesterday. I'm sorry if it spoiled your costume ball, Pearl.'

Pearl suddenly reached out and hugged her. 'Don't worry about it, sweet, it was wunnerful. I tell you, that ball is gonna be the talk of the town. Whoopee!'

Pearl's voice was so deliciously New York that Elsie couldn't help but feel a little better. 'Good. Well.' She nodded towards the house. 'Telling the parents. You know. Before MC does. Jolly good.' She nodded briskly and clutched Louis' hand more tightly. 'So if you'll – um – excuse us ...' She tilted her head towards the door.

'Sure. Yes. Of course.' Pearl cleared her throat and took Holly's hand. They stepped back and waved Elsie forward. She curtsied to them jokingly and they smiled, but their eyes were still concerned.

'If you need us—' Holly waved her other hand around vaguely '—we'll be out here. Probably in the rose garden.'

'Thank you.' Elsie smiled quickly at her friends, and then looked up at Louis. 'Come on. It's time.'

And they walked together through the doors of Pencradoc.

Elsie was still clutching Louis' hand as they made their way to the study.

Fabian was outside the room, smoking a cigarette and looking nervous. He raised his eyebrows at Elsie and Louis. 'Good talk? Head better?'

'Good talk,' Elsie confirmed. 'Head – and heart, actually, too – much better.' She stopped and looked up at Louis. 'So. Jolly good. Louis, Fabian. Fabian, Louis. Although I think you probably both know of each other quite well by this point.' Her cheeks turned crimson, but she held her ground and her composure didn't slip at all. She was still an actress at heart, Louis thought, although he knew by the fact that her grip tightened on his that she wasn't as breezy as she made out to be. The stilted way she slipped into those funny little speech patterns gave her away to anyone who knew her as well as he did.

Louis felt himself flush. 'I owe you an apology, sir.'

Fabian looked puzzled. 'Why? I can't think of any reason you've offended me or upset me. I've only been here a day or so, and our meetings have sadly been too brief.' He flicked a glance at Elsie then back to Louis and tilted his head on the side, his brows drawn together in confusion, apparently waiting for Louis to explain.

'I thought you were here to declare your intentions to Teague and marry Elsie. I'm sorry. I didn't want anyone to ... to do that. So, I could have been more pleasant to you on those occasions we did meet.'

Louis held his hand out and Fabian took it, his eyes wide through the cigarette smoke. 'Apology accepted, but you really had no need to. Perhaps, if you don't mind me saying, it's *Elsie* you need to apologise to – the things I've been subjected to hearing about a certain "MC"! You really think she was going to sit down and accept that? Despite everything she must have told you this morning, Elsie – well. She talks about you a lot.' His gaze drifted back to Elsie. 'Usually after a glass of wine or three. I know how she really feels about you. I'm hopeful that she's damn well told you now? I can't bear to listen to her MC diatribes any longer.' He winked at Elsie, and she looked at him gratefully, something unsaid passing between the two of them that even Louis wasn't privy to.

He suddenly realised what a rock Fabian had been to Elsie all this time. He felt even more guilty for despising the man in the beginning – but really, what else was he supposed to think? Elsie had all but rejected him. It seemed to Louis that she had moved on to a dark-haired, intense young man with an artistic temperament more suited to her than Louis' frankly unartistic nature.

'Fabian—'

'It's true, Elsie.' Fabian took another drag of the cigarette and offered it to her. 'Smoke? You look like you need it.'

'No, thanks.' She shook her head. 'Is he busy? Need to talk.'

'Just waiting for him to call me in. He's getting some papers together; said he'd be with me in a minute. I think it's the commission stuff.' He pulled a worried face and Elsie matched it.

'You'll be super. But, darling, please can I go in first? I ... I really need to tell him and Mama ...' Her voice trailed away, and she looked at the floor.

'Of course. Not sure where the delightful Zennor is though. Unless she's already holed up in there with him.'

Then the door to the study opened, and, sure enough, Zennor herself peeked out. 'Fabian – oh! Oh, there's a delegation of you. How lovely.' She laughed and held the door open further. 'Come along in. It's all very exciting!'

'Mama – if you don't mind, I need to speak to you first. I know that Fabian is desperately excited, but he loves me so much that he's said I – we – can come in. First. Before him. Commissions. Yes.' She nodded. 'Jolly good.'

'Elsie?' Zennor looked at her daughter oddly. 'Is everything all right?'

'Mama. I really need to talk to you and Papa ...'

'I can wait.' Fabian shrugged and stepped away, melting into the shadows of the staircase.

'All right.' Zennor nodded, frowning a little, and watched as Elsie swept past her. Elsie tugged Louis along and he dipped his head in greeting to Zennor, looking across the room to where Ruan Teague was standing by the window, some papers in his hand.

'Papa.' Elsie stood in front of his desk and Teague turned around, smiling at her.

'Elsie. Good morning again. Less tired, are we now?'

'Wide awake. It's been a hell of a long morning.'

Louis flinched, waiting for Teague to look cross at his step-daughter's language, but he simply smiled and indicated that she should sit down. 'Go on. You too, Louis. No need to stand on ceremony at Pencradoc.' Zennor came around and sat down at the chair behind the desk, looking curiously at the pair of them, and Louis risked a quick smile at her.

'I'd rather stand, thank you.' Elsie pulled herself upright. 'Papa. Mama. There's no easy way to say this, but ...' She faltered a little and shifted. Louis looked down at her, raising his eyebrows, reluctant to speak for her but willing to do so if she bid it.

His heart was pounding on Elsie's behalf though, and he hated to think how she must be feeling. 'Elsie, do you want me—'

'No. No, Louis. I'll do it.' She took a deep breath and looked from one parent to the other. 'Louis and I ... we ... we have ...' She stopped again, released Louis from her vice-like grip and shook her hands out. 'We have decided to ... to ... go to London.' She looked at her parents again, then something changed in her eyes and she suddenly seemed calmer. 'We are going to live at Brunswick Square. Louis. Myself. And our daughter. Marigold.'

'What?' Zennor stood up, her eyes wide. 'Your *daughter*?'

'Yes, Mama.' Then Elsie did sit down and covered her face with her hands. 'She's three. She was three in March. Lily and Edwin have been helping me. She stays with them while I work. And then she comes to me. You can't blame Louis for not telling you anything because he only found out last night. I told him at the ball, in fact I told the whole world at the ball, and Holly and Pearl are out there right now waiting for me, and I know, I just *know* that Margaret and her mother and everyone else who hates me will be piling into Pencradoc just to *tell* you. To make you think *badly* of me.'

'Elsie ...' Zennor sat down again, her face pale. Then she stood up and hurried around to the other side, embracing her. 'Oh, Elsie.'

'I'm sorry. I'm so sorry.' Elsie sobbed, and Louis put his arm around her as well. 'I tried to hide it all, to make it go away so nobody here would be caught up in it, and it's all gone wrong.'

'What's gone wrong?' Louis was quick to contradict her. 'There's nothing wrong. Do you see me complaining? Elsie, I think today I'm just about the happiest I've ever been – good God, I've got you back. I've got you *back*. And I've got our little girl ...'

'I–I– it's just ...' Elsie looked up at Zennor and across at

Teague and gave an odd little twisted smile. 'I know. I know what everyone else says about me. That I'm not Ellory's daughter. That I'm *yours,* Papa. That I'm Ruan Teague's daughter, and I'm not really a Lady at all.' She looked across at Teague again. Teague's face had paled and Zennor stood up, torn between supporting her husband or her daughter. Even Louis was shocked by that one.

'Elsie—' he started, his heart hammering. This could be the catalyst which would finally cause everything to explode – it could go either way.

'Louis – no. Stop. Don't worry. I *know.* I know that it's true. But I'll pretend to outsiders until my dying day that I'm Ellory's, just to save them from knowing they're right. People like the Corringtons – they don't like the fact that half of us were born out of wedlock. They're going to dine out for *years* on the fact that I've done the same with Marigold. And I didn't want Louis or you two dragged into it. It's *my* business.'

Zennor flushed. 'What *we* do or did, and what *you* do or did, it's not anyone else's business. Do you see us worrying about it? Darling, we did what *we* felt was right. We did what was right for *us*. We never ...' She flashed a look up at Teague. 'We never felt it was necessary to be married. We were – we *are* – in love, and we knew it would be forever, and you were all our own little family. I don't quite know what made us decide to get married, to be honest. Do you, Ruan?'

Ruan Teague shook his head slowly. 'I can't recall. I think we wanted to be a little more respectable in case you and Jago's girls followed the designated route of a Society marriage. You're all deemed the daughters of dukes, after all.' He looked at Zennor. 'I can't even think how that seemed important; they were all tiny little things anyway. Why the hell did we do it?' Suddenly, he laughed. 'Society marriages. As if any of them will do what's expected anyway.'

'I'll be even more proud of them if they don't,' said Zennor.

She leaned up and kissed Teague. 'But you – you, young lady.' She turned and faced Elsie and shook her head. 'You told Lily and Edwin – and not us?' She looked sad for a moment. 'What on earth did you think we would say? With our history? Your father and I, we love you. We love you so much, Elsie Pencradoc, that all we want is for you to be happy.'

'I'll make sure she's happy,' said Louis in a soft voice. 'I'll look after them both for you.'

'And you'll make sure we see our granddaughter?' Zennor pressed her lips together and folded her arms. Despite Zennor and Teague's apparent acceptance of the situation, Louis knew that the fact they – like him – had missed three years of that little girl's life, was something that would hurt them for a long time.

'Yes. Of course.' What else could Louis say? It was the truth after all.

'Do we have a picture of her at least?' Zennor's eyes drilled into Elsie.

'Yes. She's in here.' Elsie raised her eyes to Louis, then took her locket off, handing it to Zennor.

Zennor opened it and gasped. 'Oh, what a little treasure. She looks just like you did at that age. Oh my.'

She handed it to Teague and he looked at it silently. 'Technique. Quite good. Yes.' He nodded. His voice was gruff, his speech pattern exactly the same as Elsie's when she was emotional. It made Louis hide a smile and pull Elsie closer to him.

'Louis – in there too.' It was her turn to nod abruptly. 'My two best people. All together. Quite.' Then: 'Oh God. I really am sorry.' Elsie's voice suddenly hitched and she looked around at them, then burrowed her head in Louis' shoulder. Louis held her closer still, on one level still hardly daring to believe that this was real and he was finally going to have a future with Elsie. 'You should know ... Fabian knows about Marigold as well. And it's Elsie Teague. *Teague*. I'm going to add it into my name, I *am*, I've decided, because even though I'm supposed to be Ellory's, I'm *proud* to be Elsie Teague!'

Zennor took the locket gently from Teague and passed it back to Elsie. 'You're still as imperious as a Pencradoc. Never change, darling. You'll *always* be Lady Elsie Pencradoc. And Fabian!' Zennor stared at Elsie as her daughter took the locket and fastened it safely around her neck again, then she suddenly laughed. 'I might have known. He looks like the sort of boy one could talk to.'

'He's one of my best friends. Like... like Holly and Pearl. Only he's a boy. I have to see Holly and Pearl after this. They're outside. Waiting. Before Margaret gets to them. Oh! You're still going to help Fabian, aren't you, Papa?' Elsie looked at Teague in horror. 'He was good enough to come down here with me. You'll not punish him for me confiding in him?' She shot a look at Zennor. 'Paris. He wants to go to Paris, you see. He needs to go to Paris. Do you understand? After our next two Slade years are done ... so he needs to make money here while he can.'

'Why would I punish Fabian, Elsie?' Teague looked confused. 'Some secrets simply make you closer as a family, even if you're not *blood* family. I'm sure you've both shared plenty of secrets between one another. And not just about my granddaughter's existence.' He smiled quickly, then it disappeared just as quickly. 'The chap deserves some help. So I've got a commission for your friend. A good one.' He picked up the papers. 'He's going to paint your mother. Go from there. It will look awfully good if an artist like Ruan Teague entrusts a portrait of his wife to a young, up-and-coming talent.' Teague shrugged. 'Then, after that, you have two sisters, an aunt and four cousins. Once he's done those, he can paint the boys, if he has time before he travels. By then, your brothers might be able to sit still long enough for someone to do a decent job. That should give Fabian a pretty good start for a new life in Paris.'

'Really?' Elsie broke away from Louis and hurried over to Teague. 'Thank you. Thank you *so* much, Papa. I love you. I could *never* have a better Papa, I really couldn't.'

'And I could never have a better daughter.' The words were whispered into her hair, but Louis heard them anyway.

'My cousins – Aunt Alys and Uncle Jago. Do they know the truth though? About me? And you, Papa?'

'Your aunt and uncle know,' said Teague seriously. 'They think no less of any of us. The girls – well. No, they don't. And I think we shall keep it that way, don't you?'

'Yes. But that all means none of them are my actual relatives, doesn't it?' Elsie looked at Zennor. 'I mean, I know you and Aunt Alys are cousins, so I suppose I'm sort of a relative.'

'Enough, darling.' Zennor stroked her daughter's hair. 'They accept all of us for what we are, and, like I said, you'll always be Lady Elsie Pencradoc. To everyone.' Zennor cast a glance at Louis and smiled warmly. 'And we'll be delighted to let our daughter build a future with you. We really will, Louis. It's what we hoped for, if I'm truthful. I think you balance her out a little – she needs someone like you, Louis. She needs someone to keep her grounded. You're the ideal man for the job. We've always thought so.'

'Thank you.' Louis nodded. 'It's what I've always hoped for as well.'

And he knew, in that instant, that things were going to be all right – they really were.

Chapter Seventeen

Present Day

Coren had been lovely. And very understanding. After the bombshell that she was finally divorced and officially single again, she'd done that horrible girly thing of bursting into tears, and Coren had done that awfully English thing of heading straight to his apartment and coming back with a cup of tea.

'Are you all right?' he asked. 'Is this not what you wanted?'

'It *is* what I wanted.' She sniffed noisily. 'But it just seems so *final*.'

'It can't have been an easy decision to make.'

She shook her head. 'It wasn't. But Marco's in my past. He's not something I should be hanging onto. What we had – it was over a long time ago. I only hung on because ... because ... I was scared. But then I realised that it was an excuse. An excuse not to move on. I eventually realised that I didn't want to be committed to my past any more.'

She looked up at him, willing him to understand, and he looked concerned, his eyes full of sympathy. But, at the end of the day, he was Coren, and he had his own barriers and he'd never allow himself to believe that she was talking about him ...

So, she took a deep breath. 'The reason I pushed for it, Coren, is because, like I told you, I wanted to move on. I thought I'd found – no, I *know* I've found – someone else. I think I want to be with someone else.'

'Oh.' He looked at her, and then it was as if realisation finally dawned, and his face softened. 'Really?'

'Really.' She nodded and brushed some more tears from her eyes. 'But I don't know if he wants the same because, well, it's never been easy to read him.' She raised her gaze and locked on his. 'And now I *am* free, well. I just feel a bit ... shaky.' She smiled ruefully. 'Which is ridiculous.'

'Not ridiculous.' He reached out and drew his fingertips

gently down her cheeks, catching the tears. 'But I think you need to take a breath and take some time. Make sure it's what you really want to do.'

'I think I need to know if it's what he wants to do as well.'

'It is.' Coren leaned over and kissed her gently. 'But he's not going to take advantage of a woman who's only been single for twenty minutes. He's going to promise her something though. He's going to promise her that he's going to wait until she's less shaky and make sure that they are both really ready to do this. He's pretty sure he is, by the way.'

'I'm glad about that.' Sybill reached up and covered his hand with hers. 'And he's right, of course. I'd better go. I think I need to take some time to sort my head out.'

Before she went, there were more tender kisses that were really rather nice, but eventually Sybill got into her car and drove away. She kept driving, without really being aware of where she was going, and found herself on a direct route to the cemetery; the cemetery where they'd buried Lucia. It seemed to be the final thing that she needed to do – to explain to her daughter what had happened and why.

She wound her way through the peaceful pathways to the little plot that was Lucia's, and then knelt down beside it, tugging a couple of weeds out of the grass and laying down a posy of wildflowers she'd brought from the Pencradoc gardens.

And then she saw it as she pulled some long grass away from the tiny headstone – one little plant flowering brightly against the white marble. A marigold in full bloom, warm orange and cheerful, nodding gently in a breeze as if it was kissing the words carved there.

A marigold.

Sybill smiled gently and touched one of the petals. 'Do I need to explain, darling, or do you think you're a big enough girl to understand?' There was no answer, of course, but that was fine. 'I think you know though, don't you? You know that Mummy and Daddy love you very much, and we always will. But we don't love each other in that way any more, although we care very, very deeply for one another. We made you and that was the best thing we ever did. We'll always be here for you, if you ever need to talk to us. I hope you know that and if we see you or hear you, we'll know how special it is and how special you are.' She paused and laid her hand on the cool marble. 'Maybe one day I'll bring someone else who is special to me here to see you, and you can meet him.' She smiled and touched her fingertips to her lips, then pressed the kiss onto the marble. She closed her eyes for a moment, saying a little prayer for Lucia – and wasn't surprised at all when she felt a little hand in hers, ever so briefly, squeezing it, then a kiss on her own cheek.

Lucia knew, and she was giving Sybill her blessing.

The next fortnight was a whirlwind of activity, as it so often was when these events began to consume the inhabitants of Wheal Mount and Pencradoc.

"Inhabitants" was a funny word, Sybill mused, as she put the finishing touches to a press release about the exhibition and emailed it off to the *Mid Cornwall Times*. Merryn had done the same, targeting some other publications and coming at it from a different angle – the Pencradoc angle – where Sybill had gone for the "come and see how many fabulous paintings we've got by all these famous people" angle. It was more in keeping with what Wheal Mount was renowned for. The only static exhibits they had were the living quarters of Jago and Alys, but the rest of the place changed around regularly with travelling exhibitions from bigger galleries, and places like the Tate in London, or the National Portrait Gallery. Pencradoc was more in keeping with the work of local artists, but they'd staged another very popular joint exhibition comprising Laura Knight pictures and other work by the Lamorna Cove Group.

It was during the run up to exhibitions like this when she lived and breathed Wheal Mount, where she genuinely did feel as if she was inhabiting the place. Her dreams around this exhibition – when she did manage to sleep, that was – were weird, tumbling affairs incorporating everyone she knew and loved at both sites. It wasn't odd for her to dream about Coren anyway, to be fair. But now when she saw a little dark-haired girl dancing around, she realised it may well have been Marigold coming to say hello as well.

She knew the display room was looking pretty good, with the portraits in and most of them up on the wall in position. She always changed her mind countless times before she was happy, but now she thought she might have cracked it; which is why, after she'd pressed "send", she took a draft information leaflet upstairs and began to double and triple check that the numbers matched with the display.

Today, Tammy was in the room supervising the workmen as they put the final touches to the standing display boards, and Sybill greeted her with a smile. The girl was wearing dungarees that were turned up at the hems, a tight, nautical-style striped top beneath it and Birkenstock clogs. Her short hair was pulled back off her face with a colourful scarf and she had a screwdriver in her hand.

'We've got professionals working in here, Tammy, you don't need to take their jobs off them!' she teased.

'Ha! No, I just wanted to tighten up a loose screw on the display stand for your clipboards. Can't have them all collapsing on the visitors, so I said I'd do it quickly.' Tammy nodded into the next room. 'It's looking pretty good in there. It's almost like a real bedroom. You should have a look.'

'Yes, I'm heading there next – one thing though.' She pointed at Fabian's picture of Elsie, pride of place in the centre of the room. 'Make sure there's plenty of space around that one with the barriers, and get some benches set up in front of it – I think it's one that will capture the visitors' imagination, and we want to keep the flow going.'

'Agreed.' Tammy nodded smartly and went over to the

wheeled benches which were currently jumbled in the corner. 'I'll get that sorted.'

'Thanks. You're the best.' Sybill grinned as Tammy laughed and set to work, then she walked over to the connecting door to the next room.

As she pushed it open, the breath caught in her throat. 'Wow. Just wow.' She stood, staring around her at an almost perfect replica of Elsie's bedroom. It was incredible; so much so, that she could well imagine Elsie's deepest emotions as she feverishly drew all the tiny bits and pieces of her life scattered around her – almost as if she was trying to save them for posterity before the inevitable changes that would occur come the spring, when she brought her daughter into the world. It must have felt as if she was leaving her happy childhood and family home behind forever – not counting the fact she must have thought she was leaving Louis and their bright future together behind as well. Sybill's heart went out to the girl. Yes, she was twenty or so, but she was little more than a child herself, really – very young to be dealing with all of that.

But there was no room for sadness in the re-imagined bedroom today. It was splendid, down to the last detail – even incorporating a fake window with the view of Pencradoc estate beyond, and the photograph of Elsie and Fabian together before they went to the ball. A few discreet information boards would come in here tomorrow, and they would explain the set-up to visitors – and hopefully make them eager to see the portrait in the next room that had basically started Fabian's career.

They had originally wondered if Elsie's "bedroom" should be at Pencradoc instead – but they had agreed it sat better at Wheal Mount, because of the static exhibition they already had. It was possibly going to become a permanent feature, linking the two arts centres together, just as the houses had been linked together all those years ago.

That was all still to be decided, but now Sybill could smile at the thought of the future. She had a good feeling that the two places *would* be linked – she wasn't quite sure how, but she was very excited to imagine the way they could be.

Finally, the exhibitions opened at Pencradoc and Wheal Mount. Both sites were selling joint tickets valid for the length of the exhibition, and Merryn had gleefully relayed the figures for advanced sales to Coren the week before.

'This one is a huge success. You and Sybill ought to be proud of yourselves,' she said, putting a print-out on his desk. 'Well done.'

He smiled. 'It's not just us. You put together the puzzle about Fabian and that's really helped to ground it, I think. It's great that he appears at both sites – ties it all in well.' Merryn had said how impressed she was at Coren's knowledge of what the room was like, and he had, thinking quickly, passed that off as a lucky guess, based on the detailed drawing they'd discovered in Elsie's sketchbook.

That drawing was also in the exhibition at Pencradoc, carefully set in a display case with Elsie's other sketchbooks showing Louis dressed as King Arthur. Sybill had, of course, changed her mind and decided they should be displayed at Pencradoc. With them, were enlarged reproductions of a few other pages, and also Elsie's locket. It seemed the safest place for it at the minute – hopefully even Elsie couldn't get the locket out of the display case and leave it lying around somewhere else.

Coren privately thought that she'd settle down, now she'd got her point across. Even in the afterlife, it seemed she was extremely proud of the little family she'd started, and was happy for people to marvel over Marigold's cheeky little face and the handsome portrait of her husband.

The wedding photograph was also there, just to complete the exhibit, and he had to admit that it was a perfect display. Sybill had been invaluable – they'd spoken to one another often, sometimes on the silliest little pretexts but kept their blossoming relationship secret from their friends, just in case. Although he knew that neither of them had any doubts, and they could hardly be accused of rushing into anything, it just seemed the right thing to do at the minute. There was too much going on with trying to get Merryn's replacement employed, and if, by any chance, Sybill decided to try for it, he didn't want anyone to say it had been a case of nepotism.

'I'm not applying for it, Coren,' she'd told him before, laughing. 'I've already explained it to you. I can't leave Wheal Mount and I won't leave Wheal Mount.'

'Is it because I'm here? Can't you mix business with pleasure?' he'd asked, teasing.

'No, I cannot,' she'd responded briskly. 'And anyway, why would I want you to be my boss? There'd be a mutiny.'

'Very true,' he'd agreed. 'No, it's best for me that you're at Wheal Mount.'

'Professionally or personally?'

'Professionally, of course.'

'Hmmm.'

He knew that they'd both hung up the phones smiling. But now, today, he had to face Merryn and her grand plan for her replacement. He didn't know if he had a good feeling about it or not. But, at the designated time, Merryn burst into his office and headed towards him like a terrifying ship in full sail.

'Woah. Merryn.' He stared at her, slightly taken aback by her fierce expression.

'Let's get down to business.' She sat down and thrust a CV at him. 'What do you think about this candidate?'

'Candidate?' He was surprised. 'Are we ready to interview then? I wasn't aware that we'd finalised the job description.'

'*We* haven't. *I* did.' She pushed the CV closer to him. 'Read it.'

'Okay.' He looked at her, previous warnings about treading carefully around hormonally raging pregnant women ringing in his ears. He pulled the paper closer and read.

It seemed the candidate had a wide range of transferable skills

– organisation, prioritising, leadership, working independently and also as part of a team. Their personal statement was impressive enough. It was when he flipped to the second page and scanned the list of previous jobs that light began to dawn.

'Hospitality and tourism expertise, including barista and waitressing experience. Chalet girl in Switzerland. Gift shop attendant. Tour guide. Nannying. Gallery event planning.' He looked at Merryn and raised his eyebrows. 'Lemon picking in Sicily. And that's just to name a few. This is your sister, isn't it? Tegan?'

'It is.' Merryn folded her arms across her baby-bump. 'She's perfect. She's enthusiastic, and she'll do a great job. She's got loads of experience in tons of jobs – so you can use her where you think she's best placed; in the tea room, in the gardens, in the workshops, wherever. She's got me to ask if she ever needs help, and the job is only a short-term contract. It's ideal for her.'

'And?'

'And.' Merryn pulled a face. 'She's coming to Cornwall for a year while she decides what to do with her life, and I'd much rather know the place was in her hands than a stranger's.'

'Okay.' Coren tossed the CV back on the desk and threw his hands in the air. 'I'll trust you to make the right decision. It's your job at the end of the day. You've made it into what it is, and, to be honest, if you can guarantee Tegan can do it even half as well as you, I'm willing to take a chance on her. On the proviso, of course, that if it doesn't work out, I can get someone else.'

'Of course. Shake on it?'

'Shake on it.'

And they did.

After Merryn had, very unprofessionally, stood up, leaned over the desk and kissed him on the top of the head, she headed outside, already dialling Tegan's number to tell her the good news.

Coren watched her walk past the window, chatting

excitedly into the phone and couldn't help but grin. He reached for his own phone and was just about to dial Sybill yet again, when he looked up and saw a man standing inside the doorway to his office, half in shadow.

'Oh – good afternoon. Sorry, this isn't part of the public area. It's the staff offices.' He was used to visitors accidentally wandering into his office, but once they'd realised their mistake and he pointed them in the right direction, they were usually happy to shuffle apologetically away. On the basis of this tried and tested formula, he pointed vaguely to the left, meaning for the visitor to turn around and head back the way they'd come. 'If you just head back along—'

'Oh, I know my way around the place.' The man came out of the shadows and walked towards Coren, coming to a halt a little way away from his desk. 'It was you I wanted to talk to. Seen you here before now, but the time was never right.'

Coren stared disbelievingly as the man hooked his thumbs in the waistband of his smart, old-fashioned trousers and looked back at him, amused. 'Just thought you needed a bit of a talking to. She told me to tell you. Always did as she asked. Still do, to some extent.'

'Who – what …?' Coren couldn't get any more words out. In fact, his heart was pounding so much that he briefly wondered if he was going to drop dead on the spot from a heart attack – or maybe he had already done that, and this was some weird between-life where he was seeing—no. No! It couldn't be …

'Hmmm. All right, man. Let me help you. I think you're trying to ask who I am, and what I'm doing here. But I also think you already know. God, you look so much like me. But I can see her in you too. Incredible.' His grey eyes crinkled at the corners as he smiled, his fair hair looking more dishevelled than it had in the wedding picture, but less dishevelled than it did in the locket. 'Your brother got her artistic talent though. Sorry about that.'

'*Louis*?' Coren choked the word out, still not believing it. His office felt weird; sort of hot, yet cold at the same time, and everything he knew that was real and solid in the room was blurred and shimmering around the figure. In fact, in the hazy aura around the man, he could make out shapes of furniture that were not his, had never been his and, to his knowledge, had never been in the room as far as he could remember; shelves of ledgers, a table with a Tiffany lamp on it. A desk with a green, leather-bound blotting pad on it ... a typewriter.

'The very same. Look, just one thing to tell you. I'll make it brief. You, Coren Penhaligon, are your own person. You are yourself. Memories can be strange, devilish things, depending on whose memories they are. But you know, demons can be defeated by the love of a good woman, and you've got that – but you need to believe it first. It took me too long to believe it, and look what I lost out on. Wasted four years or so. She told me I had to tell you that you haven't got to worry about letting anyone in, or being anyone but yourself. Got it?'

Coren could do nothing but nod. Was this real, or an exaggerated trick of his mind, now all the pressure of hiring Merryn's replacement and the intensity of running the exhibition was over – and now he finally felt he was gradually opening himself up to Sybill?

'Jolly good.' The man, Louis, grinned, and it was as if Coren himself was looking into a mirror. 'Nice to meet you properly, man. Good luck with the future.' Then he nodded and smiled again. Coren watched him turn away and start to stroll back towards the door ...

He blinked.

He opened his eyes.

And the room was empty.

As his office settled again around him, he found he couldn't move. His hands were clutching the edge of the desk and his heart was still pounding. The door slammed, and he jumped, cursing as he was shocked back into life.

Louis. Louis had been in his bloody office! Or had he been in Louis' office? His head was thumping as he stared around the room again, as if he had never seen it before.

He jumped again as his phone rang, and he scrabbled for it, fumbling a little as he pressed the "Accept Call" button.

'Hello there.' Sybill's voice was warm, and oh so welcome. 'I was just thinking about you. So I thought I'd ring you on some pretext or other.'

'Were you? God, Sybill, it's good to hear from you...' He took a deep breath and tried to steady himself. He couldn't share that experience with her, he just couldn't.

'Are you okay, Coren? You sound a bit sort of spaced out.'

'What? Do I? Sorry.' He closed his eyes briefly, opened them again, and raked his hand through his hair. *Focus*.

Focus on Sybill.

Not on his dead relative who'd just popped in to give him some life advice.

'Yeah. Sorry – a random visitor just walked into my office. Startled me a bit. It's fine. But I *am* glad you called. Really I am. In fact, I was just about to call you when he wandered in.'

'Thanks. Great minds think alike. Poor visitor, I told you that you needed better signage.' Her laugh was warm and also very welcome. 'Yes. So, my pretext is that I was thinking that our place is pretty busy, and I was hoping yours was too.'

'It is. And also, good news.' He gave himself a mental shake and tried to settle into a normal conversation. 'We've appointed Merryn's maternity cover.'

'Oh!' Sybill sounded shocked. 'Did Tammy apply for it? I'm sorry, but I hope that she didn't it. I need her here. You can't be poaching my staff.'

Despite himself, Coren laughed. 'No, it didn't get as far as that. Tegan got it. Merryn's little sister. She got a good reference from someone.'

'That someone being Merryn, no doubt.'

'Of course. Still, it's something I don't have to think about any more, so I'm fine with it. Keep it in the family and all that.'

Family! How close he'd just come to meeting another member of it. A dead one, no less, but still ...

'So when does she start?'

'Tegan? You know?' He laughed, genuinely this time. 'I actually have no idea.'

'That's good.' Sybill sounded amused. 'It'll do you good to be less controlled in your outlook.'

'Hmm. Whatever. Anyway.' He sat back in his seat, feeling much calmer now. 'Are you free Saturday night?'

'Saturday? Yes – I believe I am. You know what an exciting life I lead.'

'Great. Can I tempt you into coming up to Pencradoc at all? It's midsummer eve, and I think the moor is kind of calling to me for a picnic. Don't know about you.'

'Midsummer eve?' Sybill's voice was warm. 'And a picnic? Sounds perfect.'

'I'll come and get you,' said Coren, suddenly even more desperate to see her.

'No – I'll drive. It's fine.'

'But there may be champagne. Alcohol. You can't drive back after having that. I was going to play taxi.'

'Who says I'll want to drive back?' It was the first time since they'd tentatively started to commit to one another that the idea had been verbalised. God knew he'd thought about it, thought about asking her to stay over, but he didn't want to push things until she was comfortable.

'Well. If you're happy to drive, I'm happy to make the spare bed up. Just in case.'

'Spare bed. Just in case. Okay. I'll see you Saturday, Coren.'

'See you then.' There was a beat. 'I love you, Sybill.' There was another beat, and he dropped his forehead onto the desk, cringing. It was too early, far too early to—

'And I love you too, Coren.'

He sat back up again, blinking at the room in surprise.

It wasn't too early at all.

And that made him feel very happy indeed.

And also – he suddenly realised what Louis had meant. He was his own person.

He was Coren.

He wasn't cold, unfeeling Ellory, or the reincarnated spirit of Elsie's one great love.

He was Coren Penhaligon.

He loved Sybill Helyer.

And she loved him back.

Him. Coren Penhaligon.

1911

'Did you see Fabian's *face*?' Elsie was practically bounding out of the house, tugging Louis behind her, laughing. 'Oh my, when Teague told him what the commission was – my word! I thought I'd have to scrape him up off the floor. Louis. I am positively *buoyant*.' She stopped and spun around to face him. 'I love you, Louis. I love you and Marigold and my parents and everything. I'm just about ready to shout it to the entire *world*.'

Louis laughed. It seemed her delight – and yes, relief – was contagious. 'I love you as well, Elsie. And I love Marigold already. How could I not, when you're her mother? But there's still a hurdle in our way.' He frowned. 'My parents. We need to tell them as well.'

'Oh. Yes.' Elsie stopped. 'Fly in the ointment. Quite.' She bit her lip. 'Head over there now?'

'After you've seen Holly and Pearl and set their minds at rest, yes.' Louis nodded over to the women who were sitting in the rose garden and waved at them.

'My goodness. Of course.' Elsie flushed and let go of Louis' hand. She ran over to the girls, and they stood up to greet her. Well, Pearl stood up. Holly got stuck somewhat, and Elsie grabbed her hand and hauled her to her feet. 'Low seats – not good in your condition.' Elsie shook her head.

'Not good at all.' Holly scowled. 'Thank God you were there. I might have had to roll myself off the thing.'

'Doubtful.' Elsie hugged her. 'A gardener would have been along before too long. Anyway – I've spoken to Mama and Teague. They took it surprisingly well.' She turned and looked at Louis who was sauntering over, his hands now in his pockets. 'We're all set. Louis is moving to London to be with us. Fabian has a super commission to paint the bulk of my family, and we just need to head MC and her ilk off before they start invading Pencradoc.' She shook her head angrily. 'But at least my parents heard it from me first, so what is the worst they can do?' She shrugged. 'They're well prepared.'

'You needn't worry about MC at least.' Holly grinned and looked conspiratorially at Pearl. 'She's *been* headed off at the pass. Their carriage pulled up not long after you went in the house.'

'My gosh, she cannot wear black quite as well as you can, sweet.' Pearl made her eyes wide and startled, and Elsie blinked.

'Black? She was wearing *black*?'

'She and dear Mama both.' Pearl nodded.

'I wondered whether she was trying to copy your good self, so that Louis would fall desperately back in love with her,' said Holly.

'I said that she was probably in mourning for a lost love. Her face was pinched too.'

'Dreadfully pinched.'

'Ugly pinched. My God, it was crazy ugly.'

'Oh.' Elsie looked from one of her friends to another and suddenly laughed. 'I don't know if I want to imagine what you said to them.'

'We asked what they were here for. Said we were next in the queue to offer our congratulations to the happy couple, and hadn't it been lovely to see you at the ball last night? Quite cheering,' said Holly.

'We smiled as we said it.' Pearl adjusted one of her gloves primly. 'And then I asked who had died and should we offer our condolences?'

'And then I made a great show of pretending that I was just about to have the baby, and they headed off the way they had come. Rather quickly.'

'You were astonishing. I said Elsie would be proud of your acting abilities.'

'I was proud of them myself.' Holly cradled her enormous bump and smiled sweetly. 'I'll just say it was a false alarm if they ever ask again.'

'Oh my. What would I do without you two?' Elsie leaned in and kissed each girl on the cheek, then hugged them. 'And for your information, I wear black because I like it, and because it suits my dark, melancholy moods.'

'Dark, melancholy moods, my foot. And without us, you'd sink, I suspect,' said Pearl. 'We'll always look out for you, you know that. Which makes it even harder to think … to think that—' She looked at Holly for support.

Holly continued the speech seriously. 'Harder to think that you couldn't tell us anything. Why not? Why couldn't you talk to us? You didn't have to do all this yourself.' She waved her hand at Elsie and Louis, encompassing them, then unconsciously brushed her hand against her stomach again, grateful, perhaps, that she didn't have to keep her own pregnancy a secret from everyone she loved.

'Oh no. Please.' Elsie covered her face with her hands, feeling dreadful. She looked at her friends, her eyes brimming with sudden tears. 'I just couldn't. I wasn't thinking straight – I didn't want anyone I associated with knowing about Marigold. There would have been too many people to keep secrets on my behalf. Louis – Louis would have found out. His parents …'

'Oh! Damn!' Pearl suddenly looked at Holly in horror. 'MC's Mother Dearest. The scheming old trout. She said she had one more call to make today.' Pearl looked past Elsie at Louis, her eyes wide. 'Ashby Court. They're heading to see your mom and pop. I'll bet my goddamn life on it.'

Margaret and her mother had indeed headed to Ashby Court. But thankfully, they'd left by the time Louis and Elsie raced up there on their horses.

Louis was pleased – he didn't think he wanted to see Margaret again any time soon. As far as he was concerned, it was over. He'd told her that at the costume ball, and he knew Elsie was prepared for a fight today, simply by her posture on the horse. She wasn't riding side saddle. She'd clambered bareback onto her mare, Henrietta – named after the artist Henrietta Ward – and galloped out of Pencradoc's grounds, heading back across Bodmin Moor. It seemed like a lifetime since he'd travelled that way this morning.

Elsie's hair was loose, as always, and flew behind her in a mass of windswept curls. Her black skirts billowed out as she focused on getting to Ashby Court just as soon as she could. She looked like a wild Romany girl, at one with the moors around her and the sky above her. Louis didn't think he had ever desired her more – it was the crystallisation of everything that had led up to this moment, everything that had gone between them before.

They sped up the driveway to Ashby Court, and Elsie dismounted almost as soon as Henrietta had stopped.

'Elsie, wait.' Louis was slower to reach the doorway, his breathing jagged from the wind rushing past him.

'I'm going in, Louis.' She turned to face him, her hair untamed, and pointed at the door. 'They have *no* right to gossip about us. This is *exactly* what I was talking about.'

'Elsie ...' He hurried after her as she marched ahead and flung the door open. 'Let me. I should tell them—'

'Tell us what?' His mother was suddenly there, standing in front of them, her eyes red-rimmed. 'What exactly do you need to tell us, Louis? Elsie?'

'Lady Ashby. Is Mrs Corrington here? Or Margaret?'

'No. No, Elsie dear.' Suddenly his mother subsided and sat on a chair, shaking her head. 'They've left. Your father, Louis, is in the study having a brandy. At this time in the morning!'

Louis hurried over to her and put his hand on her shoulder. 'Oh, Mother. I'm sorry they came here, I really am. What did they say?' He was trying to judge the situation, hoping that their better nature had won and they hadn't spread the gossip about Louis and Elsie. He knew it was a faint hope though – especially if Lord Ashby was on the brandy.

'Enough. They said enough.' Lady Ashby looked up at him, then looked at Elsie. She sighed and shook Louis' hand off before standing up. She smoothed down her dress and fixed the pair of them with a glare that made Louis cringe. 'The worst thing about it is that *they* told me. Not you two. I so dreadfully wish one of you two had told me.'

Elsie stepped forward and took Lady Ashby's hand in hers. 'Then blame me. Not Louis. He didn't know, so he couldn't tell you.' She looked at Louis, then back at his mother. 'And I'll tell you now why I kept it a secret. Because I didn't want the likes of *those people* gossiping about *our families*. That's it in a nutshell. And if you give me a chance, I can tell you *everything* right now.'

Louis moved behind Elsie and put his arm around her waist. 'You should know as well that I'm moving to London to be with Elsie and to look after her and Marigold. Marigold is my responsibility, just as much as she's Elsie's. It took both of us to make her, and I need to make up for all of these lost years with my daughter and the woman I love. And I'd rather have Elsie in *these* circumstances, no matter what people like the Corringtons say, than anybody else in any other circumstances.'

Lady Ashby nodded. 'I understand, dear. I do. I'm only sorry that they got here first. You'll be pleased to know though, that I sent them away. With a thousand fleas in each ear. I said I didn't listen to gossip, I would wait until I'd had the full story from you two, and that I was pleased my son was no longer associated with such a venomous, horrible family. There now.' She nodded again. 'I felt much better after saying that. But!' She looked at them, a hint of steel in her eyes. 'It doesn't mean I have to like the order in which you two have committed yourselves to one another. It doesn't mean I approve of what's happened. I only wanted those women out of my house, and I would back my child all the way, no matter *who* was telling me stories about them, and no matter *what* those stories were. I need to see this little girl, I need to see a picture of her at least – I want to get to know her as well. I'm more upset about that than anything, I think. Such a pretty name as well. Oh my. I bet she's beautiful.' She sniffed and dabbed her nose delicately with a lace handkerchief, then her voice hardened as she glanced at Louis again. 'But all I ask, Louis, is that before you have another child, you damn well marry the girl first.' Lady Ashby immediately looked quite astounded at herself for cursing, and Louis saw Elsie bite her lip in apparent amusement.

Louis found himself wondering whether his mother had also had a nip of restorative brandy.

'I will, Mother. I'll marry Elsie just as soon as I need to,' he said. He looked at Elsie mischievously. 'If she'll have me, that is.'

'Louis. You can't get rid of me now. I'm sorry.'

'I'm not,' he said. And he meant it.

Chapter Eighteen

Present Day

MIDSUMMER EVE

'I think it's all going quite successfully. Don't you?' Sybill was leaning against Coren as they sat on the moor, the promised picnic basket between them and a bottle of champagne open. They'd slipped out of Pencradoc's grounds and walked for a little while across Bodmin Moor, until they found the perfect picnic spot. There wasn't much champagne left in the bottle now, and she was feeling pleasantly woolly-minded. There were only a couple of hours of daylight left too, and she could think of nothing nicer than lying here with Coren and just watching the sunset on midsummer eve; it was a promise she was pleased they'd kept to one another, despite all the strange things that had happened over the last month. There was nowhere else she'd rather be right now.

She realised that this was also almost exactly the day when, over a century ago, Elsie had travelled to Elton Lacy and attended a costume ball. In more recent weeks, there had been a steady stream of visitors to Pencradoc to view Elsie's gown, beautifully displayed on Tilly, as well as Elsie's artwork, and it was a similar story at Wheal Mount. Sybill had loved reading the feedback in the visitors' book and felt that Elsie would have been preening at some of the comments if she'd been watching. "*The most beautiful woman of her time.*" "*So talented and how lucky to have known all those fabulous artists.*" "*I saw her dress at Pencradoc and I want it.*" "*Elsie's bedroom. I have no words.*"

'I'm loving the midsummer vibes,' Sybill said contentedly, appreciating the scent of the grass and the drowsy buzzing of the bees nearby. A butterfly drifted past and she smiled. 'I wonder if this was how Elsie felt when she was heading to the ball.'

'I don't know.' Coren sounded as drowsy as the bees. 'I guess she was a bit excited. I think she'd have liked her parties.'

'I think so too.' Sybill closed her eyes and shifted position. She let herself drift, safe in the knowledge that Coren was right there next to her. It wasn't hard to imagine Elsie climbing into the carriage on the arm of Fabian, probably as woolly-minded as she herself was, all psyched up to shine at the ball. But the images that now came to her – instead of the rocking motion of the carriage and the excited buzz of the atmosphere, possibly a wry smile on the face of Fabian, along with perhaps a sip of something fortifying from a hip flask – was of something very different and all together more wild and primeval ...

It was the scent of the earth and skin, warm hands on her body, the scratchy feel of fabric wrinkling and crushing, the feel of grass against her hair, hot breath, rough kisses bruising her lips as she returned them hungrily, forcing herself closer and closer to him, as close as she possibly could get, grey eyes fixing on hers, challenging her even as she challenged him back ...

'Oh my God.' She sat up and stared at Coren, feeling the heat rush into her cheeks. It was real – it was so real that she felt groggy and lost, half in Elsie's world and half in hers. She could still feel the weight of his body on hers. 'Elsie!'

'What? What about Elsie?'

'Her memories. Right here. I know it's here. She – she made love here. Right here.' She looked around her, the heat rushing back into her cheeks as more images poured into her mind. She squeezed her eyes shut then opened them again, sensing the faint shadows of bodies entwined fading back into the shadows ...

It was more than she wanted to see and, disorientated, she stood up.

'Sybill? What's wrong?' Coren reached up and touched her hand. She was sure he meant to pull her back to the comfortable position they'd been sitting in, surrounded by their picnic – but instead it was like an explosion went off in her mind, and she was no longer herself; she was Elsie Pencradoc, and two midsummers, four years apart, had held some of the most defining moments of her life.

Coren jumped as the electricity crackled up his arm, but instead of letting go of her hand, he clutched it tighter. A myriad of images flooded into his mind and he gasped. He was here, but not here. It *was* him, but not him ...

Before he could think, he pulled her back down and she was in his arms, kissing him like there was no tomorrow; more urgent and desperate than he had ever been kissed before – or maybe not. Maybe he had been kissed, once upon a time, just that urgently, and as the thought flashed into his head, he saw it and he felt it all again.

'Sybill—' With a great effort he pulled himself away from her. 'What are we doing?'

'Coren. We're doing what we've probably needed to do for a very long time.' She looked at him, studying the depths of his eyes. 'Elsie and Louis – this place was special to them, I know it was. It's going to be special to us as well – don't ask me to explain. This is *right*. This is what we need to do. We just have to believe in it.'

'I agree, I know. I *know*. But are we not getting mixed up? Are we them? Or are we us? Are we feeling what we are feeling, or what they felt?' It was a jumble of words and thoughts, despite Louis' other-worldly assurances, and he could barely make sense of them himself; but Sybill seemed to know exactly what he meant.

'We're us. But their spirits are here; part of them is still here, and it's burnt into the ground and they've saturated this place with everything they ever felt for each other. It's like magic. Can't you feel it?'

A shiver ran up his spine, which was partially to do with her holding his face in her hands and her dark eyes staring intently into his, and partially to do with the fact that, yes, he *could* feel it. And unlike before, unlike the time they'd come close to doing this very thing at this very same place a month or so ago, he knew it was the right thing to do at this moment, and he was powerless to resist.

It seemed they both felt the same. He couldn't tear his gaze away from her, and he covered her hands with his and brought her face closer …

And anything that happened beyond that was a secret between them and the moor, and no other living person at all.

1911

The locket had been opened again and wept over by Lady Ashby. Elsie had joined in the weeping and apologised all over again, then flung her arms around Louis' father and soaked his shoulder as she wailed her apologies to him as well. She knew she was fortunate that Louis' family had a particular soft spot for her. It could so easily have turned out differently. She was thanking her lucky stars and her guardian angels and everyone who loved her for the way things had happened today.

'I don't know how I thought my decision to keep Marigold secret was ever a good one,' she confessed to Louis as they rode back across Bodmin Moor towards Pencradoc. He was travelling halfway back to Pencradoc with her. Then he'd go back to Ashby Court, pack what he needed for a short stay, and travel to London with her and Fabian later that afternoon. Now he knew about Marigold, he didn't want to waste any more time by not being in London with Elsie and his daughter, and he was planning on making the move more permanent in a few weeks. The main thing was to get him there and bring her little family together for the first time.

Knowing that everything was more or less resolved now, and hoping beyond hope that Marigold would take to her father, they rode at a much more leisurely pace. Elsie was enjoying it – much more than she had the mad flight over to Ashby Court, despite the wild feeling of freedom she'd experienced as she'd gripped Henrietta's reins and leaned forwards into the wind.

'Did Lily and Edwin never try to convince you otherwise?' Louis asked, drawing up beside her, his horse falling into step with hers.

'Many times. Especially when we had to organise it and lie about things so that Marigold was with me when they saw any of my family, and vice versa.' She pulled a face, hating the memories and hating herself for putting them all in such an awful position. 'But I'm bloody stubborn. You know that more than most.' She cast a glance up at Louis. 'Have I apologised to you yet? How can you still love me now you know what I've done?'

'I love you *whatever* you do. I can't exist without you. I perhaps haven't made myself clear – you should know all that, Elsie Pencradoc! Why do you think I came to Brunswick Square? Like I told you, I had no business to attend to. I just wanted to see *you*.'

She brought her horse to a standstill and faced him. 'Are you sure? I've been deemed a loose cannon before now.'

'Then I'll be the one to steady you.'

'Will you now?'

'Yes.' He moved his horse right next to hers, and she leaned over and kissed him.

'I … think I might need steadying now. Just a little.' Her heart was hammering. She knew what she was offering, and she also knew that he would understand exactly what she was thinking.

'Just a little?' The corners of his lips turned up in a small, crooked smile.

'A little. Yes.' Without breaking eye contact, she dropped the reins and slid off the horse. 'Here seems a good place. Quite ... secluded really.'

'I agree.' Louis slid off his horse too and came to stand beside her. He took her in his arms and pulled her close. 'Is this steady enough for you?'

'It's quite steady. It'll do for now.'

'Will it?'

'Yes. But give me a little while longer doing *this*.' She leaned up and kissed him on the lips. 'And *this*.' Then she moved her mouth to the crook of his neck and kissed him again, delighted to feel a tremor rushing through his body; a tremor that, it had to be said, matched the one racing through her heart and mind at that very moment. 'And maybe *this*—' She moved her hands to the top of his shirt and began to unfasten it. 'And I'll feel much steadier.'

He grabbed her hands and stilled them and bent down and kissed her, stilling the words on her lips as well. Then, all of a sudden, he picked her up tenderly and walked across the moor to a pleasant little glade that was awfully familiar, and a different place altogether to where they'd made love the previous morning.

'Here. This is even more secluded,' he murmured into her ear, and he placed her gently on the ground. 'Can you remember the last time we were here?'

'I *can* remember it. It was almost exactly four years ago,' she whispered, smiling against his kiss. 'How the hell could I ever forget it?'

'You can't.' And he kissed her again, and his hands found the fastening on her bodice, and she didn't think about much else for quite some time afterwards ...

Chapter Nineteen

Present Day

SEPTEMBER

September and the autumn rolled around, and with it the end of both the "Midsummer Ball" exhibition at Pencradoc and the "Lady Elsie Pencradoc in Portraiture" exhibition at Wheal Mount.

Sybill smiled to herself as she supervised the packing away of the pictures, deciding which ones could – and should – be left out on display as she went along. There was no reason for the Wheal Mount walls to display the same pictures year in, year out – apart from, she acknowledged, the portraits of Jago, Alys and the rest of Elsie's wider family in the main drawing room. They were sacrosanct, and she wasn't going to be the one responsible for moving them.

Sybill's phone rang, and she glanced at it. *Merryn*. Merryn, who couldn't quite leave her job behind, even though she was supposed to be on maternity leave now.

'Hey, Merryn.'

'Sybill! I've just had a thought. It's about the next exhibition. We could sort of swap around a bit—'

'We?'

'We—'

'Merryn! No. You've left work. Stop it.'

'Sybill! I'm bored. I am absolutely bored.'

'Shouldn't you have your feet up?'

'I have.'

'Good.'

'They're up in the Tower Tea Room.'

'*Merryn*!'

'Please. Let me just run this one by you.'

Sybill raised her eyes to heaven and shook her head. 'Merryn. I've just got some bits to finish up here, then I'm coming up to Pencradoc anyway. I need to speak to Coren.'

'Great. I'll just wait then. I'm sure I can make myself useful.'

'I'm sure you can. Look – give me an hour and I'll be there, okay?'

'Okay.'

They said their farewells, and Sybill, as good as her word, eventually set off on her journey.

It was by far one of the strangest trips to Pencradoc she'd had to make. She felt sick the whole way there, and her stomach churned at the reception she might get. But it had to be done and it had to be said. And there was no getting away from it.

She pulled up and saw Merryn talking to Kit as he raked up some fallen leaves into a neat pile. She parked the car and then approached them. 'Hello. Spotted you.'

'I'm not hard to miss.' Merryn was only a couple of weeks away from having the baby, and, in all honesty, her comment was not far from the truth. The cheerful patchwork dress was pulled taut across her stomach now, and it didn't look like it had much more give in it. The pretty trainers had also given way to flip-flops – easier, Sybill assumed, to shove one's feet into when you couldn't see them any more.

'You're not hard to miss at all.' She smiled. 'Come on. Let's go for a wander, and you can tell me about your grand idea. I guess it'll be up to Tegan to implement it though?'

'Sadly, yes.' Merryn kissed Kit, and then she and Sybill walked towards the waterfall. 'My idea was that we do a World War One theme across the two sites. We could have the artwork – Fabian did some incredible pictures, and I'm sure we could source some of those. And you had the Land Girls at Wheal Mount, helping out on the estate and such-like. I knew the Women's Land Army was set up in 1917, and I've already checked that you definitely had the girls there and you did – so it was just a thought, really.'

'It's a good thought. I'd love to give Fabian some wall space somewhere, and I think he'd like the fact he was celebrated at Pencradoc for all the right reasons. And we know Louis didn't go off and fight. He had some health problems that prevented it, so it would be good to continue Elsie and Louis' story ...' Sybill didn't continue. It wasn't a story she was fully willing to discuss right now. She decided to change the subject and took a deep breath. 'Anyway. You pass all that on to Tegan and we can work with her. You need to be thinking about other things. Like, for example, decorating the nursery?'

'Ha! Yes. I suppose you're right. I can't quite let it all go though, you know? Pencradoc has been part of me for so long.'

'I know. But believe me, once that baby is here, all of this will seem of very little consequence for a while.'

'Yes.' Merryn walked in silence for a little while, her hands in her deep pockets, her brow furrowed, seemingly deep in thought.

'So. Have you thought of any names yet?' It was an old chestnut, the age-old question designed to distract most mothers-to-be from other issues they may be thinking about.

It had the desired effect and Merryn instantly brightened. 'Oh! Yes. For a girl, we're considering Rosie Loveday. Rosie after, well, Duchess Rose, and Loveday after Kit's great aunt – the one who left him and Coren this place. It's also a bit of a tradition that the Pencradoc children on Jago and Alys' side were given two names. One Cornish, and one not so Cornish – then they could decide what they wanted to be called as they grew older.'

'That's so sweet. And what about for a little boy?'

'You know, I have no idea.' Merryn laughed, almost embarrassed. 'Which is why I'm sort of hoping it's a girl.'

'It may well be then.' Sybill thought of her own experience

– she and Marco had prepared no names at all. Marco had decided on Lucia after his grandmother, and Sybill had gone along with it, too distraught to think of anything else. Privately, she always thought of Lucia as a bright star in the sky nowadays, and, perhaps crazily, regretted not adding Stella or Star or something like that to her name.

'I like Isobel.' The words were out before she could stop them, and she flushed furiously. 'It's a witchy name. Like mine. There was a Scottish witch called Isobel Gowdie in the seventeenth century, and apparently she talked at length about meeting the Queen of the Fairies. I've always loved that idea.'

'And we know Elsie was dressed as a witch for her ball.' Merryn smiled. 'The pair of you have much in common.'

'We do.'

And more than even you know, thought Sybill, flushing again.

'Anyway. I need to see Coren.' She swallowed another wave of nausea down. 'Pretty quickly. Where is he?'

'Oh ... I think I saw him disappear across the walled garden.' Merryn nodded. 'Towards the moor. No idea why he's headed out there. Usually we can't winkle him out of the office, but when I told Kit you were coming, he said he'd seen Coren go that way. So it looks like we've already lost him to the moors. Sorry we couldn't catch him for you.'

'It's fine. I'll go after him. I think I know where he'll be. Thanks, Merryn.'

'No problem.' Then Merryn turned to face her and smiled. 'You two are made for one another, you know. I can tell whenever you're near each other. There are literally sparks.'

'Hmmm. Slow burning embers, perhaps.' Sybill laughed, then, surprising both of them, she moved towards Merryn and hugged her, the hard contours of Merryn's tummy pressing into hers. 'You take care. Take it easy, and I'll see you soon – hopefully not at work. Okay?'

'Okay.' Merryn laughed and returned the hug. 'Good luck, honey.'

'With what?'

'With whatever you have to tell Coren.'

There was a beat, and the two women looked at one another. Sybill knew in that moment she had a kindred spirit, and also realised that Merryn knew exactly what she'd come to see Coren about. She exhaled slowly. 'Thanks. I'll keep you posted.'

'Make sure you do.'

They hugged again briefly, and Sybill turned towards the walled gardens and the exit onto Bodmin Moor.

She knew exactly where she would find him. But not exactly how she would tell him ...

Coren was striding across the moor with no clear direction. He was just letting his feet take him wherever they wanted to go. He was barely taking any notice of his surroundings, but strangely wasn't surprised when he looked up and noticed where he was.

He needed to think about the future and he knew that, after the first rush of passion between them, there was no guarantee Sybill would hang around for him. They'd already known each other for years now, and he knew deep in his heart that she was the one for him. But she was so incredible – what if their wild affair just burned itself out after summer and she moved on? Had they both just needed to get themselves out of each other's systems? What if that was it – the intense few weeks they'd just experienced, ever since midsummer eve – and then perhaps nothing after that? A sort of drawing away. Was she already distancing herself? What if she was already getting bored of him? Was it even possible to keep this feeling alive? Because he, for one, never wanted to let her go again.

Perhaps rather than the fear of him being too like Ellory, it was simply a different sort of fear that held him back now.

The fear that he, Coren Penhaligon, wasn't good enough for someone like Sybill Helyer. The fear that what she needed, after the things he'd found out about her, was not just him, but another family. Another baby. And he was more than willing to give her all of that, but was she willing to accept it? Was she willing to take the chance again after what had happened with Marco and Lucia? It was a decision he knew he would never be able to make for her, but it was one that would shape the rest of his life, and the rest of hers.

Would either of them consciously be able to make that decision, to take that step?

'But you know what?' he said out loud to nobody in particular as he stood on the moors and looked around him. 'Did that ever stop anyone else? Doesn't everyone just do things they don't think about too much, and take risks and see what happens?' There was no answer of course, but he was aware of something just behind him; a soft breath, a whisper, and he turned around quickly.

A little way away, coming across the moor, was a figure. She certainly wasn't close enough to have breathed or whispered in his ear, but he knew without a doubt who the figure was and his heart turned over.

He began to walk towards her, and then found himself breaking into a run. There was a little hesitation on her part, it seemed, but then she began to run towards him as well. They met in the middle and his arms were around her and, before he really knew it, he was kissing her.

'Sybill. How did you find me?' he asked when they eventually pulled away. All his doubts and fears seemed to have dissipated into the ether, all in that one moment of togetherness – just like the last time they had been here; the last time they had been alone on Bodmin Moor.

'I knew where you'd be. Merryn said you were heading over to the moor.' She shrugged. 'It wasn't hard to guess where you'd gone.'

'Am I that predictable?'

'Predictable is … nice.'

'Just "nice"? I'd rather be exciting, I think. You'd find predictable boring after a while.'

'I'd rather we made our own *quiet* excitement, Coren, if we're going to be together.' Suddenly she was serious. Her hands moved away from his shoulders, and she clutched two handfuls of material from his shirt. 'I've had too much of the wrong sort of excitement in my life. My time with Marco was unreal. I experienced huge highs and huge lows. It's a time I don't want to repeat. I'm at the point now where I want to be settled and happy and, well, grown up. Coren …' She took a deep breath. 'I have to tell you something. If you don't want anything else to do with me, that's absolutely understandable. I mean—' she laughed awkwardly '—we've never really been a couple, have we? Beyond these last few weeks. We've never really made that commitment to each other, and this has all happened rather fast. But I have to say this. I'm pregnant, Coren. That night, up here. Midsummer. Well. There we go. I'm keeping it. As I say, I understand if it's not what you want – but it's what I want. And it wasn't planned and I never expected it, but it's happened. And I'm happy. I'm actually happy.' The words tumbled out of her mouth and Coren stared at her, his heart racing.

'Woah – what? You're pregnant? Are you sure?' His hands tightened on her shoulders.

She was sobbing now, hiccoughing as she spoke, nodding. 'I am. Yes. Fourteen weeks, or so they tell me.'

'Sybill!' He pulled her closer and leaned his head down, resting it on top of hers. 'That's incredible. That's wonderful news. Honestly. I'll not pretend it's not a shock, but …'

There was a muffled laugh through her tears, her shoulders shaking. 'But it's not entirely unexpected. Not with what we know about midsummer liaisons. I didn't know how to tell you. But I'm glad I did.'

'I'm glad you did too.' His mind was whirring. He realised he was ecstatic. He'd never been so elated in all his life. Now, *now* he understood what Kit had felt on the day he'd burst into the office and announced his and Merryn's news.

And he couldn't help it. He shouted with laughter and picked Sybill up and swung her around, before setting her gently on her feet again. Then he tentatively pressed his hand to her stomach as Sybill, sobbing and laughing at the same time, took his wrist in her hand and guided it there.

'It's real, Coren. It's a baby. Our baby. All warm and safe.'

Her stomach felt surprisingly firm and slightly rounded, and he had such an overwhelming feeling of love and gratitude and protection that he swore to himself, and to her and to the baby and to the earth and sky and the moors between, that he would never, ever let anything happen to the pair of them, and he would love and protect them as fiercely as he could for the rest of his life.

And as they kissed again and held each other, laughing and crying and making plans, he looked over her shoulder and saw, not entirely unexpectedly, a shadowy group of three people – a little girl skipped and danced away in front of her parents, who chased her until, laughing, they caught her, and then finally faded away.

A memory. A happy memory of an infinite love that had reached out across the generations to touch them both here today.

Coren was sure that, in years to come, people would see him and Sybill here as well, the emotions and joy from today etched into the world around them, everlasting.

As eternal as love.

October, 1911

'Faster, Papa! Faster!' The little girl was hanging onto the small passenger seat on the back of Louis' tricycle.

'I can't go any faster!' Louis laughed and turned slightly

to see his daughter holding tightly to the edges of the wicker seat, her eyes bright and the ribbons already coming adrift from her hair.

'I'm sure you can, Papa,' said Elsie, riding behind them as they pedalled back to Brunswick Square from Edwin and Lily's home. 'You just – what do you do, Marigold?'

'Pedal *quick*!' Marigold laughed, and Louis turned his attention back to the road ahead of him.

'All right – just a little quicker then.' He obliged and was gratified to hear Marigold cry out in delight.

He was still amazed at her – every day, it seemed, he was learning more about her quirks and foibles and, in the end, it had been easier than he'd thought to introduce himself into her life.

That first evening in London, he and Elsie had rediscovered each other in Elsie's bedroom, and the next morning Fabian had done as she'd asked and made her excuses to the Slade for her. Louis and Elsie had walked to Primrose Hill together, and it was there he had met his daughter for the first time.

'Marigold,' Elsie had said, taking the little girl on her knee as the child ran in to greet them. 'I want you to meet a very special person. This is your papa. He's been very busy in Cornwall, working very hard, and he hasn't been able to see you until now. But he's missed you very much.'

'All right.' Marigold had looked at him curiously, her thumb in her mouth for a couple of minutes, and Louis had felt himself grow hot and cold at the potential reaction. Then, finally: 'Hello, Papa. Mummy has you in the house. I know you. It's all right.' She shrugged and took her thumb out of her mouth. 'I see you on the table. Oh. And in Mummy's bedroom.' Then she'd grinned and clambered off Elsie's knee. She'd surprised them all by toddling over to Louis and demanding he lift her onto his knee. 'Are you coming to live with us at home?'

Louis had been stunned and looked at Elsie for help. 'Of

course,' he said. 'I'll be living at ... home ... with you and Mama. It will be fun.'

'Good,' she'd said. And that was the end of the conversation as far as Marigold was concerned.

Elsie had been trying not to laugh, even as she blushed scarlet. 'She means the pictures of you. You might have noticed I've got them all over the house. There *is* one in my bedroom. Framed. Sorry about that. I ... draw. A lot. Hid it last night. That's all.' She shrugged and that, again, was an end to it.

Marigold had easily accepted Louis as an extra feature in her life and, even though she was still devoted to Edwin and Lily, she often chose Louis' lap when they were all together. Louis still marvelled at it all – although if he thought about it too much, it made his head spin. In a few short weeks, he had essentially gained a new life. Margaret Corrington and Ashby Court were a lifetime away. His world now revolved around Elsie and Marigold and his work in the London offices for his family's business. They were currently in the process of changing Marigold's surname to Ashby, and he couldn't be happier to be doing so.

Both Zennor and Teague, and Louis' own parents, had come to London to meet her and she had enchanted them all. She'd also had her first trip to Pencradoc, and there were plans afoot to take her back at Christmas and have a big celebration there with all their friends and families. Holly and Pearl had fallen in love with her as well, and Marigold loved her new little "cousins", so all was going well – she especially loved Aunt Holly's tiny new arrival, Joe, and had to be gently removed from his crib as she enjoyed nothing more than climbing up the side, hanging over it and talking to him.

And moments like the moment right now, when it was a beautiful October day, with the leaves turning golden and orange and red, could not be traded for anything better in the entire world.

Except ...

'Louis.' Elsie came up beside him and indicated that he should stop the tricycle, which he did, much to Marigold's protests and grumbles.

Elsie moved over to her and rested her hand on the curly hair, seemingly deliberately avoiding Louis' eyes for a moment until he ducked down and caught her gaze, prompting her further. 'Yes, Elsie?'

'Can you remember what your mother said to us back in the summer? About getting married?'

'Yes.'

'How we had to promise to do it before we had another baby?'

'Yes ...' His heart started pounding.

'Well, then.' She nodded briskly. 'I think you need to ask me to marry you.' She blinked and looked up at him. 'Sooner rather than later would be splendid, by the way. Well, before June. Summer off work at the Slade. Back in the autumn. Should work out all right, I think.'

'Elsie ... are you sure? About June?'

'Yes. Yes, I am.' She shrugged, her cheeks scarlet. 'Got away with it at midsummer. Didn't in September. That's life.'

He felt joy and laughter bubbling up from somewhere deep inside him, and he took hold of her, looked into her eyes and saw the faintest flicker of concern there. 'So, you're saying I should really ask you, shouldn't I?'

'You really should.'

So he did.

And she accepted.

And so it was.

Epilogue

Present Day

THREE WEEKS LATER
MID CORNWALL TIMES – FAMILY NOTICES

Penhaligon
Kit and Merryn are delighted to welcome Rosie Loveday into their family. Born 30th September, weighing 7lbs 14oz, much loved and cherished already.

SIX MONTHS LATER
MID CORNWALL TIMES – FAMILY NOTICES

Penhaligon
To Coren and Sybill, a daughter. Isobel Elsie Star, born 21st March, weighing 8lb 11oz.

Penhaligon/Helyer
Coren and Sybill are delighted to announce their engagement. "She said yes" on 21st March. Isobel approves.

MID CORNWALL TIMES,
SEVEN MONTHS LATER
PENCRADOC "HEARTS" CENTRE

Brothers Coren and Kit Penhaligon, co-owners of Pencradoc Arts Centre, are pleased to announce that the house and estate is now a licensed venue for weddings. Catering can also be provided on-site by local girl Sorcha Davies, owner of the award-winning Tower Tea Rooms.

Wedding packages are available to suit all budgets and all sizes of events, and the estate itself provides some phenomenal photographic opportunities for the wedding party, from atmospheric shots in the Gothic rose garden, to less formal poses by the tumbling waterfall and tranquil stream. The Mill House is a delightful retreat and honeymoon destination for newly-weds, and the estate can also be booked simply as a destination for the reception, if the couple so wishes.

Coren Penhaligon, manager of the venture, advised us that he and his fiancée Sybill Helyer, manager of Wheal Mount Arts Centre, would be the first couple to wed at Pencradoc, with their wedding taking place on the summer solstice. "It seemed appropriate," he said with a smile, "that as our daughter Isobel was born on the spring equinox, we should get married at midsummer. It's always been a special day in Pencradoc history, and we have evidence that Lady Elsie Pencradoc, who Kit and I are descended from, made some life-affirming decisions on midsummer night in 1907, and then again at a midsummer ball in 1911. Let's just say that if none of those decisions had been made, then neither of us would be here today."

And with that intriguing thought, we must leave Coren and Sybill to plan their wedding – and of course to pay some attention to little Isobel, who is already showing signs of being a much-loved daddy's girl. We wish them all the best in the future.

Thank You

Thank you so much for reading, and hopefully enjoying, *Summer's Secret Marigold*. It's the fourth book in the Pencradoc *Cornish Secrets* series and I loved bringing Elsie and Louis' story to life, and finally, *finally* getting Sybill and Coren together! I do hope you enjoyed taking the journey with them.

However, authors need to know they are doing the right thing, and keeping our readers happy is a huge part of the job. So, it would be wonderful if you could find a moment just to write a quick review on Amazon or one of the other book reviewing websites to let me know that you enjoyed the book. Thank you once again, and do feel free to contact me at any time on Facebook, Twitter, through my website (details on following page), or through my lovely publishers, Choc Lit.

Thanks again, and much love to you all,

Kirsty

xx

About the Author

Kirsty Ferry is from the North East of England and lives there with her husband and son. She won the English Heritage/Belsay Hall National Creative Writing competition in 2009 and has had articles and short stories published in various magazines. Her work also appears in several anthologies, incorporating such diverse themes as vampires, crime, angels and more.

Kirsty loves writing ghostly mysteries and interweaving fact and fiction. The research is almost as much fun as writing the book itself, and if she can add a wonderful setting and a dollop of history, that's even better. Her day job involves sharing a building with an eclectic collection of ghosts, which can often prove rather interesting.

For more information on Kirsty visit:
Twitter: www.twitter.com/kirsty_ferry
Facebook: www.facebook.com/kirsty.ferry.author/

More Choc Lit

From Kirsty Ferry

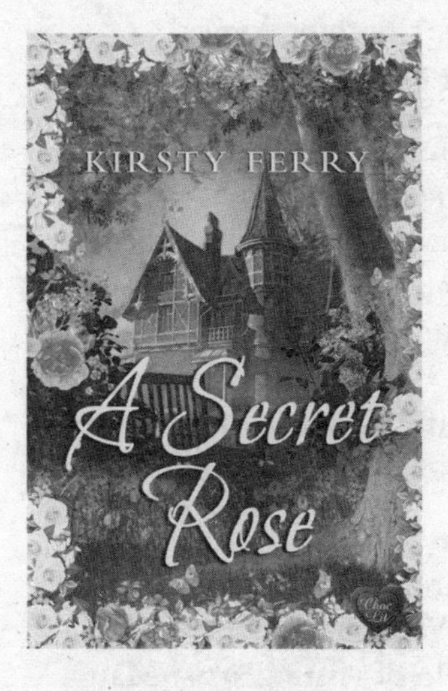

A Secret Rose

Book 1 in the Cornish Secrets series

"Wherever you go, I will follow ..."

Merryn Burton is excited to travel down to Cornwall to start her first big job for the London art dealers she works for. But as soon as she arrives at Pencradoc, a beautiful old mansion, she realises this will be no ordinary commission.

Not only is Pencradoc filled with fascinating, and possibly valuable artwork, it is also owned by the Penhaligon brothers – and Merryn's instant connection with Kit Penhaligon could be another reason why her trip suddenly becomes a whole lot more interesting.

But the longer Merryn stays at Pencradoc the more obvious it is that the house has a secret, and a long-forgotten Rose might just hold the key ...

Visit www.choc-lit.com for details.

Lily's Secret

Book 2 in the Cornish Secrets series

'There's nothing logical about Pencradoc!'

Aspiring actress Cordelia Beaumont is fed up of spending summer in the city. So, when the opportunity presents itself, she jumps straight on a train to pay a visit to Pencradoc – the beautiful Cornish estate where her friend Merryn works.

But far from the relaxing break Cordy imagined, she soon finds herself immersed in the glamorous yet mysterious world of Victorian theatre sensation, Lily Valentine. Lily was once a guest at Pencradoc and, with the help of visiting artist Matt Harker, Cordy comes to discover that the actress left far more than memories at the old house. She also left a scandalous secret …

Visit www.choc-lit.com for details.

Holly's Christmas Secret

Book 3 in the Cornish Secrets series

Once upon a Cornish Christmas ...

It's almost Christmas at the Pencradoc estate in Cornwall which means that, as usual, tea room owner Sorcha Davies is baking up a festive storm. And this year Sorcha is hoping her mince pies will be going down a treat at 'The Spirit of Christmas Past' exhibition being organised at the house by new local antiques dealer, Locryn Dyer.

But as Locryn and Sorcha spend more time together, they begin to uncover a very special story of Christmas past that played out at Pencradoc more than a century before, involving a certain 'Lady' Holly Sawyer, a festive dinner party and a magical secret encounter with a handsome author ...

Visit www.choc-lit.com for details.

Christmas of New Beginnings

Kirsty Ferry

Book 1 in the Padcock Village series

Not all festive wishes come true right away – sometimes it takes five Christmases …

Folk singer Cerys Davies left Wales for the South Downs village of Padcock at Christmas, desperate for a new beginning. And she ends up having plenty of those: opening a new craft shop-tea room, helping set up the village's first festive craft fair, and, of course, falling desperately in love with Lovely Sam, the owner of the local pub. It's just too bad he's firmly in the clutches of Awful Belinda …

Perhaps Cerys has to learn that some new beginnings take a while to … well, begin! But with a bit of patience, some mild espionage, a generous sprinkling of festive magic and a flock of pub-crashing sheep, could her fifth Christmas in Padcock lead to her best new beginning yet?

Edie's Summer of New Beginnings

Kirsty Ferry

Book 2 in the Padcock Village series

Can Edie rediscover her artistic mojo and become a 'Watercolour Wonder'?

Edie Brinkley went from rising star on the London art scene to hiding out at her gran's cottage in the little village of Padcock after a series of unfortunate circumstances leave her almost too panicky to pick up a paintbrush.

When celebrity artist Ninian Chambers rocks up in the village to film Watercolour Wonders, a new TV art competition, Edie is horrified – especially as he played no small part in her decision to leave London.

But, with the support of the Padcock community, and one very special fellow contestant, could Ninian's show ultimately offer a fresh start for Edie and her art career? Or will Annabel the sixties' style stealer, along with make-up artist Tallulah and her 'Caravan of Hell', sabotage her summer of new beginnings?

Visit www.rubyfiction.com for details.

The Schubert Series

A series of quirky romcoms set in Edinburgh and featuring a big black cat called Schubert!

***Every Witch Way* – Book 1**

***A Christmas Secret* – Book 2**

***It Started With a Giggle* – Book 3**

***It Started With a Pirate* – Book 4**

***It Started With a Wedding* – Book 5**

Visit www.choc-lit.com for more details.

The Hartsford Mysteries

A series of atmospheric time-slip romances, all set in the same beautiful mansion house in Suffolk.

***Watch for Me by Moonlight* – Book 1**

***Watch for Me by Candlelight* – Book 2**

***Watch for Me by Twilight* – Book 3**

***Watch for Me at Christmas* – Book 4**

Visit www.choc-lit.com for more details.

The Rossetti Mysteries

A series of compelling time-slip romances set in the art world in Yorkshire and London.

***Some Veil Did Fall* – Book 1**

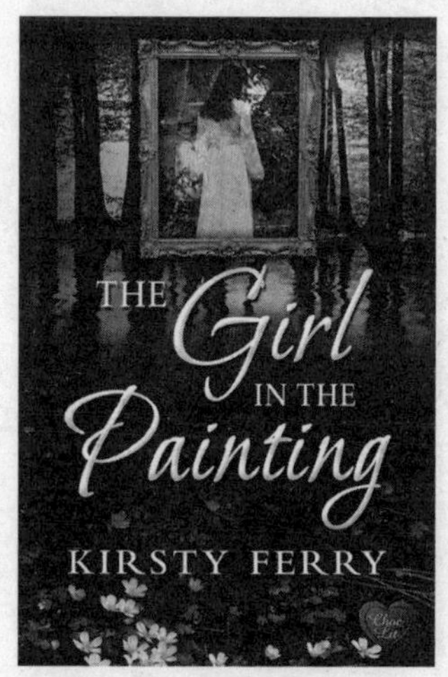

***The Girl in the Painting* – Book 2**

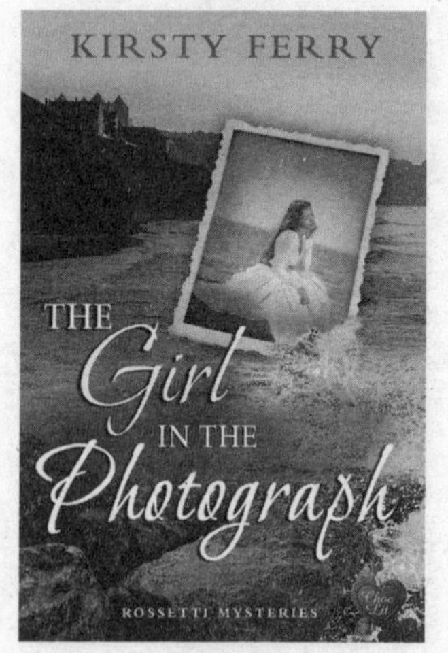

***The Girl in the Photograph* – Book 3**

***A Little Bit of Christmas Magic* – Book 4**

The Tempest Sisters Series

Cosy contemporary romances set in Scotland and on the North East coast.

***Spring at Taigh Fallon* – Book 1**

***Jessie's Little Bookshop by the Sea* – Book 2**

***Summer at Carrick Park* – Book 3**

***Christmas on the Isle of Skye* – Book 4**

Visit www.choc-lit.com for more details.

Introducing Choc Lit

We're an independent publisher creating
a delicious selection of fiction.
Where heroes are like chocolate – irresistible!
Quality stories with a romance at the heart.

See our selection here:
www.choc-lit.com

We'd love to hear how you enjoyed *Summer's Secret Marigold*. Please visit **www.choc-lit.com** and give your feedback or leave a review where you purchased this novel.

Choc Lit novels are selected by genuine readers like yourself. We only publish stories our Choc Lit Tasting Panel want to see in print. Our reviews and awards speak for themselves.

Could you be a Star Selector and join our Tasting Panel?
Would you like to play a role in choosing which novels we decide to publish? Do you enjoy reading women's fiction? Then you could be perfect for our Tasting Panel.

Visit here for more details...
www.choc-lit.com/join-the-choc-lit-tasting-panel

Keep in touch:
Sign up for our monthly newsletter Spread for all the latest news and offers: www.spread.choc-lit.com.
Follow us on Twitter: @ChocLituk,
Facebook: Choc Lit and Instagram: @ChocLituk.

Where heroes are like chocolate – irresistible!